LEARN

NYT & USA TODAY BESTSELLING AUTHOR

KAYLEE RYAN

USA TODAY BESTSELLING AUTHOR

LACEY BLACK

Cover Design: Y'all That Graphic
Photographer: Furious Photog
Model: Brendon Charles
Editing: Hot Tree Editing
Proofreading: Kara Hildebrand, Deaton Author Services, Sandra Shipman & Joanne Thompson

watch and LEARN

NYT & USA TODAY BESTSELLING AUTHOR

KAYLEE RYAN

USA TODAY BESTSELLING AUTHOR

LACEY BLACK

chapter

1

NATE

I DON'T BOTHER TO GLANCE in my rearview mirror as I leave the stadium and the city lights of downtown Nashville. I'm not interested in sticking around. Broadway Street is something I'm not interested in tonight.

My cell phone sits in the cupholder with half a dozen text messages from my teammates asking where I am, one of those my best friend, Jax. I didn't tell him I wasn't coming, but it's been long enough now he's gotten the hint. He knows me well enough to understand what my lack of reply means.

I press a little harder on the accelerator of my Audi RS e-tron GT. It's a sweet car, but it's not really mine. It's not that I can't afford my own. I'm the highest-paid quarterback in the league. That means I have more money than I know what to do with. I have local car dealers sending me cars that cost one hundred and fifty g's just to drive around in their model for the season. It's pathetic, really. My parents worked two jobs and lived paycheck to paycheck to keep a roof over our heads, and here I am, capable of buying a small island and still having money to burn, and all the luxuries in life are handed to me because I'm good at throwing a football.

My phone beeps again, alerting me to a new message, but I ignore it. Preseason games start next week, and my team is out living it up. The press around this season has been brutal. We're coming off back-to-back league championships, and everyone wants to know if we can do it again.

In case you were wondering, fuck yes, we can. I'm Nate Vaughn, best fucking quarterback in the league, and my team, the Nashville Storm, is stacked with an O-line that has my back and a defense that dominates the field. We've got this. However, I don't have patience with the media. The naysayers and all the fucking football groupies. Yeah, I know, first world problems and all that, but I just want a little peace. Is it too much to ask to just have a drink at the bar with my buddies and be Nate? Not Nate Vaughn the quarterback?

I just need one fucking night to breathe before this season kicks off next week.

As I reach the outskirts of town, I see a small dive bar. The neon sign in the window says The Bar, and it makes me laugh. Making a late decision, I turn into the parking lot and kill the engine. This place is dead from the looks of the empty parking lot. I send up a silent prayer I can grab a drink and finish it in peace.

As I pull open the door, the lights are dim, and the jukebox in the corner plays a slow country tune. Shoving my keys and my phone that I'm still ignoring into my pocket, I saunter up to the bar and perch my ass on one of the old, rickety wooden barstools.

"What can I get ya?" she asks, her tired gray eyes on me.

I smile at the older lady. She has jet-black hair that doesn't even remotely look like her natural color. She's wearing bright red lipstick, bright blue eyeshadow, and a T-shirt that says The Bar is tight across her chest. The best part of this lady? There's not a single ounce of recognition in her eyes as to who I am.

"Coke, please." It's a last-minute choice. I have to drive home, and the last thing I need is a DUI or an accident. The press is already up my ass.

"You want some Jack in that Coke?" she asks, her voice raspy as if she's smoked one too many cigarettes.

It's on the tip of my tongue to say yes, but we're in season, or close enough, and I want this win. My body is my temple, and I need to keep it that way. There will be time for Jack when we bring home Nashville's third consecutive win in the league. "Nah, just the Coke, please."

She nods and gets to work, pouring me my plain, old, boring Coke.

The lady behind the bar slides my glass in front of me, along with a small bowl of peanuts before moving on down the bar. I take a sip of my cold drink and stare up at the television screen. I expect to find sports or maybe the news that I'll have to tune out, but I'm surprised to find one of those romance movies that my mom loves to watch playing. I chuckle and allow myself to get sucked into the movie. They're all the same, the plots similar, but my mom loves these things, and I admit, I've watched far too many in my lifetime.

The movie goes into a commercial, and I inwardly curse when I realize I was riveted by the cheesy rom-com. I glance around the room, just waiting for a reporter to jump out and start grilling me with questions or a photographer to give me a sleazy grin as he or she snaps my picture and makes a run for it to the nearest tabloid for their payday.

That's when I see that I'm no longer the only customer of The Bar. There's a woman sitting a few stools over. Her dark hair is pulled up in some kind of messy knot on her head. My eyes scan what I can see of her, and she's wearing scrubs. A nurse, maybe? I watch her as she reaches for a bowl of peanuts to her left, and her stool wobbles. I'm on my feet and rushing toward her, catching her just before she face-plants on the dirty floor.

"I got you," I tell her. My voice is deep and raspy, even to my own ears.

The dark-haired beauty opens her eyes, and they are the most alluring hazel I've ever seen. A gorgeous mix of greens and browns, and I can't help but stare. "I'm so sorry," she says. "Thank you for saving me." She moves to stand. I don't let go of her until she's steady on her feet. She takes a deep breath and smiles up at me. I wait for the recognition to hit her. For her claws to come out, thinking she can sink them into the great Nate Vaughn, but neither happens.

"I'm sorry. Thank you again." She climbs back on her stool, and I reach for the bowl of peanuts and slide them her way. She gives me an embarrassed yet thankful smile.

"Long day?" I ask. I don't know why I'm engaging this woman in conversation. Is she being coy? Pretending she doesn't know who I am?

She huffs out a breath. "You could say that."

"Nurse?" I guess.

"Doctor. Well, working on it. I'm in my first year of residency at Heartland Community Hospital."

"Nice. Good for you."

A small smile tugs at her lips. "Thank you." She glances down at the bar where I was sitting. "Can I buy you another for saving me?" A red tint coats the skin of her porcelain cheeks.

"I'm all set," I tell her. "But you can keep me company. You look like you could use it." I'm intrigued that she's yet to mention my career. Could she really not know who I am?

"Sprite," the bartender says, setting a glass in front of my new friend.

"Hitting it hard, I see," I tease.

Another blush colors her cheeks. "Yeah, I have to drive home, and I have to be back at the hospital bright and early in the morning. I don't need to be kicked out of my residency program because I'm hungover and can't get out of bed."

"Another Coke?" the bartender asks me.

I lift my half full glass and drain it before nodding my approval to the bartender.

The beauty smiles up at me. "Seems I'm not the only one playing it safe tonight."

"Like you said, I'm driving home." I shrug. Grabbing my fresh glass, I take a sip and place it back on the counter before sitting on the stool next to my new friend. "I'm Nate," I say, offering her my hand.

"Oaklyn." She takes my hand in hers, and her skin is silky soft. "Nice to meet you, Nate."

I nod and take another drink. There is zero recognition in her eyes. "So, what's got you sitting in a bar all alone sipping Sprite?" I ask.

"Tough day."

"Want to talk about it?" I'm shocked that I asked. I'm not a complete asshole, but I'm not one to take on other's problems, but there's sadness in her eyes, and I want to know what put it there.

"I lost a patient today. Well, not me specifically, but I was working on the case, and yeah." She blows out a heavy breath. "It's part of the job. I knew that, but damn, it's hard, you know? Knowing that you did everything you could but still couldn't save them. This man was a father, a grandfather, a husband, a son, and a brother. There are a whole host of people who are mourning him tonight, and I might not have known him, but I'm one of them."

I don't know what I was expecting her to say, but it wasn't that. I thought maybe she was having man troubles, or she needed money to fix her car or some shit. "I'm sorry." I place my hand over hers where it sits on the bar. "I can't imagine dealing with that day in and day out."

"I know that we help more than we lose. It's just… this was my first loss. It's one I'll always remember." She takes a sip of her Sprite and turns to look at me. "What about you? What's got you sitting in a bar all alone sipping Coke?" She gives me a small grin as she tosses my question back at me.

"Work." I'm hesitant to tell her what I do. Either this woman is an incredible actress, or she really has no idea who I am. It's… nice. Refreshing even. This is exactly what I wanted. To just be Nate for a night.

"Want to talk about it?" she asks, chuckling.

"My job comes with expectations and lots of media," I confess. I watch closely to see if her expression gives anything away.

"So, are you some kind of celebrity or something?" She studies me under the dim lighting as if she's trying to place me.

"Some might say that."

"I'm sorry."

My shoulders stiffen. Here it comes. Her confession that she knows who I am. I knew she was too good to be true, that this moment of anonymity was a lifeline.

"That has to suck. Being watched. I imagine it feels like being a fish in a bowl."

Well, fuck me. "Yeah, it's actually very similar to that."

She glances behind her at the empty bar before her eyes come back to mine. "Looks like you found a good place to hide."

"Yeah," I agree. "So, why a doctor?"

"My best friend, Natalie. She's an asthmatic. When we were little, she was hospitalized a few times, and I felt helpless. I wanted to do something for her. I wanted to learn how to support her." She shrugs. "I decided when I was ten that I was going to be a doctor, and well, here I am." She pops a couple of peanuts into her mouth. "What about you? What made you want to be kind of a celebrity?"

"I never wanted to be. Not really." I pause. My gut tells me I can tell her what I do, and it's not going to change a damn thing. Besides, she's a stranger in a bar, and it's not like I'm proposing marriage. "All I ever wanted to do was play football."

"Is that what you do? Play football?"

I smile. "Yeah, I play for the Nashville Storm."

"Are you any good?" she asks, taking a drink of her Sprite.

I choke on a laugh. "I'm pretty good."

"What position do you play?"

"Quarterback."

"That's the one that tosses the ball, right?"

"Throws the ball, and yes."

"Throw, toss, it's the same thing." She shrugs.

"Do you watch football?"

"Nope. I barely have time to sleep. My dad does, though. He's a fan of the Storm. I'm sure he probably knows who you are."

I wait for her to ask for an autograph or a picture to send to her dad, but the request never comes. What are the chances the one night I wanted to be me, just Nate, that I meet a beautiful woman in an old, run-down bar, and she doesn't know and doesn't seem to care what I do for a living?

"Do you love it?"

"Yeah, I love the game. I don't love all the media and the groupies."

"Oh, come on now." She smiles. "Big sexy man like you has a problem with women throwing themselves at you? I call bullshit. Your nose is growing, Nate."

I love the sound of my name on her lips. "You think I'm sexy?"

Her head falls back, and her laughter wraps around me like a warm embrace. "That's seriously the only thing you heard?"

I lean in close. "Oaklyn, when a beautiful woman tells you that you're sexy, you pay attention."

"To the fact that she claims you're sexy."

"If it helps, I think you're fucking gorgeous. Sexy. Beautiful. Intoxicating. Take your pick." I reach for my glass because it's not often I toss out those words. With the groupies, you give them a compliment, and they start looking at wedding invitations.

If I thought she was blushing before, it's nothing compared to the red hue that's covering her cheeks now. I can't help but wonder if that blush coats other parts of her skin.

"Dance with me." I climb off my stool and hold my hand out for her. I've made the situation awkward, and all I can think about is getting my hands on her.

"Here?"

"Where else would we dance?"

"There's not really a dance floor."

"Do we need one?" I lean in close, placing my lips next to her ear. "I want to hold you close, Oaklyn. We don't need much space for that." I stand back to my full height and smile. "Come on."

"We can't just dance where there's no dance floor."

I grab her hand and pull her to her feet. "Watch and learn, baby." I lead her to the jukebox and feed in some cash, choosing a few songs before hauling her into my arms. My hands rest on her hips, and she hesitates before she presses hers against my chest.

"Do you always get what you want?" she asks.

I smile down at her. "Most of the time."

"And you wanted to dance?"

"I wanted to dance with you." I tug her a little closer. She has to move her hands to hold around my neck. There's no room between her body and mine, and I know she can feel my hard cock against her stomach, but that's okay. I want this woman to know what she does to me. I want her to know that I want her.

Fuck me, do I want her.

"I can't tell you the last time I danced with a man."

I raise an eyebrow. "You usually dance with women?"

"No." She laughs. "I don't have time for dancing or dates. I work a shit-ton of hours and practically live at the hospital."

"So, what you're telling me is when I ask to see you again, you're going to turn me down?"

"Yes. I mean, wait. What?"

Unable to resist, I press a kiss on her nose. "You're cute when you're flustered."

"You want to see me again?"

"Yep."

"I don't really date."

"Because of your schedule."

"Yeah."

"I understand that. The preseason starts next week, and I'm going to be busy, too, but there's something here. Something I think we should explore."

"We don't know each other."

"That's what dating is for."

"You want to date me?"

"I want you." It's the most real I've been with a woman in a long damn time.

"You want me?"

"Don't pretend like you can't feel what you in my arms does to me."

"That's just men. I'm a doctor. I know it's attraction. You can't control it."

"Not with you."

"I don't have time for dating or relationships. I'm stretched thin as it is." Her mouth is turned down in a frown, and I hate it.

"I understand you're career-focused. I admire that, and I understand it. What about your needs, Oaklyn?"

"My needs?" She peers up at me under long lashes.

My hands roam up and down her back. "Sex, beauty."

"I—well—it's been a minute."

"A minute?" I ask, amused. I know what she's trying to say, but I'm enjoying the pink in her cheeks.

"A year. Maybe longer."

"Let me take care of you." It's a request that I don't have to think about. I want her beneath me, on top of me. Fuck me. I want her any way I can have her. That she's not the normal groupie is her biggest appeal to me. Not to mention she's fucking gorgeous, and she's saying all the right things. She doesn't want anything from me. No time for dating and relationships, but I know she can carve out a few hours a week to let me worship her body.

"Take care of me?" she repeats, and it's a cute habit of hers. She's unsure, and I love that. She's not throwing herself at me, but I can see in her eyes that she's interested.

Dropping my head, I place my lips next to her ear. "Sex, Oaklyn. Hot, sweaty, soul-shattering sex. You and me. Anytime you need a release from that stressful job of yours, I want to be the man to give it to you."

I watch as she swallows hard. "When?"

"Now. Next week, next month, whenever you need me."

"Just sex?"

I nod. "Not just sex. The best sex of your life."

"Cocky," she murmurs.

"Not if I have the skills to back it up."

"No one can know."

That is not what I was expecting her to say.

"If I agree, it's just between us. I don't want to be a notch on your bedpost in the tabloids."

"We'll be discreet."

"I have to be back at the hospital at six, and it's just after seven, so we only have a few hours before I need a full night's sleep in order to function. There are lives on the line."

"Your place or mine?"

"Mine."

I nod and link her hand with mine. Leading her to the bar, I pay our tabs, leaving a hefty tip for our bartender, and guide her outside. This night is unexpected. I wanted a night to be just me, and I got that and so much more.

chapter 2

Oaklyn

My hands are practically shaking with anticipation as Nate leads me out the door of the dive bar.

Before this evening, I'd never been to The Bar, but as I was leaving work, I just couldn't force myself to go home. I drove aimlessly for close to thirty minutes before coming upon the worn-down building with old neon lights in the dingy windows and a nearly empty parking lot. My car was pulling up before I even considered what diseases lay beyond those doors. My keys were dropped in my purse, and I slipped out of my Honda and went inside.

While the room was dark and dreary, it wasn't hard to spot the only other customer in the bar. I didn't intentionally choose a seat so close to him, but I'm damn glad I picked that one. Not because it wobbled and I almost fell on my ass, but because he turned out to be the hottest man I've ever seen in person, and that's saying something because Luke Bryan was recently visiting at the hospital I work for, and he's one of the sexiest men I've ever had the privilege to gawk at.

But even Luke with his magical pelvic thrust dance moves doesn't hold a candle to quarterback Nate who plays for the Nashville Storm.

Mental note to Google him later.

Now, I'm being escorted from the bar with said hot guy. Our destination predetermined. Our intent clear.

Sex.

And while I don't usually judge a book by its cover, something tells me sex with Nate is going to be memorable.

"I'll follow you?" he asks, pausing as I unlock my car.

Nodding, I slip inside my warm car and give him a wicked smirk. "Try and keep up."

He chuckles, low and gravelly, and the sound goes straight to the apex of my legs. "Watch and learn, baby." With a wink, he shuts my car door and jogs to his own vehicle, a fancy sports car that screams "looking to get laid."

I start my car and back away from the bar, heading toward the exit. Traffic is practically nonexistent here, but I know it'll be short-lived. We're headed toward the north end of the downtown area where the hospital is located. I was lucky enough to find an apartment within walking distance nearby, thanks to a tip from my best friend, Natalie. She lives in the same building, and when a single-bedroom apartment became available one floor below hers, she put in a good word for me.

I worm my way through town, feeling the headlights of the car behind me like a warm caress. Maybe it's the fact it's been longer than anyone should have to admit since I last had sex. I've always been a fan of it, but with school, followed by my residency, it has fallen to the wayside. At the end of the day, it just hasn't been as important as sleep.

That changes tonight.

For the first time since Daniel Masterson and I had a short three-week fling our first year of med school, I'm taking the bull by the horns. Or specifically, one particular bull and his bigger-than-average-sized horn.

I felt it against my stomach while we danced.

I crank up the AC, even though it's plenty cool in here now, because I feel a little flushed. I'm sure it has nothing to do with the anticipation racing through my veins. I also realize that's probably a lie. The eagerness I feel to spend time with Nate is overwhelming. This is the point where I should be second-guessing myself. I mean, I'm taking some random home with me. If that doesn't scream desperate, I don't know what does. But the more I wait, the less guilty I feel. Something tells me a night with Nate will beat any night I've had with any previous man.

And yes, I'm making that assumption based on the horn.

Please, God, let him know how to use it.

The moment we reach a stoplight, I pull out my phone and connect a call to Natalie.

"Hey." Her greeting echoes through my speakers as soon as the call connects.

"Do you know Nate Somebody from the Storm?"

"Nate Vaughn? Girl, every woman with a functioning uterus knows Nate Vaughn."

I glance in my rearview mirror and find him exactly where I left him. The light turns green, so I slowly edge my car out into traffic and continue on my way. "Can you send me a picture of him?"

Yes, I could just Google, but this seems easier, considering I'm driving.

"I can. Why?" She gasps. "Oh my gosh, did something happen to him? Was he in the hospital today?"

"No, no, nothing like that. Calm your tits," I tell her as I approach the turnoff for our neighborhood.

"Okay, just sent it. It's the first one that popped up on the internet. Did you know he did *Playgirl* last fall? Holy shitballs, I think that football barely covered his man bits. No wonder he was smirking like that," she says, almost absently. I'm sure she's combing through images of him now thanks to Google.

My phone vibrates, so I carefully pick it up and click on the message she sent. My mouth drops open. The first image that popped up was his *Playgirl* photo? Jesus, that football looks small in his hands. Are his hands really that big?

"You know what they say about big hands," Natalie chimes in. Okay, obviously, I didn't just think that. "Why do you ask, anyway? You don't like football."

My brain spins, grappling for an answer. I hate lying to my bestest friend, but there's no way I can tell her I'm about to do the nasty with Nate Vaughn. She'll have a brain hemorrhage, and then I won't get to the enjoyment part of the evening, because I'll have to take my best friend to the hospital.

No bologna pony for me.

"Someone was talking about him at work. His stats or something."

Liar!

"Oh, damn. I was hoping it was something juicy," Natalie grumbles.

As I start to near our apartment, I know I need to get her off the phone so I can register Nate as a guest. "Listen, I'm gonna hop off here. It's been a long day."

"Want me to grab a pizza and bring it down?"

"No," I reply too quickly. Taking a deep breath, I add, "No, that's okay, but thanks for the offer. I'm exhausted." *Fake yawn.*

"I have to be back at the hospital by six, so I'm just gonna hit the bed."

Oh, am I…

Guilt hits me hard, but now isn't the time for this conversation. I can have it with her tomorrow, after I've had a round or two with Nate's hammer. Something tells me one time won't be enough. I just pray he's got the stamina I envision he has as a pro football player.

"All right, but if you change your mind, text me."

"Sounds good. Love ya," I sing. The moment she replies, I click the phone button on my steering wheel and disconnect.

Checking my rearview mirror once more, I confirm the football Adonis is behind me and pull into the parking garage for my building. I pull my visitor's pass from deep inside my purse and jump out before reaching the security station. When I approach his car, he rolls down the window. "Here, you'll need this to get in the gate."

He nods, taking the small card and setting it on the console. Without another word, I return to my vehicle and scan my own card, opening the gate so I can enter. I pull forward and wait while he does the same. It doesn't go unnoticed by me that he's the first person to ever use my visitor's pass. With my parents relocated to sunny Florida, and not having any siblings, the only person to stick with me through the craziness of med school lives in the same building, so it's not like she needs a second one.

Once he enters the garage, I drive up to the second floor where my reserved spaces are located and pull into the first one. Nate parks beside me in the one labeled Guest and is out before I even have my car turned off. Apparently, someone is as anxious to get inside as I am.

Slipping out of my car, I retrieve my work bag from the back seat and lock the doors. Then, my hand is engulfed in his very big—*yes, his hands really are freaking huge*—and warm hand as we walk to the elevator. Once inside, I use my keycard a second time to engage the elevator. This was one of the selling points of this apartment building. Not only is it close to the hospital I work at, but there are security measures in place.

The door closes and the elevator begins to ascend. Nate slides in close, his woodsy, masculine scent punching me square in the clit, making it throb with need. I've never been big on scent. In my line of work, there are too many bad ones, but right now, with the mixture of his soap and shampoo dancing in my nostrils, it takes every ounce of self-control I possess not to just bend over right here and now, begging for him to take me in the middle of the elevator car.

He runs his thumb over my palm, sending shivers of desire through my entire body. My nipples pebble against my bra, leaving me grateful for wearing a lightly padded one today. At least he can't tell my nipples are standing at attention right now, begging to be sucked into his mouth.

Nate takes my bag as we exit and head for my apartment. Sexual tension hangs heavy around us, like a bubble of desire and need. Slipping my key inside the knob, I release the lock and open the door. Before we cross the threshold, I place my hand on his forearm, pausing our motion. "I just need you to know," I start, clearing my throat. "I don't take football players home with me."

His eyes burn dark with heat as the corner of his mouth curls upward in the most devilishly gorgeous smirk. "I don't either."

The nervousness building in my chest bursts like a balloon as laughter spills from my lips. "I suppose that's good to know."

He cups my cheek with his free hand and holds my gaze. "I'm not going to lie to you and say I've never done this before, but it's as unexpected for me tonight as it is for you. I didn't go to that bar to find a hookup. If I wanted to do that, I would have gone with my teammates to whatever club or bar they're at this evening."

I nod, appreciating his honesty.

"But when I saw you, the moment I had my hands wrapped around you to prevent you from falling, I knew you were someone I wanted to spend a little more time with."

My eyebrows pull together as I grin. "Naked time?"

He snorts out a laugh and runs his hand down the column of my neck. "I won't say no to that. In fact, that sounds like the best thing I've heard all night. All week, even."

Nate reaches for my phone, which is still in my hand, and when he touches the screen, it comes to life, revealing the image Natalie sent me. A wide grin spreads across his face as he gazes down at his naked body. "Doing a little internet browsing, were we?"

I shrug, refusing to get embarrassed. "I called Natalie and asked her to send me a picture so I could confirm you were who you said you were."

He sobers a bit. "That's actually very smart of you."

"A woman can never be too careful in the city," I reason. "Some gorgeous guy claims to be a big-shot football player, I should verify it before I proceed to get naked with him."

"Brains and beauty," he says, offering me a wink as he slips my phone into my purse.

I push the door open, and we step inside together. It happens so fast, I don't even realize what's transpiring until the door slams, my bag and purse are tossed onto the floor, and I'm pressed against the hard wood. His mouth is on my neck, his lips trailing hot and hungrily down my skin.

"I've never found scrubs as sexy as I do right now," he whispers, sending all my blood rushing to the apex of my legs. His hand moves to my side, his fingers gripping me through the blue material of my top.

"They're not sexy at all," I counter, angling my head to give him better access.

"I beg to differ. I suddenly have all sorts of doctor-patient fantasies I'd love to act out."

"Don't all men want the hot nurse?"

He shrugs, moving his hand from my side to my ass as he presses his erection into my stomach, making me moan in anticipation. "No way. This is much sexier," he insists, rubbing himself against me. I hitch my leg around his thigh and grind my pussy against it, reveling in the zaps of pleasure streaking through my veins.

Suddenly, he pulls back and locks eyes with me. "You can still stop this, you know. Just say the word. I don't want to pressure you," he states.

I'm already shaking my head. "I don't want to stop. I want this. I want *you*."

Keeping me pinned against the door, Nate slowly lifts my scrub top, the cool air-conditioning kissing my skin and sending goose bumps across my body. He takes in my simple blue bra before reaching out and pulling the material down. A groan spills from his lips as he drinks his fill and licks his lips. "Fuck, you're beautiful."

He bends down and sucks one nipple into his hot mouth, causing me to gasp as pleasure races through me. My fingers dive into his hair as he pinches my other nipple, rolling it between his talented fingertips. If this man plays my body half as well as he plays football, I'm in for a real treat.

An orgasmic one.

"Let's get these pants off you, shall we?" he murmurs without removing his mouth from my nipple.

"Yes, please."

Before I can slip my fingers beneath the elastic waistband of my scrub pants, his big palms grip the material, and he pulls it down to my ankles. I've never been more grateful for wearing a pretty pair of comfortable underwear than I am right now, but there's no time to praise the panty gods because his mouth is there, his tongue pressing against the wet cotton material between my legs.

"Spread your legs, Oaklyn," he instructs, helping me step out of my scrubs and lifting my left leg up onto his shoulder.

My leg falls open as he pushes the material of my panties to the side, exposing my pussy. I'm riveted in place as his tongue snakes out and swipes between my folds. I jerk back, my shoulders knocking against the door, but he doesn't relent. His tongue moves, alternating between flicking and licking my clit and delving deep inside me. The combination is quickly driving me straight toward the edge of release.

My fingers tighten their hold on his hair, and the action seems to spur him on more. He sucks my clit into his mouth, groaning, causing shock waves of pleasure. I spread my legs as far as I can without knocking my heel off his shoulder, searching for the building orgasm. When he presses a single finger up into my pussy, I know I'm close.

"Oh, God," I whisper, closing my eyes and rocking my hips against his face.

"You're close." It's not a question. He knows I'm ready to explode. "I want to taste your cum, Oaklyn. I want to feel your pussy spasm around my fingers." That's when he adds a second one, stretching me almost painfully around two large fingers. "Now, beautiful. Come now."

And I do.

It's pure magic as I fly high above the clouds, blinded by the bright white light of my release. Wave after wave of pleasure courses through me. I grind myself against his face, rolling my hips in time with his movements and drawing out every sliver of euphoria I can. I don't feel an ounce of embarrassment at how needy I am.

All I know is I want more.

"That was fucking beautiful," he mutters, wiping the sides of his mouth as he stands up. Nate towers over me with a possessive gleam in his dark brown eyes. Normally, this look might turn me off, but when I see the desire reflecting back at me, I feel nothing but longing for more.

Like a craving I'll never satisfy.

A shiver sweeps through me as I anticipate what's next.

"We're not even close to being done yet, beautiful." He lifts me up effortlessly, my legs wrapping around his waist as he carries me toward my bedroom.

Something tells me this is just the beginning of a night I won't soon forget.

chapter

3

NATE

MY HANDS GRIP HER ASS as I carry her down the hall—I'm assuming toward her bedroom. Oaklyn has her head buried in my neck, her hot breath causing goose bumps to break out across my skin.

"Which door?" I ask, my words raspy. In my entire twenty-nine years of life, I've never been this turned on. My cock feels like heavy steel in my jeans. I'm certain the imprint of my zipper will be embedded into the skin.

"Last on the left," she mumbles, her lips next to my ear. She nips at my lobe, and I groan, gripping her ass even tighter.

I didn't want this tonight. I wanted a quiet night to enjoy an ice-cold beverage and then I was going home to crash, but then I caught this beautiful woman in my arms, and there was a spark, an instant pang of desire that couldn't be ignored.

Thankfully, the beautiful Oaklyn felt it, too, and well, here we are.

We finally reach her bedroom door. It's already open, paving the way for me to carry her inside. The smell of vanilla and something else, lavender maybe, assaults me as soon as we enter. Lifting my foot, I kick the door closed. I assume she lives alone — we didn't get that far — but I don't want anyone to walk in and interrupt us.

The room is dark, but I manage to make my way to the bed. I turn so that I can sit with her still in my arms. My hands move to cradle her face as I kiss her. I take my time, letting my tongue trace over her lips. I suck on her bottom lip, and she gasps, opening for me. I take the opportunity to slip my tongue inside and taste her fully.

The kiss isn't awkward, as some are when you kiss someone new. No. Kissing Oaklyn feels as though we've done this thousands of times before. Her tongue slides against mine in a well-practiced stroke. She doesn't seem to mind that she can still taste herself on my lips, and that is hot as fuck.

Leisurely, I explore every inch of her mouth. My hands begin to roam over her body. I find the hem of her shirt and lift it. Her arms rise into the air, allowing me to pull it over her head and toss it to the floor. I don't break the kiss as I reach around and unclasp her bra.

She pulls away, and I groan, which makes her smile as she makes quick work of discarding the piece of fabric that's keeping me away from her tits. She leans over, and I hold her tight to keep her from falling. Before I can ask her what she's doing, the room is filled with a soft glow from the bedside lamp.

Once she's settled back on my lap, I reach up and roll a hard, perky nipple between my fingers, and this time Oaklyn is the one groaning, but hers is more of a moan that has my cock twitching in my jeans. Bending my head, I latch on to her nipple, sucking and nipping, then soothing the ache with my tongue.

Oaklyn arches her back, which gives me full access to her breasts.

"Skin," she rasps.

I lift my head. "Tell me what you need."

"Take this off." She pulls at my T-shirt as she sits up straight. "I need to feel your skin."

Reaching behind me, I grab the neck of my T-shirt and pull it over my head, letting it fall to the floor. "Come here." I wrap my arms around her and tug her into a hug. It's not something I've ever done. Usually, my hookups are a get in, get out, and get home kind of situation. Don't get me wrong, they get off. We both do — that's kind of the point. But there is something about Oaklyn, about her request to feel my skin, that I can't deny.

Actually, I think it's her that I can't deny. Either she's a really good actress, or she really doesn't give a fuck about my job. That's hot as hell and not something I ever thought I would say, but here we are.

Oaklyn sighs, and that sound has something flipping over in my chest. "You're all hard and sculpted, yet your skin… it's so warm. And your hands, they're rough and calloused, but they feel like silk when you touch me."

"That's all you, beautiful. I don't know that I've ever felt skin as soft as yours." I'm not just feeding her a line of shit. Her comparison to silk is actually perfect. That's how she feels beneath my fingertips.

When she pulls back, my hands stay wrapped around her, and my fingers lock at the small of her back. I can't seem to get her close enough. "It's been a while for me." Her voice is soft, but there is something in her eyes, something that resembles a plea for me to take this slow.

"We stop when you say stop, Oaklyn. No pressure. No expectations." I'll be disappointed, and my cock will scream in protest, but I'd never force this on her. She needs to decide where this goes tonight because me, I'm all in.

"No." She's quick to answer. "I don't want to stop. I'm just… out of practice."

I can't hold back my smile. "It's just like riding a bike."

She tosses her head back in laughter. My eyes follow the slender column of her neck. "I can't say that I've ever had someone refer to sex as riding a bike."

"You know what I mean." I tickle her sides, and she squirms in my lap, and I moan as her pussy rocks against my jean-covered cock.

"Oh."

"That's all for you," I tell her. Bracing my hands on her hips, I guide her to rock against me once again, and the moan that falls from her lips is the hottest fucking sound I've ever heard before in my entire life. "You're gonna do just fine," I croak.

"Too many clothes, Nate."

"You want me naked?"

"I want us both naked."

"Is your pussy aching?" I reach between us and gently trace over her clit with my thumb.

"You have no idea," she murmurs.

"Yeah, I think I do," I say as I run my fingers over her pussy. She's wet and ready for me. I tap her thigh. "Stand up and strip for me, gorgeous."

Not needing to be told twice, she scrambles off my lap and removes her panties, kicking them to the side. As for me, I'm still sitting on the bed, my cock screaming to be set free as I take her in. Her tits are a nice handful, perky nipples that I know taste as good as they look. Her hips flare, giving me just enough to hold onto, and her legs look like they're nice and strong—strong enough to wrap around my head or my waist, depending on which position we're in.

She reaches up and crosses her arms over her chest while at the same time, she crosses her legs. "Why are you just staring at me?" There is a little bite in her tone but also a slight quiver.

"Just memorizing the moment."

"Less memorizing and more stripping." She nods toward my jeans.

I'm a smart man. Yeah, I'm a jock, but I'm not stupid. When a gorgeous woman looks at you like you're her next meal and tells you to strip, you do it. Standing from the bed, I hold her gaze. Her hazel eyes are pools of desire. She swallows hard, and her eyes travel to where I'm making quick work of the button on my jeans. Once the zipper is down, I dip my thumbs into the waistband of both my jeans and my boxer briefs and pull them off in one go. A soft gasp reverberates in the quiet room.

I'm watching her.

She's watching me.

My cock, specifically, as it bounces against my abs once it's set free from the confines of my clothes. I step out of my clothes one leg at a time before kicking them to the side. Oaklyn is still staring at my cock, which twitches under her gaze. Wanting to see her reaction, I wrap my fist around it, starting at the base, and stroke up, then back down.

She licks her lips.

Licks. Her. Fucking. Lips.

"Oaklyn." Her name is a warning. My voice is gravelly and filled with want for this woman.

"I guess you're big everywhere, huh?" she says, her eyes still glued to my cock.

"Eyes on me." It's a command. My voice is sterner than I intended, but fuck me, I'm about to come just from her staring at me. I'm not fifteen.

Her eyes immediately snap to mine. "Good girl."

She drops her arms to her sides, which allows me to see that her chest is heaving. With each breath that she pulls into her lungs, her tits rise and fall, and I have to force myself to look away.

"Tell me what you need, Oaklyn."

Her eyes flash to my cock once again before she swallows hard and locks eyes with mine. "You." She bites down on her bottom lip. "But, uh, Nate... hell, I know the anatomy of it all. I've studied the logistics, but I'm not quite sure that's going to fit."

My head falls back in laughter. This fucking girl.

"I'm serious. I mean, I know you're a big guy, and you toss that football around with other big guys, but this" — she waves her hand toward my dick — "I wasn't expecting — I don't know. Something average. Like a large dill pickle. You know, the ones you can buy at the grocery store or the gas station in individual bags? Instead, I get... an eggplant."

"I'm not sure if I should be flattered or concerned that you're comparing my cock to food."

"Nate!" Her voice pitches. "That thing can do damage. Permanent damage."

Releasing my cock, I step toward her. I don't stop until I have her wrapped in my arms, with my dick pressed tight against her belly. "I promise you it's going to fit." I bend and press my lips to hers. "I'll take care of you. Trust me on this." She peers up at me, and I don't know that I've ever seen a more beautiful woman.

"You're in control here, Oaklyn. I'll do the work to make this a night you'll never forget, but I need you to trust me to do that. I need you to trust that if it's too much and you want me to stop, that I will. I need you to relax and let me control your pleasure."

"O-Okay."

"Give me your eyes, baby." She blinks a few times before she captures my gaze. "I'll take care of you."

I don't know what I'm expecting, but it's not for her to reach out and palm my cock, giving it a gentle squeeze. "Fuck," I hiss.

"I had to touch it." Her mouth tilts into a small grin, and I huff out a breath.

"Turnabout is fair play," I say, reaching down and sliding my fingers through the lips of her pussy.

"Nate," she moans as she grips my cock tighter.

"On the bed." I remove my hand and take a step back. She releases my cock, and scrambles on the bed, just as she's told.

Good fucking girl.

I sit on the side of the bed and lean over, pressing my lips to hers. I get lost in the feel of her tongue sliding against mine. When I finally pull away, we're both breathing heavily, and her eyes are hooded.

Slowly, I trace my index finger down her cheek. I continue on, taking my time as I pass over her neck and her chest. I massage each breast, nipping, being sure to give them equal amounts of my attention before I continue on my journey. Her belly quivers as I trace over her belly button, and when I slide my fingers between the lips of her soaking wet pussy, she expels a heavy breath.

"Nate," she breathes.

"So wet for me," I say as I slide one long, thick digit inside her. She's tight, but that's okay. We've got time. Nothing another orgasm can't fix. "Open those legs, baby. Let me in." Like the good girl she is, she spreads her legs wide, and suddenly my seat on the edge of the bed isn't close enough. I need to be front and center to see all of her.

Climbing on the bed, I slide my legs beneath hers and move in close. I watch my hand with rapt attention as I push in and out of her. My fingers are soaked, and her legs are quivering.

"Ready for more?"

"Please."

Damn. She's perfect.

Needing this just as much as she does, I pull out, add another digit, and push back in. I lazily pump my fingers in and out of her. She moans, and her back arches. I watch as she grips the sheets, and I know she's close. Leaning forward, I run the pad of my thumb over her clit while the other hand still plunges two fingers inside her over and over again. When her walls start to grip me tighter, I bury my fingers to the hilt and make a come-here motion. I repeat the motion until she's crying out for me and comes all over my hand.

When her body falls lax onto the bed, I remove my fingers and immediately suck them into my mouth.

Fuck me. Her taste is so damn addicting. "You did so good," I praise.

Climbing to my knees, I lean over and kiss her. She doesn't hesitate to return the kiss with vigor, even with the fresh taste of her cum on my lips. When I move to snag a condom from my wallet, she reaches out and grabs hold of me.

"Where are you going?"

"Condom."

"I have one." She reaches over into the drawer of the nightstand and pulls out a new box, handing it to me. "They're good," she says. "I just replenished them."

I raise my eyebrows, and she grins.

"It's been a while, but a girl never knows when her luck is going to change."

"Ah, so I'm your good luck?"

"Depends."

"On what?" I ask as I tear open the box and pull out a condom. I rip the packet open with my teeth and sheath my cock.

"On whether or not that monster cock of yours rips me in two."

I chuckle as I settle over the top of her. "You won't be ripped in two, but I can promise that you'll still feel me tomorrow." It's with those words that I reach between us and guide myself to her entrance. I take my time, pushing in a little at a time, allowing her body to get used to me. When I'm fully sheathed, I have to fight to stay still and keep my eyes from rolling into the back of my head.

"Oh. Oh, wow," she hisses.

I brush the hair out of her eyes. "Breathe," I whisper. It's taking everything I have not to move, but I don't want to hurt her.

"I'm good," she says. "You can move."

"Are you sure?"

She answers by lifting her hips and locking her legs around my waist. "I'm sure. Show me what you've got."

"My. Fucking. Pleasure." I pull out and push back in. She moans. It's deep and throaty and sexy as fuck. Her pussy is already squeezing the hell out of my cock, and I send up a silent prayer for small favors. I'm not going to last long. She's too sexy, too hot, too wet, and my need for her is too strong.

Her hands slide beneath my arms, and her nails dig into my back as she holds on. With each thrust, she digs deeper into the skin, and it only urges me to thrust harder and faster. I want her to feel me tomorrow. I told her that this would be the best night of her life, and I've always been a man of my word.

I lose track of time. I'm lost in her. In the feel of her body pressed to mine, the way her pussy cradles my cock, taking every inch as if it were made just for me. The sounds of her moans, the way she calls out my name. All of it, everything in this moment, everything about her consumes me.

Tingling starts in the base of my spine, and I'm not going to last much longer.

"Nate — I'm — Nate!" she screams as her orgasm crashes over her like hurricane waves crashing onto the shore.

I try to hold out, but her pussy is milking my cock in the best possible way, and I have to let go. I still as I lose control and find my own release.

Careful not to crush her, I balance my weight on my forearms as I rest against her, kissing her softly. We're both breathing heavily, and I can't help but think that this night, this woman, has just given me the best sexual experience of my life. I've never come this hard. I've never wanted a woman again before I've even pulled my cock free and disposed of the condom, but here we are.

I want her again.

Carefully, I pull out of her and climb off the bed to take care of the condom.

"Bathroom is through there." She points to a door in her bedroom.

Taking a minute to dispose of the condom and clean up, I pull open cabinets until I find a washcloth and run it under warm water. I take it back to the bed and sit next to her. "Open for me," I say, and there is no hesitation as she does as I ask. I take my time cleaning her up as best as I can before tossing the wet rag into the bathroom. It lands with a loud flop on the floor.

"That's a good toss. I guess you do pretty well with a football too, huh?" There's a smile gracing her lips and sated happiness in her eyes.

"Something like that." I smirk.

"Hey, Nate?"

"Yeah?" I give her my full, undivided attention.

"Do you think you could do that again?"

"What? Toss the washcloth?"

She shakes her head. "Me."

A slow smile tugs at my lips. "Watch and learn, gorgeous." I reach into the box, grab another condom and proceed to show her twice more before we both fall into a deep sleep, wrapped in each other's arms.

chapter 4

Oaklyn

IT'S BEEN THREE DAYS SINCE my incredible night with Nate, and I still feel him. Not between my legs — though the two previous days were a totally different story — but everywhere else. My skin keeps heating up as if it can still feel his touch. His hands may have been calloused, but they took care of business expertly as if he was made to play my body as well as the game of football.

Pushing Nate and his monster cock and magical hands out of my head, I drop my personal belongings off at my locker in the employee lounge and make my way to the labor and delivery section on the first floor. Today starts my thirty-day residency in that particular department, and I'm pretty excited about it. I'm hoping I'm able to help deliver my first baby before the end of my shift.

Using my keycard, I enter through the double security doors and walk straight to the nurses' station. "Good evening, I'm Dr. Schmidt," I tell the first nurse who looks up.

She gives me a pleasant smile, but there's no missing the hint of relief in her eyes, which tells me things are a little hectic right now. "Hi. Dr. Jonas requested your assistance as soon as you arrived. She's in room fourteen right now," the nurse states.

Nodding, I turn and make my way toward room fourteen, where I'm instantly greeted with the sound of a woman having a contraction. I pause outside the door, not wanting to interrupt, and once the laboring woman's contraction passes, I knock on the door.

"Come in," the familiar voice of Dr. Jonas filters through the slip of space of the cracked door.

I step inside, happy to see this physician. Not only is she my personal gynecologist, but I've heard amazing things about her from former residents and OB patients. She's always pleasant, even when she's stressed, and never barks orders. There are a few older men here who seem more annoyed with having a resident follow them around, but she's not one of them.

"Good afternoon," I greet as I enter the room, offering the laboring patient a small smile.

"Hello," the attending physician replies, looking over to the woman on the bed. "This is our resident, Dr. Schmidt. She's going to be assisting me this afternoon, and if she's lucky, she'll help deliver your perfect baby boy before the end of her shift."

The woman gives me a tired grin. "Hi. I'm Greer, and this is my husband, James." She places both hands on her belly and exhales loudly. "First baby here, and he's being a little stubborn."

James leans over and kisses his wife's forehead after picking up the washcloth draped across it. "He's not stubborn. You've just made such a comfortable home for him these last nine months, he doesn't want to leave."

She snorts. "Well, it's time to go," she insists, just as another contraction begins.

I move to the monitor to watch her readings as she breathes through the painful contraction. Dr. Jonas stands beside me as we wait for the mother-to-be to relax once more. "You're very close, Greer. It won't be much longer," Dr. Jonas states. "You're a rock star. Not many of my patients can do this without medication."

Greer flings her head back against the pillow and groans. "It was a stupid decision," she mutters, closing her eyes and taking a short breather.

"I'll get this wet again," James says, scurrying into the small bathroom and rewetting the washcloth.

"I'll be back to check on you again shortly, but if you need anything before, use the call button," Dr. Jonas reminds the patient before moving toward the doorway.

Following her, we step out into the brightly lit hallway, where she gives me a grin. "Are you excited for your first night in OB?"

"Most definitely," I reply, stepping up beside her as she turns to walk down the hall.

"Well, you'll probably help deliver two, maybe three babies today."

My eyes widen. "Really?"

"Mmhmm. We have six women in labor right now. Two are approaching ten centimeters, including Greer back there. I'm going to take you with me to finish rounds on the others in labor, but we'll want to keep a close eye on Greer and a woman named Loree Gallow. She's in room ten, and I was with her before I checked on Greer. She's on baby number three and progressing quickly."

I nod. "I'm excited to learn," I tell her, even though I'm sure she can read it all over my face.

"Good. I hope you're wearing comfortable shoes. We've got our work cut out for us today," she replies with a beaming grin.

The moment she reaches the nurses' station, she says, "Ten and fourteen are both close, vitals looking good. I'm going to check to see how the rest of the patients are doing, but keep me posted once they finally hit ten, please."

"Of course, Dr. Jonas," the nurse, Jackie, replies.

Then, we're off to the races.

By the time the end of my shift has come and gone, I'm exhausted. While I'm smiling from ear to ear, I'm worn out, nevertheless.

When I reach the staff break room, I finally pull my phone from the pocket of my scrubs. I always keep it on silent while working, refusing to not give one-hundred-percent of my attention to every patient I see.

And today was one for the record books. I helped deliver three babies, all healthy and perfect. All boys too. I assisted with the first two deliveries but took a more active role during the third. The woman, Alicia, did beautifully and didn't seem to mind that I'm a first-year resident. Of course, Dr. Jonas was right beside me, talking me through every step and making sure I was comfortable and relaxed.

The phone in my hand vibrates, and my breath catches in my throat when I see the name on the screen.

Nate Vaughn.

I haven't talked to him since he left in the very early hours Tuesday. But before he slipped out of my bed, he put his number in my phone. He also sent himself a text so he had mine. Three whole days without so much as a peep. Not that I expected it.

We have an agreement. A sexual one. We established that with my crazy schedule, and his, we would have a "benefits" arrangement of sorts for as long as it was gratifying for both parties. And based on our first night together, I imagine it to be *very* gratifying throughout our time together.

I tap in my code and pull up the messaging app.

> **Nate:** Just thinking about your thighs wrapped around my neck while my face is buried in your pussy.

I glance around the room, grateful it's empty and no one is witnessing my blush. Or the fact I'm squirming where I sit, my core flooding with wetness at his dirty words.

> **Me:** I'm sorry, who's this?

I almost laugh when I set my phone down on the bench and retrieve my bag from my locker.

> **Nate:** Don't toy with me, naughty girl. I've been thinking about you all damn day, and no amount of jacking off is working.
>
> **Me:** Sounds like a YOU problem.
>
> **Nate:** It is a YOU problem. I keep picturing YOU coming on my cock, wondering what YOUR mouth would look like stretched around my dick.

Again, I squirm, especially since his words are followed up with a photograph. Not just any photo. A dick pic. Nate Vaughn just sent me a photo of his hard monster cock with his hand wrapped around the base. Not the first one I've received, but definitely the first to make me actually want to jump on said cock.

Tossing my bag over my shoulder, I grab my phone and head out the door.

> **Me:** Looks like you're about to remedy your pesky little issue.
>
> **Nate:** Not likely. I thought I took care of it an hour ago, yet here we are.

A shiver sweeps up my spine, and I start to tingle in all the right places. I should probably be a bit appalled, and perhaps disgusted at his confession, yet that's not what I feel. I'm excited to know he's masturbating to thoughts of me.

Nate: Whatcha doing?

I wait to reply until I'm sitting in my car and have it running. Then, I reread our exchange and send him a quick response, despite it being almost midnight.

Me: Just got off work.

The bubbles appear almost instantly, and instead of pulling from my parking spot and heading home, I wait for his reply.

Nate: Hungry?

Just then, my stomach growls angrily. It was a busy shift in the labor and delivery department, and my dinner consisted of a bottle of water and a granola bar I keep in my locker. That's okay, really. I knew my eating and sleeping schedule would be a mess once I started my residency, and it has been. We're paid for our work, but it's a fairly small wage, all things considered. I often pick up extra shifts when I can, which is part of the reason I barely sleep anymore.

Me: I could eat, but it's almost midnight.

Nate: Come here. I'll order food.

Goose bumps pepper my skin. Do I want to go to Nate's house? I'm pretty certain I know what my visit will lead to, especially with that photo so fresh in my mind. Do I mind? Nope. My body is already responding to the idea of getting naked with him again. For three days, I've replayed our night, and now I get to experience it once more.

And bonus, he's going to feed me first.

Me:	Something greasy, like burgers and mozzarella sticks.

Nate:	Done. I'll send you a pin of my location.

When the notification pops up on my screen, I input it into my map app and put my car in reverse. Before I move, I fire off one final reply.

Me:	20 minutes

Nate:	Code is 16410

Nate:	Be safe. See you soon.

Placing my phone in the cupholder, I back up and drive for the exit. The roads aren't very busy at this time of night as I make my way past my own neighborhood and toward one I know is exclusive and ritzy. With each mile I pass, the houses become bigger and more glamorous. Many musicians live in this area, thanks to the gated communities, high safety ratings, and neighboring private schools.

As I finally approach the address on the screen, I can't help but look around me. I can't see any of the houses, thanks to the gates and tall landscaping, but I'm certain this is where some of the biggest names in entertainment and sports live. It doesn't surprise me Nate resides here. If I had the status he seems to have, I'd want privacy and protection too.

"Your destination is on the right."

I pull into the driveway and stop at the security box. Instead of paging the house, I input the code he sent me and watch as the elaborate black iron gate slowly opens. As I pull forward, the house comes into view. "Holy shit," I mutter, making sure I've cleared the gate before pausing to take it all in.

The driveway is paved with gorgeous landscaping on both sides and leads to a huge brick home with a three-car garage. Wait, no. Four car, and the last one is huge, like it could fit a camper or something. The porch is lit with the soft glow of yellow lighting and looks about as welcome as they come. I can see myself sitting on the swing, enjoying a cup of coffee and watching the sun rise over the trees.

Don't go there. This isn't a relationship. It's a hookup.

I park my car in front of the first garage bay and climb out. As I close my door, movement catches out of the corner of my eye and I find Nate standing on the porch watching me. He has his arms extended up, hands on the top of the railing. He's also shirtless, wearing only a pair of basketball shorts that do absolutely nothing to conceal his erection.

Nate Vaughn is positively scrumptious.

"Are you ogling me?"

Shrugging, I grab my bag out of the back seat of my car and walk toward the front steps. He meets me there and gently grabs my head before placing his lips against mine. The kiss is soft, more like a caress. A tease of what's yet to come.

When he releases me, he reaches down and takes the bag from my hand. "Come on, beautiful. Let's get you inside. Food should be here soon."

Nodding, I follow him into the massive house, taking in the beautiful space. "Wow," I mumble as he closes the door behind us.

"Wanna tour now or later?"

My gut tells me to take the tour now. I have a feeling we'll be a bit busy later. "Now."

He places my bag on the floor beside the entry table while I toe off my shoes. I catch a glimpse of his bare feet, and that single image causes something to stir inside me. I've never been a foot person, but the sight of him so casual has my heart thumping in my chest.

We walk through the foyer to the stunning dining room and kitchen. There's a cute little breakfast nook, and I can picture him sitting there, overlooking his backyard, and reading up on current events. Wait, no. He'd be catching up on sports scores and highlights from the night before.

We move through the built-to-entertain kitchen and toward the back of the house. There's a beautiful office space with floor-to-ceiling bookshelves and a large wall of windows. Through the double glass doorway, I find just enough lighting to see an inground pool and pool house, as well as a firepit and sitting area.

"Do you sit out there often?"

"Yeah. A few teammates come over on the nights off and hang out. We'll watch whatever game is playing on the TV that's hidden on the side of the pool house, swim, and drink a few beers. Well, unless it's during the season. Most of us don't drink then."

I nod before turning my back on the yard and following him out of the room. We move through the living room, which consists of big, leather couches and chairs and the biggest television I've ever seen. There are a few pieces of art on the walls and a couple of framed photographs on the end tables I'll check out later, but not a lot of personal touches that scream Nate. If anything, it screams professional decorator.

Finally, we're moving toward the stairs. The staircase is wide, big enough for multiple people to walk side by side as they ascend, and when we reach the second floor, I find several doorways spanning the hall to the left and right, most of them closed.

"Four bedrooms and six bathrooms in total, but what sold me on this place was the view," he announces as we slowly make our way down the hallway to the right. "Three guest rooms here, each with their own bathroom. I have two set up for guests and the third as a workout room."

He opens each door so I can peek inside. The guest rooms are pretty standard, with comfortable bedding and plenty of space for someone to relax and get comfortable. The workout room is exactly as I'd expect a professional athlete to have. Lots of equipment I wouldn't know what they're used for, with the exception of the treadmill, but those things and I don't see eye to eye. In fact, I despise any sort of running, inside or out.

When we've looked inside the last room, he takes my hand and leads me back to where we started, only facing the left hallway. This one is shorter and has a single door at the end, but something tells me it consists of the entire master bedroom.

The door is open and as we step inside, a small gasp slips from my lips. This room is huge and magnificent. To the right, the sleeping area faces a wall of glass. There's even a sitting area with comfortable, plush chairs facing the view. And he's right; the view is spectacular. You can see all of downtown Nashville from here, lit up like fireflies dancing in the night.

"See what I mean?" he asks.

I didn't realize I'd walked to the windows until he said something. "It's stunning."

"It is. I had my bedroom designed around the view."

"There's so much glass, though. How close are your neighbors?" I quip, wondering if they get to enjoy the view of a naked Nate walking through his bedroom every morning and night.

His lips spread in a wide grin. "Custom glass. You can see out, but not in."

"Ahh," I reply, turning my attention back toward the lights. "I can see why you love it."

"Beautiful." I can feel the heat of his gaze, and when I glance to my right, I find him watching me, not the scenery.

His phone pings, and he quickly pulls it from the pocket of his shorts. "Food's here," he announces as he reaches for my hand once more. "Bathroom and walk-in closet are that way," he says, pointing to the two remaining doors on the opposite side of the space. "I'll show you those later," he adds with a wink.

Nate taps away on his phone as we return to the foyer, and within a few minutes, a man is standing at the door with a bag of food. "Thanks," Nate says as he hands over cash for a tip.

"Hey, thanks, man. Enjoy," the delivery person replies as he pockets the money and turns to leave.

Once the door is secured behind him, Nate turns and nods toward the living room. "Let's get comfy."

The scent hits my nose the moment he starts to pull food from the bag, and my mouth waters in anticipation. "I didn't know what you liked on your burger, so this one has everything, and this one's plainer with some stuff on the side."

"The plainer one, please," I reply, taking the offered container of food.

Nate grabs the two bottles of water off the end table and joins me on the couch. We're both silent as we devour our food, the sound of the television providing a little white noise as we eat.

Finally, when I'm unable to take even another bite, I push my container away and flop back on the couch. "I'm stuffed."

He snickers and reaches over, stealing the last few bites of my burger and the last remaining mozzarella stick. He smiles widely as he finishes the food and pats his own belly. "Growing boy."

I snort in reply, shaking my head. "More like burns a million calories a day."

His grin is wolfish as he winks. "That too."

He gets up and tosses the containers in the trash before returning to the couch. I feel the weight of the day starting to settle on me now that my stomach is full, and my eyes start to grow heavy. I wonder how I'm going to stay up for sexy times, despite the fact I'm eager to get naked with the man.

"Lay back on the couch." His words startle me, mostly because I hadn't realized my eyes were closed.

I do as instructed, bringing my legs closer to him. He moves them onto the couch and pulls off my socks before slowly digging his thumbs into the underside of my feet. "Oh, God," I groan, realizing my words could be confused as orgasmic, but not caring in the least.

He chuckles but doesn't stop his masterful massaging. "Close your eyes and relax."

I want to argue, to suggest we move this party up to his bedroom, but my eyes seem to close all on their own. He rubs my feet, pressing his thumbs and fingers into all the right places on my tired, sore feet, and all I can think about is how amazing it feels.

How comfortable.

How much I'm enjoying being with him, even though our arrangement is supposed to be sex and we have yet to start that portion.

How right it feels to be here, in his space and lounging on his couch with his hands on me.

That's the last thing I remember before letting the exhaustion take me.

chapter 5

NATE

I CAN'T STOP WATCHING HER. Oaklyn fell asleep almost as soon as she took her last bite. I knew the minute she stepped out of her car that she was exhausted, yet here she is. She still came to me. She wanted me as much as I wanted her, but her body needs the rest.

I stare at her for far too long, which moves me into creeper status, but I can't help myself. She looks like an angel with her dark hair splayed out on my couch pillow. An exhausted angel, but an angel all the same.

Her feet are still in my lap, but I've stopped kneading her tired muscles. I don't want to wake her, but I can't just leave her down here on the couch either. I don't know if she has to work tomorrow or not, but I know missing a day of residency isn't something that's on her to-do list.

Carefully, I stand and manage to slide my arms beneath her and lift her into my arms. She snuggles into my chest, and I smile at the act. She feels good in my arms. With careful steps, I make my way upstairs to my room. I manage to place her on the bed without waking her up. I pull the comforter over her.

I second-guess letting her sleep in her scrubs, but I've heard they're comfortable, and I don't want to risk waking her up. I decide to let her stay as she is. Stripping her down would cause even more temptation, and I'm battling with needing her as it is.

Unable to resist, I bend down and place my lips against her forehead. "Sweet dreams," I whisper. This night didn't turn out as I'd hoped, but I'm not mad about it. I got to see her, something I'd been dying to do since leaving her place three days ago. Sure, my cock is still raging, begging to be inside her, but he'll have to wait until next time.

I could go to one of the guest rooms to sleep, but I don't want her to oversleep just in case she has to work tomorrow, and I have practice early. So, in the darkness, I make my way to the opposite side of the bed and crawl in beside her. Reaching over, I set my alarm. I'm pretty sure she's working noon to midnight shifts. I'll wake her before I go to see if she has to work. Otherwise, she can hang out here until I get home from practice, and we can take care of the benefits we agreed to.

Kicking off my shorts, leaving me in just my boxer briefs, I slowly slide beneath the covers and close my eyes. It's not often I sleep with a woman in my bed. In fact, it's been years, probably college, and those were drunken hookups as we passed out. I don't allow people in my home or in my bed. It's my place. My hookups are few and far between these days, but when they do happen, it's at their place or a hotel. I don't know why I invited her here. My gut tells me that Oaklyn isn't like any other woman I've met before.

Closing my eyes, I drift off to sleep to the sounds of her even breaths.

I don't know how long I've been asleep when I'm startled awake. My eyes pop open, and I take a minute to get my bearings. That's when I remember Oaklyn is in my bed. Not just in my bed but snuggled up against me. She's got one arm and her head resting on my chest while her leg is thrown over my waist. My hard cock is pressing against her knee.

That must be what woke me up.

Even in my sleep, this woman does things to me. Makes me want her with the burning passion of a thousand suns. She's sleeping soundly, but I'm wide awake. Turning to glance at the clock, I see it's just after five. My alarm is set for six thirty. I still have a good hour-plus sleep I can get, but I know there is no going back to sleep with the sexy Oaklyn draped over me.

I'm debating how to handle this. Should I slip out of bed? Will that wake her? She needs her sleep, but if I continue to lie here with her draped over me, I'm going to be hurting.

Who am I kidding? My cock is already so hard it aches. I need to slide out of bed slowly. Just as I start to move, so does her hand. I freeze, waiting to see what happens next. I'm not even sure I'm breathing when her hand travels over my abs and finds its way to my cock.

She moans, and my cock twitches beneath her palm. One hand is gripping the sheets while the other rests on her hip. I should push her away or wake her up, but I do neither.

"Nate," she murmurs, and I squeeze my eyes shut.

"Oaklyn." My voice cracks. "Babe, are you awake?" It's a dumb fucking question. I know she's sleeping, but my brain isn't exactly firing on all cylinders at the moment. Her grip tightens, and she squirms, trying to get closer. I'm not sure, but she's practically lying on top of me now as her hand strokes my cock through my boxer briefs.

Son of a bitch.

"Oaklyn." My hand that was once gripping her hip begins to trace up and down her back as I try to wake her up. She needs sleep, but fuck me, I need her. I move her hair out of her face and peer down at her. The room is dark, but the moonlight shows her angelic features.

"Oh, Nate," she moans as she rocks her hips.

"Fuck," I mutter, and her eyes pop open. Slowly she lifts her head, and there is just enough light to make out her surprised expression. "Hey, beautiful." My voice is husky. I've been with my fair share of women. I've had thousands throw themselves at me, and Oaklyn, at this moment, blows them all out of the water. She takes my breath away, and it has nothing to do with the fact that she's still gripping my cock.

"Did I wake you?" she asks as she continues to stroke.

"Something did," I tell her, bending to place a kiss on the top of her head.

"Did you wake up like this?" she asks, her hand taking another leisurely stroke of my cock.

"Did I wake up hard or with your hand on my dick?"

"Both."

"Both," I agree.

"Hmm," she purrs. Yes, it sounds like she's fucking purring as she strokes me. "How much time do we have?"

"I have to be out of the house by seven."

"I'm off today."

"I wasn't sure. I was going to wake you before I left, just in case."

"So we have time?"

"We have time." Fuck me. I'll make the time. I'll pay the damn fine for being late to practice. Nothing and no one is pulling me out of this bed until I've felt her come on my cock.

"Condom?"

"Nightstand. My side."

She climbs over top of me, settling her pussy just over my waist, and reaches into the nightstand. She grabs a condom and tosses it on the bed. Before I can suggest that she undress, she lifts her scrub top over her head and throws it behind her.

She's wearing a sports bra, and although it's not lace and silk, she still looks hot as fuck. Maybe it's because I know what's waiting for me underneath. "Not sexy, I know," she says, pulling the bra off and letting it fall to the bed.

"You're sexy, Oaklyn. Every fucking inch of you."

"You're good for my ego." I can hear the smile in her voice. She moves to the side and lies on her back until she's wiggled out of her scrub pants and panties. "Take care of these for me, will you?" As she says the words, she reaches over and slides her index finger beneath the waistband of my boxer briefs. "They're kind of in my way."

I open my mouth to tell her to do it herself but think better of it. I'd love nothing more than for her to strip me down, but right now, I just need to be inside her, and I'm not going to do or say a single fucking thing that will delay that from happening.

Once my underwear is gone, I reach for her. She moves toward me, and I expect her to straddle my hips. However, the beauty surprises me when she moves to lie between my legs. I automatically open them, welcoming her in. I know exactly where this is heading.

I'm. Here. For. It.

I grab the pillow that she was using, the one that smells like her, and prop it behind my head on top of my own. I don't want to miss a single second of this. I'm tempted to turn on the lamp, but the sun is starting to rise, and there's a soft glow of the morning as it greets us through the bedroom windows.

She wraps both of her hands around my cock and takes me into her mouth. There is no teasing. Just her hot wet mouth, taking me down her throat. Her hair falls over her face, and I can't have that. I need to see her. So I gather it in one hand and hold it back. I keep my grip light, not wanting to hurt her.

When she removes one hand from my cock, and grabs my other, placing it on her head and pushing down, I almost lose it. "Baby," I grit. "I'm about to come down your throat." My words are husky and raw.

She hums her approval of my words and gets back to work. Her head bobs with my assistance, and my balls tighten. I'm close. So fucking close, but this isn't how I want this to happen. I've been dreaming about her pussy milking my cock for days. Four, to be exact. I need that.

"Oak—" I start, but she takes me deep, to the back of her throat, and I suddenly lose my ability to speak.

When she comes up for air, I release her hair, slide my hands beneath her arms and pull her up to me. My mouth crashes with hers as my hand grips her ass, one long digit sliding inside her.

She's wet.

Hot.

Dripping for me.

"Condom," I say the words against her lips.

"I wasn't done," she murmurs back, her tongue swiping across my bottom lip.

"That's not how I want to come." I add another finger, and she bites down on my lip.

"H-How?"

"I want your pussy to milk my cock."

"If you insist."

Before I know what's happening, she's sitting up and moving back. She once again has my cock gripped in her fist, only this time, she's hovering over me as she guides my cock inside her. She sinks down, just the tip, and I feel as if my fucking head is going to explode.

"Oak-lyn," I breathe. "Condom, baby."

"Just once, Nate. Please. I just need to feel it once. Then we'll suit you up."

It's a bad idea. I know it is. I already feel like I'm addicted to her, and just the tip of my bare cock is inside her, and I'm already feeling feral when it comes to this woman. Oaklyn is quickly becoming an addiction I never saw coming. Then again, I guess that's how most addictions start. Something good that makes you see stars barrels into your life, and you chase the high.

Oaklyn is my high.

"It's risky." It's not a no from me, but it's not a yes either. She feels so fucking good, I don't want to say no, but I feel as though I need to try to at least be the voice of reason.

"Just once." She's still hovering as my cock rests barely inside her. At this point, it's been longer than it would have been had she just sunk down on me and pulled off.

"One I'm willing to take," I tell her. That's all she needs to hear as she sinks all the way down.

"Oh, God. I—" She rocks her hips. "I never knew it could feel like this." She's lifting up, and my cock falls free from heaven far too soon, but I know it's how it must be. "I'm on the pill," she says as she reaches for the condom.

It's on the tip of my tongue to tell her that's all we need, but the words never release. That's not the responsible thing to do. We agreed that we were going to hook up. This isn't a relationship, not really. We're two people seeking release, and the risk we took, yeah, we can't do that again.

My hands roam over her thighs as she sheaths me with the condom and sinks back where she needs to be. She moans and rocks her hips just as she did before, but she's ruined me. I know what it feels like without anything between us. Oaklyn gave me a little slice of heaven, and now I'll never be the same.

Never. Be. The. Same.

"Nate."

My name on her lips has me sitting up. I need to be closer to her. Why can't I get close enough? Wrapping my arms around her, I hold her naked body against my own. Her skin is so fucking soft, almost as soft as her wet pussy was around my bare cock.

Almost.

Oaklyn moans as she begins to bounce on my dick. My hands find her hips, and I assist her as we chase our release. Her hands dig into the back of my head, her nails scraping my scalp, but I welcome the pain. I need something to distract me. I can't come until she does.

That's the rule. My rule.

One that I live by, but this sexy little minx is pushing me to my limits.

"What do you need?" My voice is raspy and desperate.

"Ri-Right there," she moans. The sound is sexy as fuck, as it emits from the back of her throat.

I lift my hips as she falls on my cock, and she cries out my name. "Nate!" Her pussy quivers, and I can't hold back any longer. With a grunt, I spill inside her while she's still in the midst of her release.

We come together.

It's a thing of beauty as we settle back on the mattress. I'm still inside her as she snuggles into my chest. My arms hold her tight, and I try to remember but can't pull up a memory where sex has ever been better.

I can't.

"I need to take care of the condom," I say once our breathing is back to a regular synchronized rhythm.

"Damn condoms," she mutters, but she lifts off me and snuggles back beneath the comforter.

Dropping a kiss on her forehead, I climb out of bed and make my way to the bathroom. I clean up and grab a cloth, run it under warm water, and come back to her. I sit on the edge of the bed. "Open for me."

"I can do it." She reaches for the cloth, but I pull it just out of her reach.

"Don't deny me this." I don't know why it's so important to me, but it just is. I usually let the woman I'm with handle this on her own, in the privacy of the bathroom, but there is this primal need for Oaklyn to stay in my bed.

The sun is now higher in the sky, and I can watch her as she rolls those beautiful hazel eyes at me. I also know that I need to get moving. "I need to head to practice."

"Oh, okay, let me get dressed." She starts to get up, but I place a hand on her shoulder, stopping her.

"Stay. Rest. This is a short practice. Then I have to be back again later this afternoon to watch game tape. You sleep. I'll bring us home some lunch." It's not a lie. We have two sessions that I usually just stay for. I lift in between instead of driving home, but today, I have a reason not to.

"Really?" She seems surprised.

I'm surprised too. This is my home, my safe haven, and I don't bring women here, let alone let them stay here while I'm gone. "Yes, really." Bending, I kiss her lips. "What do you want for lunch?"

"Anything. I'm not picky."

"All right, I'll handle it. I expect you to still be in bed when I get back." How quickly she fell asleep last night comes to the forefront of my mind. She got a handful of hours at best, and I know how hard she's been working. She needs to rest.

When she smiles and settles back onto the pillows, I stand and make my way to the shower. It's a quick rinse. There is still water on my skin and water dripping from my hair when I climb into my car and head to the stadium.

I don't bother looking in the rearview mirror. I can feel the smile that spreads across my face and the relaxed set of my shoulders. A man could get used to waking up next to the sexy doctor.

chapter 6

Oaklyn

"SO WHAT'S YOUR PLAN THIS weekend?" Nate asks, his voice husky and sleepy in the early Saturday morning light, as he runs his hand up my bare back.

"I'm not sure. I don't get a lot of weekends off. I won't know what to do with myself," I state.

"I can think of a few things," he teases, the innuendo thick on his tongue. A tongue that woke me up just two short hours ago by licking my clit until I came. Somehow, even after only sleeping a couple of hours after a long twelve-hour shift, I didn't seem to mind being woken up.

For the last two weeks, we've spent countless late nights and early mornings entangled in the sheets at either my place or his. My crazy work schedule, along with his intense practice, workout, and preseason schedule doesn't always leave us a lot of time, but we've somehow managed to carve out small chunks here and there.

A couple times a week, we'll crash at each other's houses, while other times, we steal thirty minutes for mind-blowing orgasms and a few shared meals. We even managed sex in his fancy car in the hospital parking lot, despite knowing we were probably caught on camera. He insisted we weren't, that he was parked out of the way of security, but I'm not sure if I believe him, especially if it was his little head doing the thinking and not the big one on his shoulders.

But surprisingly, I wasn't too upset.

In fact, there was this extra thrill coursing through my veins. I've never been one to do anything so risky — something so naughty — especially when there's a chance of being caught, but the risk only seemed to heighten the pleasure.

Shifting so my leg is hanging out of the comforter, I return my thoughts to the conversation at hand. "I have about fifty-two loads of laundry to do, and my fridge has nothing but a bottle of ketchup and some questionable cheese in one of the bottom drawers."

He snorts. "Good thing you let me feed you most nights. I'd hate to think of you eating questionable cheese."

Flipping over, I curl onto my side against the pillow, not bothering to cover my breasts. Nate notices right away, his eyes cast down as they drink their fill. "You have a preseason game at home tomorrow afternoon, right?"

"Yeah," he replies, moving close so we're practically face-to-face. "About that," he adds before clearing his throat. "Would you like to go?"

My eyes widen and my heart lurches in my chest. "What? Why?" I ask, unable to hide the shock from my voice.

"Well, you don't know much about the game, so this would be a good one to attend. Less crowds and a slightly more laid-back experience."

My mind is spinning. "But… we're just sleeping together."

"I know, but that doesn't mean you can't go to a game. I wouldn't put you in a suite with the wives and girlfriends, Oaklyn. Nothing about you going tomorrow would raise any red flags. You'd just attend, and that's it. You can take Natalie with you. Or anyone else, really."

I nibble on my bottom lip, considering his offer. Casual friends don't go to work events, but I don't think this can be considered a true work event. Yes, this is where he does his job, but it's a football game and there would be no harm in me attending, right?

"Umm," I start, but he cuts me off.

"Think about it. I can leave tickets for you at the Will-Call counter in the morning. Game starts at three, but I suggest getting there by two. A lot of the players do stuff with the fans beforehand."

"Like what?" I ask, more curious about his job than I ever have been.

"Photos, tossing the ball around with kids, signing stuff, things like that."

"What if I want a photo with you?"

He smiles that heart-stopping grin that makes my chest feel tight and sends a flurry of tingling between my legs. "I can make that happen."

"What if I wanted you to wave at me when you score a basket?" I ask, knowing I'm getting the terminology wrong, but there's something fun and carefree about goading him just a little bit.

Nate laughs hard and shakes his head. "We score touchdowns, babe, not baskets. And if you want me to score one for you, I will."

My eyes narrow just a bit. "Cocky, aren't we?" I tease, even though I'm certain he could do exactly as he stated.

"Not cocky, confident. Watch and learn, baby. Watch and learn," he replies, his voice husky as he reaches for my hip and draws me close. "You want me to wave at you during the game? I'll come up with a special signal just for you."

"Like what?" I ask, my breath hitching as he lazily glides his thumb down my chest, right between the valley of my breasts. My nipples pebble hard, begging to be touched.

"How about this?" he asks, raising his hand and making the hand job motion.

I can't stop the giggle. "Oh my God, not that. You'll have everyone talking for sure," I state with a gentle slap to his hard forearm.

"Well, that's what I want when I think of you. It's fitting," he mutters, bringing his mouth to my neck and gliding his lips across my flesh.

"You want hand jobs?"

"I think of sex, baby. Phenomenal sex," he whispers, licking down the column of my neck and drawing a gravelly groan from my lungs.

"Come up with something else, Nate," I mumble, the pleasure taking hold as I rock my hips forward and come in contact with his muscular thigh.

"How about this?" he starts, snaking his other arm around my hip and drawing me against his body. "When I'm signaling you during the game, I'll touch my lips and hold up two fingers."

"How will you touch your lips when you're wearing a mask?"

"It's called a helmet, Oaklyn," he responds with a tsk. "And I can still touch my mouth. I use it to call plays."

"Okay, so you're going to point to your mouth through your *helmet*? Why two fingers?" I ask as he applies pressure with his leg where I need it the most. I'm certain he can tell exactly how wet I am for him.

"Because that's how many orgasms I'm going to give you with my *mouth* the first chance I get after the game."

Suddenly, we're moving. I'm flat on my back and Nate is positioning himself between my legs. His mouth hovers over my pussy, his warm breath tickling in the best possible way.

"Every time I point at my mouth and hold up two fingers, that's two orgasms for you. That's a promise to feel my mouth against this pussy, Oaklyn. That's how you'll know I'm gesturing you, wanting you, even when I'm working," he states.

My mind blanks completely as he slides his tongue across my clit and sucks it between his lips. All I can think about is the pleasure. The way he makes me feel. My body, despite being tired from working the night before, is suddenly alive once more. No one has ever done that to me. No one has ever had the ability to drive me wild with just one look. One touch. One kiss. I go from zero to sixty in half a second, ready to rip my clothes off and chase the orgasms I know he's good for. And let me tell you, Nate Vaughn is *very* good at orgasms.

So maybe I'll go to the game tomorrow with Natalie, and maybe he'll score a goal… or whatever. Maybe he'll touch his lips and hold up two fingers. No one in the entire stadium will know what it means. No one but me.

And I know he'll deliver on his promise.

Two orgasms with his mouth for every time he signals for me.

Yes, this little arrangement we have is proving to be quite beneficial.

As I close my eyes, he takes me over the edge with said mouth before sliding on a condom and giving me one more.

"I can't believe you're here," Natalie says as we find our seats in the half-filled stadium.

"Why?" I ask, pushing the bottom down and having a seat on the hard plastic.

"Uhh, well, let's see. How many innings are in a football game, Oaklyn?"

My eyes narrow at my best friend, mostly because she's about to successfully prove her point. "Four," I state, lacking any sort of confidence and turning my attention to the field.

"Ha! Yes, there are four, but they're called quarters. Innings are in baseball."

"Oh," I reply with a shrug, my eyes continuing to scan the players on the field until they finally find the one they're looking for.

Number ten.

He's sitting on the ground and chatting with a small group of players while they stretch their legs. I've never been into the whole jock scene, but I can see why women lose their ever-loving minds. He's wearing blue football pants, a tight, white undershirt, and his hair is already damp and unruly. He's not even doing anything, but I'm getting wet as I watch him and practically panting like a dog in heat.

"Damn, no wonder you're spending all of your free time naked. That man is pure sex," Natalie mumbles softly so no one around us overhears. "I bet the orgasms are epic," she adds, shoving popcorn in her mouth.

"Totally epic," I murmur in confirmation, keeping my eyes focused on the field. "And you promised not to say anything," I add. The truth is, I've shared a lot about the unique relationship Nate and I have with her, even though I refrain from getting into the dirty details. Not that she hasn't been jonesing for the juicy parts; I just prefer to keep those private.

"Your secret is safe with me, Oak. You know I'd never tell a soul. Oh my God, he's looking up here," she whisper-yells.

She doesn't need to tell me, because I'm aware. My eyes have been glued to him for the last thirty seconds, following his every move. Nate is scanning the stands where we're sitting, and I swear I feel my core clench the moment his eyes meet mine. His mouth curls upward, but he doesn't do the little signal he mentioned yesterday morning, and I can't help but feel a little saddened.

I was really hoping for a two-pack of orgasms courtesy of his mouth after today's game.

Nate walks over to the sideline with his teammates and grabs a ball. I lean back in my seat, keeping one eye on him, and steal a handful of Nat's popcorn. "I may not understand what they're doing, but I can appreciate the view," I quietly tell my friend.

"No shit. There's candy as far as the eye can see. Maybe I need to see if Nate has a teammate looking for a little no-strings sex like you two."

"Shh," I hiss, glancing around to see how close others are to where we sit. Fortunately, the nearest group of guys is a few rows back and to the right, and they're not paying us any attention.

"He's coming this way!"

I look out to the field and see him approaching the stands. Of course, he's considerably lower than the first row, but he's still far enough out I can see him point over to my right. I look over and see a young boy, probably ten or twelve years old, running down the stairs to the edge of the stands. Nate stops about ten yards out and tosses the football to the boy. He catches it before throwing it back. They continue to throw the ball back and forth for several minutes, while who I assume are Dad and Mom takes pictures off to the side.

Nate gives the kid his attention the entire time, complimenting him on his arm and giving him a few pointers for the perfect spiral. My heart seems to turn all mushy as I watch their exchange. When someone hollers for Nate, he grabs something off the bench behind him and runs toward where the kid stands.

"He's signing that football for the boy," Natalie deduces as he tosses the ball back up to the kid one final time. The young fan waves ferociously and cradles the ball to his chest before following his parents back up the steps to their seats. "That was the sweetest."

I nod in agreement, finally returning my gaze to the field. The players have gathered around a group of men, assuming the coaches, and are listening intently. The clock on the big screen is counting down, only three and a half minutes before the start of the game. My blood starts pumping as excitement courses through my veins, and I find my left leg bouncing in anticipation.

Finally, the clock strikes zero and we're instructed to stand for the playing of the national anthem. Then, it's time for kickoff. Well, at least that's what Natalie says. Players run onto the field, but my eyes search the sideline for the number ten jersey. I find it over by a coach and the number seven, and all three are looking at a binder as the whistle blows and the ball is kicked high into the air.

"Nate's up first," Natalie announces over the cheering crowd.

"Huh?"

My best friend rolls her eyes. "We received the ball during the kickoff, so our quarterback — *Nate* — will have four chances to advance the ball ten yards."

So many questions swirl around in my brain. "They only have to go ten yards?"

Nat just stares at me, her mouth slightly agape. "Jesus, you're hopeless. I'm getting you a *Football for Dummies* book."

"Whatever," I mutter, watching Nate take the field. He's sliding his helmet on his head, and my mind automatically goes to his mouth, and I'm wondering if he can touch his mouth as easily as he said he could.

The players line up, and Nate yells something that causes them all to move. The entire thing is fascinating to watch. He throws the ball through the air and straight into the hands of another player on his team. The crowd goes wild, and I jump up and cheer right along with them. Unfortunately, he's knocked down hard before he can make it too much farther.

"That's a thirty-yard completed pass from quarterback, Nate Vaughn, straight into the hands of receiver, Isaiah Jones. First down, Storm!"

"Beautiful pass," Natalie cheers, extending her arms above her head as she claps.

I watch, completely mesmerized, as he throws two more times and then hands the ball off to a player behind him. We're very close to the end zone — at least, that's what the guy over the intercom system called it — and I'm practically holding my breath as they line up once more.

"He's going to run it in."

I glance to my friend for a moment before looking back at Nate. "You think?"

"Definitely. A preseason game is the perfect time to work on these kinds of plays, and Nate was the leader of quarterback sneaks for touchdowns last season. He'll want to practice once or twice before they take him out."

"Take him out?" I ask, unsure why they'd do that. He's the starting quarterback, so why would they take him out of the game?

As if reading my thoughts, Nat says, "They'll let him play the first half, but then put the backup QBs in for the second half. They don't want to risk Nate getting hurt before the season officially starts."

The whistle blows and they line up once more. I cover my mouth with my hands as I await to see what he does. When the ball is hiked, he curls the ball into his stomach and runs straight forward. The big guys in front of him seem to move the opposing players out of the way, creating the perfect hole for Nate to slip through.

"*Touchdown!*"

The stands erupt into cheers, and I'm right there with them. I'm yelling, clapping, and jumping up and down, all while my eyes are glued to the man who just scored the first touchdown of the game.

That's when I see it.

He slips his fingers into his helmet, touches his lips, and then raises two fingers high in the air, all while his teammates celebrate around him. My cheeks burn and my core clenches with need as I look up and catch the replay on the big screen. Yep, there it is. I can see his actions much better now that the camera is zoomed in on him. He slips his hand through the guard on his helmet, touches his mouth, and then holds those two fingers above his head.

For me.

"I wonder what that means. I've never heard of him doing that!" Natalie hollers at me over the noise.

Shrugging, I choose to keep that piece of information to myself. Not because I don't want to share with her, but because it feels like something that's ours. Just him and me. And that's an incredibly exciting prospect.

For the next hour, I watch him play. It's like nothing I've ever witnessed. The only sporting events I went to were a couple of boys basketball games in high school, and only because I had a friend who played in the pep band. Other than that, I preferred books to balls and spent all of my time reading or studying.

Now, I'm starting to see the appeal.

Of course, it could be the man. There's been something incredibly appealing about him since we first met in that dive bar at the edge of town, and it's not just the orgasms he administers. I enjoy chatting with him too. Late at night, while I'm eating dinner, we sit and talk about anything and everything. I'm quickly learning that Nate Vaughn isn't just a pretty face who can throw a football. He's smart, funny, charming, and loyal to his family, teammates, fans, and the city.

He's the whole package.

And he's all mine.

At least for tonight.

NATE

I'M JOLTED AWAKE WHEN THE bus comes to a stop. We had a one o'clock game today in Indianapolis. The game was brutal, but we still came out on top. As soon as I settled into my seat and the bus started rolling down the highway, I put on my noise-canceling headphones and crashed.

Digging my phone out of the pocket of my sweats, I turn off the playlist I was listening to and see that I have a message. I grin when I see who it's from.

Oaklyn: You kicked ass out there today, Vaughn. Way to make the home team proud.

She follows it up with a heart emoji. I stare at the red heart for far too long while my teammates shuffle past me, exiting the bus. In the past, something as simple as a red heart from a woman would annoy the hell out of me, and I'd cut her loose. With Oaklyn, I'm just not ready to do that.

I'm enjoying this arrangement that we have. It's the first week of October, and we've been casually sleeping together since August. I'm not sick of her yet. Not even close. Oaklyn is cool as hell to be around, sexy as fuck, and she gives just as much as she takes in the bedroom. Or the front seat of my car. She's adventurous, and best of all, she's not clingy.

She has a hectic work schedule and understands the demands of my career, even if she doesn't understand my career. A smile tilts my lips when I think about the lazy Saturday afternoon we had a few weeks ago. It was pouring down rain in Nashville, and Oaklyn wanted me to teach her more about the game. We ended up naked on my living room floor. That is an afternoon I won't soon forget.

Glancing at the time, I see it's almost eleven. I know she starts a new rotation in Pediatrics tomorrow, so I don't want to risk texting and waking her up. I hate that I missed her message. There is a heaviness in my chest when I think about her sitting on her couch, waiting for a reply that never came.

We're just hooking up.

Exclusively.

It shouldn't bother me.

Yet, the heaviness is real. Standing, I stretch, shove the headphones in my bag and my phone back into my pocket, and make my way off the bus. Most of my teammates are already in their cars and driving off. I wave to a few as I reach my own. My bag is tossed into the trunk before unlocking the door and sliding behind the wheel.

I don't know exactly how it happens, but ten minutes later, I'm scanning my guest card and pulling into the parking lot of Oaklyn's apartment building. I park next to her Honda and kill the engine. I stare up at where I know her window is, but there are no lights on.

I should stay in the car. I should drive away, but I know what awaits me up there. The temptation is so strong. I can practically feel her soft skin beneath my fingertips. I can smell the subtle hint of lavender and vanilla, the scent combination that I will only ever associate with her.

I can imagine curling up in bed, with Oaklyn wrapped in my arms, and falling into a deep, restful sleep. Something I need after days of travel and a brutal game today. Before I can talk myself out of it, I climb out of the car, lock the door, and make my way inside her building. I take the elevator up to her floor and quietly rap my knuckles against the door.

I tell myself that if the soft sound doesn't wake her up, I'll go home. I'll go back to my car and back to my place, where I should be anyway. I shouldn't be here knocking on her door at this hour. I know that, but I knock again, just as soft as the first time. Lifting my arms, I brace my hands above her door and bow my head and wait. The knock is soft, and I know she's not going to hear it if she's asleep, yet I still stand here.

I'm just about ready to force myself to turn around and go back to my car when the door opens. A fresh-faced, sleepy-eyed Oaklyn frowns when she sees me. "Nate? Are you okay? What's wrong?"

I'm silent as I take her in. She's in a tiny pair of sleep shorts and a tank top. Her hair is a messy bunch on top of her head, and I don't know if there has ever been a moment when she's looked more beautiful to me.

My chest tightens again. Dropping my hands, I rub at the ache to try to get it to subside. "Hey, Oak." My voice is gritty.

She steps forward and rests her hand against my cheek. "Are you all right?"

"I got your text."

She tilts her head to the side. "So you drove over here to reply?"

"I didn't see it. Not until the bus pulled back in at the stadium, and I felt bad for not replying, and I was driving home but ended up here."

"You ended up here," she repeats.

I shrug, because that's the only answer I have to give. I didn't intend to come here, but this is where I ended up. I tried to stay in my car, but here we are. I can't explain why. Deep down, I don't really think she needs me to.

"Do you want to come in?"

"Yes." I don't bother denying myself entrance into her world.

"Are you hungry? Can I get you anything?"

I shake my head. "Did I wake you?"

"No. I was just lying in bed, trying to fall asleep."

Lifting my hand, I tuck some wayward hairs behind her ear. "You have to be up early?"

"Yeah, I have to be at the hospital by seven."

Reaching behind me, I lock the door and hold my hand out to her, and she doesn't hesitate to slide her palm against mine. With my other hand, I flip off the light, bathing the room in darkness. "Let's go to bed."

She doesn't argue. Instead, she leads us down the hall to her room. I don't release her hand until we're standing next to the bed. Kicking off my shoes, I strip down to my boxer briefs and reach for the blanket. "After you." My voice is soft, partly from exhaustion, and the other part, that's all for her. For Oaklyn. There is just something about this woman that brings that side of me to the surface. The soft, caring side that I've never really wanted to show anyone but those closest to me. It's too late, and I'm too tired to try and examine if Oaklyn makes that short list. Besides, actions speak for themselves, and I can't seem to help myself where she's concerned.

She crawls into bed, and I move in after her. She starts to scoot to the other side, but I'm not having any of that. I want her close.

Something else I refuse to examine. While we're making a list, I should also point out that I've never slept better than the nights she's in my arms.

She snuggles into my chest, and I wrap my arms around her. "Night, beautiful," I whisper, placing a soft kiss against her temple.

"Night, quarterback."

I'm not sure if it's her calling me quarterback or the fact that the woman is warm in my arms, but I don't need a mirror to know that I'm smiling as I drift off to sleep.

I wake up alone in her bed, which smells like her. Looking over at the nightstand, I see it's a little after ten. Damn, I was exhausted. Thankfully, we're off today. Usually, when we travel on Sunday, we get Mondays off. I had planned to get up when Oaklyn did and hit the gym, but that obviously didn't work out.

Tossing off the covers, I search the floor for my sweats and find them folded along with my shirt and my phone sitting on top of the dresser. Grabbing my cell, I smile when I see I have a message from her.

> **Oaklyn:** You were out for the count, QB. I didn't want to wake you. Make yourself at home or whatever. I'll be here until seven tonight.
>
> **Me:** Just woke up. Sorry, I missed seeing you this morning. Dinner tonight?

I toss my phone back onto the pile of clothes and make my way to the bathroom to handle business. I find a spare toothbrush in the bottom drawer. Not the first time I've had to be in that particular drawer. This time when I'm done, I place the blue piece of plastic into the holder on the sink next to hers. Seems like a waste to keep tossing them each time.

I need to shower and shave, but first, I need to see if Oaklyn got back to me.

Oaklyn: My place or yours?

I think about that for a minute. I'm off today, and she's working. I'm sure she'd much rather come home and relax.

Me: Yours. I'll take care of dinner. You just bring your sexy ass home.

Oaklyn: Oh, is QB on the menu tonight?

Me: Is that what you want?

Oaklyn: Is that even a real question? That's what we do, right?

Me: I'll handle dinner, and we can be each other's dessert.

Oaklyn: Deal.

Me: Having a good day?

Oaklyn: It's looking better.

Her reply is followed up with a winking emoji and a football emoji. It makes me laugh. I'm glad none of my buddies are here to witness my reaction to just texting with her. I don't know how I got lucky enough to find someone as chill, as sexy, and as good in bed as Oaklyn, but damn, I'm thankful that I did. She was exactly what I needed.

Grabbing my clothes from the dresser, I quickly get dressed and make my way out of the bedroom. I search through the kitchen drawers and find a spare key. Luckily, the keychain is one of those that you can write on, and it literally says, *Spare apartment key*. This helps my plan. I didn't want to have to go to the hospital and get a key from Oaklyn. She would ask questions, and I want to surprise her with dinner.

Locking up, I head to my car and speed off to my place to shower and set my plans in motion.

I didn't make it back to Oaklyn's apartment until almost three this afternoon. I had a few things to handle at my place, and then I went to the store. I try to eat semi-healthy during the season, and I noticed that Oaklyn didn't have any kind of grill on her small patio. Grilled chicken salad is what I have planned for us for dinner, and I stopped at a local bakery and grabbed two large slices of chocolate cake.

Anyway, I knew that she didn't have a grill, so I went shopping. I ended up finding an indoor grill that's also an air fryer and a bunch of other things. Once that was secured in my cart, I made my way to grab the chicken and everything we'd need for a salad. I added a loaf of fresh bread and some of those yogurts I see in Oaklyn's fridge a lot. I don't know if she needs them, but I was pushing the cart past the yogurt case, and they stuck out to me.

On my way to the checkout, I grabbed her some fresh flowers and called it good. Now, here I am, it's six thirty, and I have everything put away. The salad is put together, minus the dressing. The new indoor grill air fryer contraption has been cleaned and is set up on her small kitchen island. I even did her a solid and tossed in a couple of loads of laundry. She's lucky her unit has a washer and dryer. I remember in college, my roommates and I either had to lug our dirty shit home or to the laundromat. Our apartment had its own in the basement, but it was dingy as hell and always smelled like wet socks after a long summer practice.

The dryer buzzes, and I check the clock. Six forty. I need to get the chicken on. I take care of that before going to the small closet that houses her washer and dryer and swap her laundry. I feel bad that I woke her up last night, and I know that she works just as many crazy insane hours as I do. She even picks up extra shifts. I need to add dedicated and hard-working to her long list of accolades I've been keeping.

Laundry swapped, and her scrubs hung up, I check on the chicken. It's grilling up nicely. There's nothing else really for me to do. I couldn't find a vase, so I have the flowers in a large cup I found in the cabinet. I make a mental note to send her flowers, ensuring they have a nice vase that she can use in the future.

Has no man ever sent her flowers before? I'm stunned if that's the case, and then there is a bigger part of me that's glad that I get to be the first. Pulling my phone out of my pocket, I set a reminder to send her flowers at her work tomorrow. I know they will put a smile on her face.

My phone pings with a message before I can shove it back into my pocket.

> **Oaklyn:** Getting out on time. YAY! I should be home right around seven.
>
> **Me:** I'll be there.

I should probably tell her that I hijacked her place, but I really do want it to be a surprise. I've never wanted to do anything like this before. I've never wanted to take the initiative. Oaklyn sparks that inside me.

I wait a few more minutes before pulling the salad out of the fridge and the three different dressings I bought. I wasn't sure what she liked, and yeah, that bothered me, but I'll find out for sure this evening.

I'm dicing up the chicken on the cutting board I found above the fridge when she walks in.

"Hey, you." I stop what I'm doing and lean over. She knows exactly what I'm waiting for as she walks toward me and pecks my lips with a kiss.

"What are you doing?"

"Making our dinner."

"Where did that come from?" She points to the grill.

"I noticed you didn't have one, and since it's getting cooler, I thought this indoor version would be better."

She nods and lets her eyes roam over everything I have spread out on the island. "There's wine in the fridge, but I know you have to work tomorrow, so I made lemonade too. I found the mix in the cupboard when I was looking for the cutting board."

"Nate." She pauses, so I turn to give her my full attention. "You did all this?"

"Yeah. Oh, and there is a load of laundry in the dryer, and your scrubs are all hung up in your closet. I assumed that's where you wanted them." I look down at what she's wearing. "You're not wearing scrubs today."

"No. Only on days that I know I'll be getting hands-on patient care, like labor and delivery and the ER. This week started my pediatric rotation."

"Got it. Well, they're clean when you need them."

"I—I'm not sure what to say."

"I had the day off. I felt bad for waking you up, and I knew I would be monopolizing all of your time tonight. It's not a big deal. It's selfish, really. I get more time with you, and the faster we eat, the sooner we can move on to dessert." I waggle my eyebrows, and she cracks up laughing.

She points her index finger at me. "I hope that's not your best move, QB."

"You know it's not." I wink, and she shakes her head, all while a smile tugs at her lips. "Grab a seat. I didn't know what kind of dressing you liked, so I bought a few options."

"Ranch is my favorite."

I nod. "Good to know."

"What are these?"

"Flowers. But I couldn't find a vase."

"You bought me flowers?"

Something like awe spills over in her voice. "I'm setting the mood." I keep my reply light and casual. That's what we are. I know I let myself get out of control today for a benefits-only relationship, but Oaklyn is a good person. She works hard, and I wanted to do something nice for her. I can afford to do nice things for her, and a little bit of my time is nothing. There are days when I wish I could give her all of it.

I shut that thought down, pushing it into the back of my mind as I place her chicken salad in front of her. Moving back to the counter, I grab the loaf of fresh bread and the butter I set out earlier, and we're ready to eat.

We're both quiet as we dig into our food. Several minutes have passed when Oaklyn wipes her mouth and gives me her full attention. "You know I'm a sure thing, right? You didn't have to do all of this."

"Can't a man just do something nice for… his friend?" I stumble over the question.

She studies me for far too long. I can feel my hands start to sweat, and I hate that she gets to me like this.

"Yeah, Nate. We're most definitely friends."

Her answer is good enough for me. The rest of the night is filled with lots of conversation, and we forgo the chocolate cake when I take her to her room a couple of hours later and show her just how delicious a shared dessert between us can be.

Decadent.

Sexy.

Sweet.

chapter 8

Oaklyn

"WE SHOULD HAVE GONE TO Dallas. It looks significantly warmer there than here," Natalie mumbles as I take a seat on my couch. "Plus, we'd get to see the game in person."

I shrug and don't reply. The last thing I want to confess is how much I really wanted to fly to Dallas for today's game. Not only is that city on my bucket list of places to see before I die, but I would have loved to be there to support Nate.

He's having trouble with a teammate. He won't give me many details, but I caught the concern in his eyes when he casually mentioned him. The guy is on the line, and from what I've gathered, he's running his mouth behind Nate's and the coaches' backs. When I asked Nate, he told me not to worry, said it's just part of the game. Sometimes teammates don't particularly like each other — there's a lot of big egos involved — but they always come together when needed on the field.

"People are wearing shorts and T-shirts there. I'm jealous," she adds, popping a handful of popcorn in her mouth as we await kickoff.

The weather has been decent here, considering it's early November, but we're no longer in the shorts and T-shirts phase of the calendar. Nashville has turned cooler with its chilly nights and falling leaves. If only I wasn't working crazy hours and could stop and enjoy it every now and again. Hoodie season is one of my favorite times of the year, but I have yet to be able to enjoy it.

Maybe I'll say something to Nate when he returns from Dallas. I know he loves to be outside, sitting around his firepit and hanging with his friends and teammates. He's done it a few times in the last two weeks, but every night I was working. Plus, there's the fact we're not exactly public with our, well, whatever we are, so it's not likely he'd invite me over to hang with his friends. Even though we're having a great time and I've really begun to care a lot for him, we've maintained our friends-with-benefits relationship. When I need to get off, which as it turns out is quite often when he's the one doling out the *O*'s, I call him.

I try not to dwell on the fact those nights usually include spending the night. I have a small drawer in his master bathroom, and he has one here. There are a few pieces of my clothing in his closet, and he has no problem leaving a couple of items here either. Of course, on the nights we're not together, I may or may not sleep in one of the T-shirts he's left. It smells like his detergent and faintly like the man who usually wears it, and I've discovered I sleep better when I'm wrapped in his clothes.

Maybe I need to request he leave a hoodie…

It would be way too big on me, much like the T-shirts, but I don't care. There's nothing better than an oversized hoodie on a cold winter night, especially one that smells like Nate Vaughn.

"Look at her," Natalie says, pulling my attention back to the TV.

There, in the middle of the screen, is a woman with incredibly large boobs and wearing a tight tank top with Nate's number on the front. Her blonde hair is perfectly styled, her makeup precisely applied, and she's holding a sign that reads *Marry Me, Nate!*

"So gross," Natalie adds, taking a drink from her glass of wine. "How desperate are these cleat chasers?"

"Pretty desperate," I mutter, thinking back to some of the stories I've heard over the last couple of months.

"How many baby daddy accusations has he had?" she asks.

"Four," I reply, recalling the latest one. About three weeks ago, a woman from Detroit went public, stating Nate was the father of her child. According to her, they spent the night together, meeting at the hotel bar before a game last season. There were even photographs of their time together—images I couldn't unsee, thanks to the fact they were published and shared everywhere. Fortunately, they were proven to be photoshopped, thanks to investigative work by Nate's PR team, but the rumors still flew. Women were coming out of the woodwork, talking about nights they'd spent with him, and it was all I could do not to hunt them all down and throttle each and every one of them.

One thing I learned through the ordeal is Nate seems to have a type.

Blonde, blue eyes, skinny, and with voluptuous curves and boobs.

I don't fit that mold. It's not the first time I've realized it, but it really hit home when Baby Gate was thrown in my face everywhere I looked. My hair is dark brown, and my eyes are a dirty-hazel color. While I have a few curves, mostly because my diet isn't very healthy thanks to my work schedule, my boobs aren't anywhere close to being surgically enhanced. I wear a combination of scrubs, comfortable dress clothes, and pajamas when I'm not at the hospital. Nothing about any of that screams sexy, that's for sure. Yet, Nate doesn't seem to mind. He regularly compliments me on what I'm wearing and tells me how sexy I look, despite the overwhelming exhaustion I tend to feel.

He's really good for my ego.

"Women can be stupid. I'm glad he's suing her for slander," Natalie replies, speaking of the lawsuit that recently went public toward this woman. She was looking to get a payout and will now do the paying.

"Football pants makes them do crazy things," I quip, trying to lighten the conversation.

"No kidding. Look at Johnson Bruniga out there. Those pants were made for his tight, sexy ass," she replies, referring to the running back.

"Who names their kid Johnson?" I wonder, reaching over and grabbing a handful of popcorn.

"I bet he has a big dick."

My eyes fly across the couch to my best friend, and I instantly laugh at the serious look on her face. "What?" I ask through my giggles.

"You'd have to have a big one with a name like Johnson. He was probably teased growing up, called Dick or Harry. The only way to combat the evilness is to whip out your cock and show the world your johnson," she reasons.

"You're nuts."

"Can you ask Nate for me? Maybe see if he could snap a pic in the shower or something?"

"What? Oh my God, no!" I bellow, laughing so hard I can barely breathe. "No way will he take a dick pic for you, Nat."

She tsks and nods. "You're probably right. I'm going to have to do it. There's nothing online about him, which is really odd because cleat chasers love to brag about the players they bang. Maybe he's gay?"

"I don't know, Nat. Sorry, but I do know I can't ask Nate to find out for you. That sounds like a line no player crosses in the locker room," I reason, wondering how we got so far off course in this conversation. Then, something else hits me. "Wait, what did you mean you're going to do it yourself?"

She shrugs. "It's probably best if you don't know the details, but I'm pretty certain it wouldn't be too hard for me to sneak into the locker room."

My jaw practically unhinges. "What? They have security stationed in front of it, weirdo. You can't just waltz in and take a snapshot of his dick."

She seems genuinely saddened. "Really? How am I going to see it then?"

"I don't know," I reply, kicking my feet up onto my coffee table. "Maybe you need to casually run into him somewhere and strike up a normal conversation."

She nods in understanding. "A meet-cute, like you and Nate."

I shrug, not adding any more response.

"I think he goes to that club with the team after games. The one where they're always photographed in the roped-off VIP section surrounded by half-naked women in barely there dresses. What's it called?"

"Alive."

"Yes! I couldn't remember the name of it, but they cater to the rich and famous for sure. You could score us an invite, you know. Give Nate a blowie and then ask him if we can go with him one night after a game. Take one for the team, Oaklyn, so I can try to snatch a peek at the johnson."

"You're going to give yourself an asthma attack if you don't settle down," I tease as the commercial break ends. "Kickoff is next."

"Look at you, learning the proper football terminology and stuff. I'm so proud of you. Good dick is helping you branch out a little from your normal medical jargon."

"I don't just talk about medical stuff. In fact, I try not to talk about it when I'm off work. You're the one always asking me for details on the weird cases I see."

"Like the guy who got poison ivy in his ass because his boyfriend didn't realize the tree they were leaning against was covered in the itchy vine?"

I pull a face. "I never should have told you that."

"You violated nothing. You didn't tell me who it was," she replies, pointing to the TV. "There's Nate!"

My eyes return to the screen, and I instantly smile when I see his gorgeous face. He's in the middle of the field for the coin toss, looking as sexy as ever. They're in their white uniforms, since it's an away game, and I have to admit, while I love him in the Nashville blue, he looks positively edible in the white.

"The Storm have won the coin toss and elected to defer," the broadcaster says as the captains from each team shake hands and jog back to their respective sidelines. *"Nate Vaughn, originally from Indiana, has quite the fan club in attendance for today's game."*

The television shows a handful of people in a small suite, looking on from their elevated position. When they realize the cameras are pointed at them, they all wave proudly.

"That's Nate's parents, Naomi and Brad Vaughn, his sister, Janelle, as well as his uncle James, head coach for Purdue, where Nate played in college. It's good to see them all in Dallas for today's game," the broadcaster continues before the camera cuts back to the field.

"Did you know his family was going?" Natalie asks, and even though I have no right to, I feel a little betrayed I wasn't told. Yet, I do.

Nate and I are casual.

Yes, exclusively so, but still. He doesn't have to tell me when his family is flying to his games. It's not like he'd introduce me to them or anything if I were there too. That's not the type of relationship we have, despite knowing in my heart it's been feeling like it could be more.

That's not what we agreed upon.

"No," I reply absently, watching as they prepare for kickoff.

Together, we watch the first quarter, munching on popcorn and drinking too much wine. Thank goodness she lives one floor above me, and I don't have to worry about how she's going to get home.

As the second quarter starts, I notice Nate over on the sidelines talking to a player who looks vaguely familiar. Even though you can't hear what they're saying, I notice the tension around Nate's eyes and mouth. The man talking to him is smiling, but there's not one hint of happiness coming from Nate.

I wonder what that's about.

"How's your mom and dad?" Natalie asks when she returns from the bathroom.

"Doing well. Mom is working for a golf course and Dad's helping build houses." My parents had always dreamed of relocating to Florida, so when I graduated med school, they took the leap and moved to Destin. They still talk about me coming down there when I complete my residency, but to be honest, I love Nashville and don't see myself leaving anytime soon.

"That's good. When are they coming up next?"

"Christmas. I'll have to work, and it's so hard to schedule anything longer than a day or two together, so they agreed it was just easier this way."

"Are you going to introduce them to Nate?"

That makes me pause. I glance her way, the wine making my brain a little foggy. "Why would I do that?"

"Well, you two have been seeing each other for a couple months now, right?"

"About three," I reply, feeling my stomach churn a little. I'm just not sure if it's from the wine or the conversation.

"Well, it seems like you're reaching the point where you'd meet each other's families," she suggests.

"But we're not in a relationship, Nat. We're sleeping together. That's all."

Her eyes narrow, and I can tell she doesn't believe me. "Keep telling yourself that."

"Stop. We agreed to keep it about sex."

"*Good* sex," she replies with a smirk.

I hold up my nearly empty wineglass and drink the rest of the contents. "We're just not there, Nat."

She sets her glass down on the coffee table and turns her attention to me. "Okay, but here's the question, and I want you to be completely honest with me. Do you want there to be more?"

I open my mouth to remind her of the fact my life isn't really my own when she stops me. "Don't give me the whole work-schedule thing. Yes, your hours are unpredictable, but you could fit in some time. You two manage to have dinner every few nights at either your house or his, so it would be no different to go out somewhere instead of eating at home. So I'll ask again. Do you want more?"

I'm about to tell her no, but the word doesn't come out. Instead, the completely opposite spills from my lips, finally vocalizing my deepest confession. "Yes." Swallowing hard, I continue, "I know what we've both said this *thing* is, but I really like him, Nat. A lot. I think… I could be falling in love with him," I whisper, tears filling my eyes.

She smiles back at me and reaches for my hand. "Are you going to tell him?"

I adamantly shake my head as I swipe away the wetness leaking from my eyes. "No way."

"Why not? What if he feels the same way?"

"He doesn't," I insist quickly. "He's been very clear on his stance. Besides, I'm the one who insisted I didn't want anything more."

"Yeah, but you're allowed to change your mind, Oaklyn. People do it all the time."

"Not about this," I state, reaching for the bottle of wine, only to find it empty.

"I call bullshit," my best friend announces. "You're human and humans change their minds. What started off as a fun, no-strings relationship can easily turn into something more when the parties have chemistry. You've said it yourself; you guys are combustible together. And you enjoy his company outside of the bedroom too. So what if you started dating officially?"

My mind is spinning.

What if…

Would he be willing to explore a deeper relationship with me? Not that we have to move in together and plan a wedding, but perhaps a few dates and maybe him introducing me to his friends wouldn't be so bad.

"Nate Vaughn is down, folks. He was just sacked in the backfield and isn't getting up."

My eyes move to the screen, and I watch in horror as Nate lies on the field, trying not to shift his leg. The agony is all over his movements as he reaches for his knee but refuses to touch it.

A gasp flies from my mouth as I stand up and move closer to the television. My heart is pounding in my chest, my breathing coming in fast pants as the coaches and medical team rush onto the field.

"Let's see what happened to Vaughn on that play," someone says before it goes to the replay. I want to yell at them to go back to Nate, but they've already switched back to the video.

My eyes are glued to the monitor as it shows the ball being snapped into his hands. The broadcasters are talking, but I don't listen. I watch the play, watch his body, so I can determine what sort of injury he's dealing with.

A defender on his left pushes off the player in front of him. That guy barely touches the man charging toward Nate in an attempt to take him to the ground. When the defender reaches Nate, he lowers his shoulder and tackles him low, pushing straight into his side and wrenching his knee.

Bad.

"Oh, God," I whisper, watching once more as they replay the tackle. The angle of the hit, mixed with the way Nate is standing doesn't look good. It's definitely a knee injury, and when the camera finally returns to live coverage, I can tell it's not good. Nate is in excruciating pain, lying in the middle of the field, as they attempt to move him onto a golf-cart-looking thing.

When he's finally sitting on it and the medical staff jump on beside him, they take off toward what I assume is the Storm's locker room. Just before he reaches the tunnel, he holds up his hand, signaling he's all right, and waves to the crowd. Then, just as quickly as the injury happened, he's gone, and the television is cutting to a commercial break.

"This is bad," I mutter mostly to myself.

"He's going to be okay, right? Probably just a pulled muscle or something," Natalie insists, reaching for my arm and giving it a gentle pat in support.

But I know the truth.

That was no pulled muscle.

I saw it on his face.

Nate is seriously injured.

Something tells me life as I know it is about to change.

chapter 9

NATE

"WHAT THE FUCK WAS THAT?" I stomp over to the bench where Trevor Thomas, one of my O-line guys, sits and smirks as he sips water. Motherfucker isn't even sweating.

"Tough play, Vaughn. Don't worry. The D will get the ball back."

"I'm getting murdered out there. Do your fucking job and block." I lean over, getting in his face, and he smiles. I've had enough of his shit. I've been trying to deal with it all season, and I'm done. As soon as we get back to Nashville, I'll be talking to Coach. The game tape will show that this fucker is missing his blocks on purpose.

"Come on, man," Jax says. He places his hand on my shoulder and leads me to the opposite end of the bench, handing me a bottle of water. "You know that's not going to fix things," he says once we're seated.

"I know, but fuck. I'm getting sacked every fucking play. He's slow or not moving at all." I can see Jax nod out of the corner of my eye. I keep mine trained on the field as I try to get my breathing and anger under control.

Thankfully the defense holds them off, and it's time to take the field again. I call out the play, step back, and before I know what's happening, I've got a linebacker's shoulder in my side, and we're going down. My foot was back, ready to throw the pass, which has me landing on my twisted knee.

White. Hot. Pain.

Searing pain in my knee. I've played sports since I was a toddler, and I know that this is bad. I try to sit up and reach for my knee, but the movement causes the pain to intensify, and I think better of it. Instead, I flop back on the field and let my trainers take a look and tell me what I already know.

I'm fucked.

Hot tears sting my eyes from the pain and the loss of the season. I feel like a pussy, but there are so many emotions — fear and anger to name a few — coursing through me. I don't know how to deal. I squeeze my eyes closed, breathing through the pain and the news I know I'm going to get. I know my body. This is bad.

"It's not looking good, Vaughn," the trainer says.

"I know." I grit my teeth to keep from going off on him.

"We're taking you in." There is a flurry of activity while they get me loaded on the cart. I manage to wave to the fans just before we make it into the tunnel headed toward the locker room.

"We're going to have you checked out," Mike Collins, the head trainer, tells me. He doesn't elaborate, but then again, he doesn't have to. This facility has everything they need. Collins sending me to the hospital tells me what I already know. My season is over. The pain intensifies as they load me into the back of the ambulance, and I swallow back the scream of pain stuck in my throat. I have a bad feeling. A very bad feeling.

"Mr. Vaughn, I'm Dr. Shannon. I've got your test results here."

I nod and try to sit up in bed. The nurse rushes to my side and helps me raise the back of the bed. My family is here, my parents, my sister, and my uncle James. I'm thankful they were able to make it to the game. None of us could have imagined that this was how the day would turn out.

"Let me have it." I nod to my family. "You can speak freely in front of them."

Dr. Shannon nods. "Torn ACL, MCL, and PCL in your knee. We need to do surgery. We need to do a full PCL reconstruction."

"What's my recovery time?" The words feel like sandpaper as they cross my lips. Full reconstruction isn't good for an athlete. I can guess the answer to my question, but I need to hear it all the same.

Dr. Shannon places his tablet on the edge of the bed and gives me his full attention. "You can expect to be up and in physical therapy soon after surgery. The normal level of activity is hard to determine. You can expect a decreased range of motion. We're looking at nine-to-twelve months for recovery and healing."

"And playing?" I ask. "What are my chances of getting back out on that field, Dr. Shannon?"

"We won't really know until we see how you progress. However, it's my professional opinion that you won't. At least not professionally. Injuries like this… they're difficult. You could walk with a permanent limp and have looseness in your knee or joints. We don't really know for sure. Each patient is different. I can say for certain with a complete reconstruction and the nature of your job, twelve months is more likely before being on the field again would even be an option."

I swallow hard as panic starts to rise in my chest. I feel a strong hand on my shoulder and look over to see my dad. "We'll get a second opinion," he says, his voice gruff with emotion.

"I always encourage my patients to do so." Dr. Shannon nods. "I'm sure you have a doctor back in Nashville that you can consult with. I'm happy to provide a list of recommendations as well."

"W-We have team docs."

Dr. Shannon nods. "Let's talk about the surgery." He goes on to tell me about how they are going to do the repair. "We are one of the top surgical teams in the country for these kinds of injuries. I assure you that you are in good hands." He waits for my nod. "Any questions?" He looks at me, and I shake my head.

"Great. I'll have a nurse come in and go over consent forms, and we'll get you prepped for surgery."

"When can he go home?" Mom asks.

"The surgery will take a few hours for each tear. This late in the day, we'd like to keep him overnight, and we'll get you on your way home tomorrow."

"Thanks, Doc." I lean my head back against the pillow and let the reality of my situation sink in. More than likely, I'm never going to play football again. There's a knot in my stomach and an ache in my chest. This is everything I've worked for. Hell, football is who I am. I don't remember a time in my life when I wasn't playing. Who am I without the game?

As promised, I was released from the hospital Monday morning. The team chartered a private plane to fly me home, and I've been holed up in my house ever since. My coach, the trainers, and many of my teammates have stopped by. My family left to go grab dinner, and the house is finally quiet.

I love them. I appreciate them and all that they've done for me, but I need a second to just breathe. My team doctors looked over my records and scans, and their diagnosis is the same as Dr. Shannon's.

My knee will never be the same.

Career-ending injury.

Sure, there's a small chance I could return to the game. However, the damage was significant, and the chance of re-injury is high. Not to mention other teams will know that my knee is weak. A second injury like the one I just took might leave me without the ability to walk. As much as I love the game of football, I want to be able to walk.

Speaking of walking. I've been talking to my parents, and I'm going to go home with them. The Storm has already set me up with a great team of doctors and physical therapists close to my parents' place. I could manage on my own. I could hire a driver and help with other things, but when Mom mentioned that it might be nice to get out of Nashville and away from the Storm and the press, I agreed.

My phone pings, and I know who it is without even looking. Oaklyn has been checking up on me every day, asking when she can see me. I've held her off until now.

Oaklyn: How are you doing? Need anything?

Me: Same. No, thank you.

Oaklyn: When can I come and visit?

Me: I have the house to myself for a few hours.

Oaklyn: I was off today, so that's perfect. On my way.

I want to see her, but I hate that she's seeing me like this. I hate that I can't toss her over my shoulder, carry her sexy ass upstairs, and show her and her pussy how much I've missed them.

I may never be able to do that again.

I'm aware that I'm being dramatic, but fuck me, I think after what I've been through, I'm allowed. My career is over far too soon. I knew I wasn't going to play football forever, but I thought I had a good ten years or more in me, at least. Fate has other plans. Fate or Trevor Thomas. I don't know what his deal was with me, but the fucker failed to do his job. I know that accidents happen. Football is a full-contact, dangerous sport, but he wasn't even trying. All fucking season he's been slacking, and I'm the one that has to pay the price for his negligence.

It's a good idea for me to get out of Nashville and distance myself from the team for a while. At this point, I have nothing left to lose. Well, there is one thing, but that's about to be taken care of too.

I busy myself, flipping through the channels until there is a knock on the door. "Come in," I call out. I know it's Oaklyn, and no way am I stumbling up on those fucking crutches to answer the door. That will just make me look weaker in front of her.

"Hey, you." Her eyes are soft as she gives me a kind smile.

That fucking smile of hers can brighten the darkest of days. She leans over and places a soft kiss against my lips. "I missed you. How are you feeling?" she asks as she places a bag on the coffee table.

"You know, hanging out." I keep my tone even, pretending as if I don't care.

I do care. Too much.

"I brought you some of your favorite snacks." She nods toward the bag.

"Thank you." I open my arms for a hug, and she comes willingly. Her lavender and vanilla scent wraps around me. I'll never forget the way she smells. She lifts her head, and I know what she wants. I bend, pressing my lips to hers. The taste of her explodes on my tongue. My hands dive into her hair as she moves to climb on her knees.

"Come here." I hold my arms open for her to climb on my lap.

"I don't want to hurt you."

"You won't hurt me. Come here, Oaklyn." She does as I ask and straddles my hips. Very gently, she settles on my lap. At this angle, I can kiss her like I really want to kiss her. It's more than a kiss. Our mouths are fucking. It's wild and messy, and frantic.

It hits me that this will be the last time I kiss the beauty in my arms. I have nothing to offer her, and I know Oaklyn well enough to know that she's going to want to go out of her way to take care of me. She is going to be a doctor, after all. She has enough on her plate right now. Her residency is what's important. I may have lost my dream, but she's still chasing hers. I won't be a burden to her.

Now I just need to find a way to tell her. I know that we're just a benefits situation, but for me, it's more than that. Somehow, this sexy, smart, beautiful woman in my arms has come to mean something to me. She means everything to me, and no way am I going to hold her back. If I'm being honest, Oaklyn is one of the main reasons I agreed to go stay with my parents for my rehab and therapy.

Oaklyn is one of the good ones. She's a born caretaker, and it's in her nature to put others first. That's why she's an incredible doctor. That's why I have to push her away. Besides, I've fallen for her, but that doesn't mean she's done the same with me. I broke the rules.

Slowing the kiss, I pull her into a hug, and we sit in silence for several long minutes. I run my hand slowly up and down her back. I want to soak up this moment with her.

"You're quiet." She moves to snuggle up to my side.

"I'm leaving." I blurt it out.

"What?" She sits up, her eyes wide. "Where are you going? Do you need me to take you?"

I shake my head. "No, I'm leaving Nashville." I point to my knee. "No more football for me."

"Oh, Nate. I'm so sorry." She places her hand on my cheek, and I allow myself a few seconds to relish the soft feel of her skin before moving her hand away and placing a kiss on her palm.

"It's a risk all players take."

"So, what's next?"

"I'm going home to Indiana."

"Indiana?" she repeats.

I nod. "That's where I'm from. My parents and little sister are still there. My uncle too. I'll have lots of therapy and rehab in my future. It makes sense to be with family."

She nods. "Family is important." She pauses. "For how long?"

I don't really know how long, but I know what I need to tell her so she understands we're through. I shrug. "Forever."

"Forever?" she asks, her voice barely a whisper.

I know my next words are going to cut her, but I also know they're necessary. They're also going to cut me because they're not true. "There is nothing here in Nashville for me." Lies. Big fat motherfucking lies. She's here, and if things were different, she would be more than enough to keep me here.

"Nate—" she starts but stops as tears well in her eyes. She takes a few moments to compose herself. "When do you leave?"

The tears in her eyes are like a knife to the chest. "This week. A day or so. I need to settle a few things with the team, and the rest can be done via email."

She nods. "So that means I won't see you?" Her voice cracks, and fuck me, I'm barely holding my own composure.

"Yeah," I say, brushing her hair out of her eyes. "You're finally free of me."

"Nate, I-I don't want to be free of you."

I pull her into a hug so that she can't see my face as I battle my own emotions. I thought I could do this. I thought I could be a hard-ass and send her away, but I just can't do it. I can't be a dick to the greatest woman I've ever known. Knowing her has changed me. I'll never forget the time we shared together. I'll never forget her. My heart tells me that this is wrong, to stay, but my head knows that pushing her away is the right thing to do. I can't be a burden to her, and the next year of my life is going to be hard. Lots of pain and anguish to get my body back in shape. Hell, I just want to walk again without a limp. It's going to be hard and grueling, and she doesn't need that stress or worry.

"Promise me something?" I ask her.

"Anything."

"Don't forget me." My voice cracks, and I clear my throat. "I'll never forget a single moment I spent with you, Oaklyn Schmidt."

She loses her battle with her tears as a sob racks her chest. I hold her tighter, trying to take her pain. Trying to show her that it's killing me to leave her, too, but I know it's what's best for her.

I'm a fucking mess. I'm pissed off about my injury, about Trevor not doing his job. I'm pissed off. I have to move back home with my parents. Yes, my choice, but it still pisses me off that I had to make it. I'm pissed off that this incredible woman in my arms is hurting. I'm fucking tortured I have to leave her just when I found her.

My head is all over the place, and I know the reality that football is done hasn't really set in yet. I don't need her to be around to see that. To see me break and battle the anger that I know will take a long damn time to recede.

I know our time is running out. My family will be back soon, and I don't want her to be here when they return. I can't handle them knowing what I'm leaving behind. They'll try to talk me out of it, but this is the right thing to do.

"You should go."

She pulls away from my embrace and wipes at her cheeks. "I can't just leave you here."

"My family is still in town. They ran out to get dinner. I insisted they all go to get out of the house, and they'll be back soon."

"Right." She nods slowly and stands. Her legs seem to be unsteady, so I reach out for her, only to remember that my fucking knee is jacked, and I can't. Silent tears stream down her cheeks, and I have to swallow hard past the lump in my throat.

"Thank you for all the good times." I try to smile, but I know she can tell it's forced. "I'll never forget you, Oaklyn."

She gives me a small, watery smile. "You, Nate Vaughn, are unforgettable." She leans over and presses her tear-coated lips to my cheek before turning and walking away.

I hold my breath until the front door opens and closes. I count to one hundred before yelling, "FUCK!" My hands grip my hair, and I fight the urge to shed tears of my own. It's not supposed to hurt like this. We were just having fun, but the pain in my chest tells me a different story.

The pain lays it out for me perfectly. I'm in love with the sexy doctor, and I pushed her away.

chapter 10

Oaklyn

I'M A LITTLE EARLY FOR my lunch date with Natalie, but that's okay. It beats sitting home, moping, and let's be honest: I've been doing a lot of that lately. Eight months' worth, as a matter of fact. Eight long months since Nate was injured and went home to Indiana, breaking off our arrangement and crushing my heart. As much as I tried to keep the pesky organ out of our relationship, it didn't work.

I fell for him hard and fast.

My heart broke just as quickly.

So many times I've wanted to reach out, to see how his recovery is progressing. Is he still doing therapy? How has his mobility progressed over the last eight months? Is he able to walk without ambulatory devices like a cane, or is he too much of a jock to use mobility assistance if it was needed? Something tells me he'd fight that tooth and nail.

Mostly, I wonder how he's doing. Is he lonely and sad, like me? Or is he out living his best life, despite the fact he lost the career he worked so hard for?

It's crazy to admit how often Nate Vaughn slips into my mind, like an intrusive memory. I picture him relaxing on his couch or curled up beside me in bed. I used to watch him sleep, watch the way his chest moved up and down in a slow, yet powerful way. If I wasn't pulled against him, his arm was always thrown over his head, his hair wild and so very perfect all mussed. Even in his sleep, he was beautiful.

God, I miss him.

I miss the way he cared, the way he always put my needs before his own. Despite the fact our relationship status was unconventional and sexual in nature, it was our own, and it fit our needs. Well, until those needs changed. Until he was injured and suddenly required care to help him heal.

I recall our final minutes together more than I should. There was no denying the happiness I saw in those dark eyes when I walked in. The heat pouring from his body wasn't just because the room was warm. His body responded the moment I straddled his lap. I felt his erection brush against my clit, sending tingles down my limbs and wetness to flood my core. Just being that close to him for a few moments had the same impact on me it always had, and that was before he even kissed me.

And what a kiss it was.

I replay it over and over again like the highlight reels on that popular sports channel. For months, it was all I saw, especially in the wee hours of the night, when I was begging for sleep to claim me. Except, when that finally happened, it was Nate who filled my dreams. It's a terrible place to be in, stuck between the heaven of longing to see him again and the hell of not being able to escape his memory.

I often think back on that day with a mixture of emotions. Sadness always leads the field, but other feelings are always still in the race. Sometimes it's anger that's battling for the win, while other times it's a weird sense of profound joy, because even though I hate the way it ended for us, I know I'm a better person for knowing him.

Then, I recall the look in his eyes. The one he tried to camouflage with bravado as he told me our arrangement had come to an end. There was something else there, a glint in those dark orbs that told me he was afraid. That what he was saying wasn't spoken from his heart, even though he said it. Every now and again, it's that particular look that keeps me company late at night, when the world feels gloomier and lonelier than it did the day before.

Those are the nights I almost call him.

But he's no longer here in Nashville.

My phone vibrates in my purse, and I quickly pull it out. It's probably Natalie, letting me know she's running a little late. Not that I'd be surprised or anything. She'll be late to her own funeral someday, unable to be anywhere on time. Definitely a good thing she works for herself from home, because she would have been long fired for her tardiness.

The notification isn't for a text, however. I click over to the email and watch as a few pop up on my screen. The first one I delete, since it's a sale ad for the site I get my bras and panties from, and I'm not exactly floating in reasons to wear pretty lace and satins right now. It's the second email that makes me pause, my finger hovering over the alert notification. I only have one alert set up on my email account, and that was done in the wee hours of the morning a few days after Nate left.

I know this particular email will contain something about Nate Vaughn, and even though I consistently tell myself to delete the alert, I can't seem to do it. It's the only piece of him I still have, and I gobble up the news like a starved animal. Most of the time, it's random stuff, like someone saw him going into his therapy session or he was seen at a convenience store buying Kit Kats. That one always makes me smile, and I like to assume he was thinking of me at that moment, since Kit Kats are my favorite. Other times, it's sport-related stories, speculating about the health of his knee and if he'll ever make a return to the sport he loved to play.

However, I'm not prepared for this one.

When I click on the alert, I scroll down to get to the heart of the reason his name is mentioned in the news article. The result brings a tear to my eye. Realization sets in and it's like a sharp backhand across my already aching heart.

He's selling his home.

"Oaklyn!"

I blink and look up, surprised to find my best friend sitting across from me. "What?"

She gives me an annoyed, yet worried look. "I've been sitting here for three minutes trying to get your attention. What the hell is wrong?" she asks, looking down at the device in my hand.

"Oh, sorry," I apologize sheepishly. "I was just… reading something…" My words trail off as I shut off my screen and set my phone down on the table. "How are you?" I ask eagerly to change the topic.

"Mmhmm, spill. What were you reading?" Her eyes narrow at me.

Sighing, I take a sip of my caramel iced coffee and shift in my seat. "I just read an article that says Nate put his house on the market."

"Where did you find that?" she asks, holding out her hand to see.

I open my phone once more and hand over the article. There's a link as well, taking you to the listing, but I didn't have the opportunity yet to click it.

When I hand over the phone, her eyes narrow. "This is an alert notification, Oaklyn. You set up a Google alert for him?"

"That's not the issue here. He's selling his house. That means he's not planning to come back to Nashville." There's no way to mask my sadness.

Her eyes fill with pity, and I'm not sure if it's because of the news or the fact I'm semi-tracking my former friends-with-benefits buddy eight months after he left the state. "Oaklyn," she starts, holding my gaze long enough to get her point across. "You're never going to get over him if you're stalking him like a psycho."

"I'm not stalking him," I argue, even though I sort of am. "I just wanted to know if there were any updates on his injury or career, that's all. It was innocent and not at all psychotic. It's not like I'm peeking in his windows or boiling his bunny while he's tied to the bed upstairs."

The corner of her mouth curls up. "Did you ever tie him to the bed?" she asks, leaning forward just a bit. "Wait, he seems more like the tie-er, not the tie-ee. He totally had you tied at some point, didn't he?"

"Stop it," I chastise, definitely not wanting to go down that particular road of memory lane.

"That's a yes," she replies, clicking the link to go to the house listing. "Jesus," she mutters after a few minutes of browsing. Her eyes are wide as she looks up at me. "That bathroom. Please tell me you got bent over the bench in that shower, Oaklyn."

My cheeks blush a terrible shade of red. I'd like to think it has more to do with the July temperatures, but we both know that'd be a lie.

"Shut up, you ho-bag! I'm so proud of you," she whisper-yells before handing back my phone.

"Anyway," I reply, placing the phone on the table once more and meeting her gaze. "I guess that means he's not coming back.

I guess, his family is all there, so it shouldn't surprise me, but I think a part of me was hoping."

"I know," she replies. "But maybe this is exactly what you need to help you get over him. He's selling his house here. As much as I know it hurts, Nate Vaughn isn't coming back, sweetie."

I nod numbly, mostly because the words are trapped in my throat. And if they are able to escape, tears won't be far behind, and crying is the last thing I want to do right now. "You're right."

"I'm always right," Natalie quips with a big grin.

"Are you ready to order food?" I glance up at the counter and notice it's starting to get busy.

"Yeah, I'll go order. You want your usual?" she asks, and as soon as I nod, she grabs her wallet and heads up to the counter.

The temptation is too much, and I'm flipping over my phone before she even secures her place in line. I tap on the internet browser and start scrolling through the photos of Nate's house. It's mostly empty, with the exception of a few staging pieces. This isn't the stuff he had in his home when I visited.

When I land on the master bedroom pictures, my heart does this painful lurch in my chest. The bed is completely different, but I can see it as it was last year. I can visualize the rumpled sheets and smell his soap and detergent hanging in the air. I can practically feel his touch, his lips against my skin.

Is this what it'll always be like?

Trapped in a constant state of missing someone who feels more like a figment of my imagination at this point than someone who actually existed.

Maybe Natalie's right. Maybe it's time I dated again.

Of course, that seems dumb, since the whole reason we entered our arrangement in the first place was because neither of us really had time to date. Between my regular work hours and the ones I pick up as often as possible for the added income, I have little time to sleep, let alone enjoy a relationship, which is exactly why the deal Nate and I made was so perfect. Everyone thinks doctors are rich, and while there are many who are, the ones who are just completing med school or their residency have a way to go before the real money comes in. A resident makes about the same amount as a nurse, which is why I'm pulling all the extra hours I can get. Med school is expensive as hell, and I'll be carrying those expenses with me for quite a while.

"Hello."

I look up and find a man standing beside the table. He's incredibly big, and not just his height. He's broad, built like a tank, and completely blocking my view of the counter where Natalie is. The man is holding a bag of food in one hand and what looks like an iced tea in the other.

"Hi," I reply hesitantly, glancing down to check the position of my chair to make sure it isn't in the aisle.

"This may be forward of me, but I saw you sitting here and thought you looked familiar. Do you work at the hospital? A nurse, maybe?"

The weird vibe I was getting is quickly replaced with something less unsettling. "I'm a resident."

He flashes me a blinding smile, and even though he's sporting a full beard in the middle of July, I can see his pearly whites and tell he has a nice smile. "Wow, that's cool. I thought that was you when I spotted you sitting here."

I want to ask if he was a patient or just visiting, but it seems awfully personal, and I'm not in the habit of talking about my work or personal life with a stranger. However, he seems to already know where I work. Instead of elaborating, I return his grin and wait for him to politely excuse himself.

"Can I have your name?"

I hesitate enough that he jumps right back in.

"I understand if you don't want to say. You don't know me from Adam. My name's Trevor," he says, holding out his hand.

I go ahead and extend my own, politely shaking his as I reply, "Oaklyn."

He beams what truly is a sexy smile, and I'm pretty sure he knows it too. "Nice to meet you, Oaklyn."

Before I can reply, Natalie returns and slides into her seat. She looks from me to Trevor, the mountain of a man standing beside our table, and there's no missing the smirk on her face. "Hi," she says to the man beside her. "I'm Natalie."

"Trevor," he replies, offering her a grin and handshake. "I'll leave you two lovely ladies to your lunch." Then he turns back to me and says, "Maybe I'll run into you again sometime, Oaklyn."

"Maybe," I answer, even though a part of me hopes we don't. I can tell he's interested, and if Nat hadn't returned when she did, I think he was about to ask me for my number. To be honest, I'm not sure I want that right now.

At least not yet.

"Enjoy your day," he states, throwing me a wink before heading for the door and stepping out onto the busy sidewalk.

"Holy shit, who was that? He looks familiar," Natalie says, taking a drink of her iced beverage. My guess is something coffee with extra shots of espresso.

"Some guy named Trevor is all I know."

"Hmm," she says, clearly racking her mind. "Big sexy thing. He has the whole beard thing going on. I hear beard burns are all the rage."

I choke on the sip of my own iced coffee and wipe my lips. "Jesus, Nat."

She shrugs casually. "Tight ass too. I don't think he's a musician. Maybe a boxer or something? With all those muscles, he has to be a jock."

"I'm done with sports players," I grumble, my mind automatically going back to Nate.

"You can't be done with all of them. There are so many other sports to sample. You've got the baseball players, hockey players, wrestlers or MMA fighters, and even more football players. You can't strike them all off the list just because the first one you dated broke your heart."

I swallow over the lump in my throat and avert my gaze.

"Besides, I bet Mr. Muscles Trevor could show you a good time. He looks like the perfect guy to help you get over your Nate slump."

"I'm not in a slump."

I'm totally in a slump.

"I don't need someone to get me over him. I'm working my way through it just fine," I counter, feeling my nose start to grow from the lie.

She points to my phone and gives me a look, clearly not buying the story.

"Fine, whatever. My point is, I'm not quite ready to date yet, but I'll get there, okay? Seeing him sell his house will help me get the closure I need. This proves he's not coming back, and I'll just have to deal with it."

After several long seconds, she finally reaches over and squeezes my hand. "I'm really sorry, Oak. I know it's been difficult, and I'm not trying to discount your feelings. I wish I could give you a timeline for getting over the hurt you feel, but let's be honest, I have no real experience with the whole love thing."

"What about Cody?" I ask, referring to the one guy she dated longer than a minute.

She snorts out a laugh. "Cody? I only kept him around because his cock was a solid nine-incher, and he had that cute beagle puppy. Remember?"

My wide eyes stare back at her. "Nine inches?"

She slowly nods. "Oh, yeah. And he was a Scorpio, and you know what they say about Scorpios and their high sex drive, right? Why do you think I walked funny those three months we were together?"

All I can do is shake my head in reply, and yes, think of Nate. I never measured his dick, but the man was seriously gifted in that department as well.

Natalie's name is called, and she jumps up to retrieve our food. We sit together and eat, the conversation moving from her work to my own, and before I know it, it's time to go.

"You're off to work, right?"

"Yep. I'm on until midnight," I tell her, checking my watch to make sure I'm not pushing it to be on time.

"Come up to my apartment when you wake up. I'll cook you waffles."

"I'm not going to say no to that," I respond, throwing my purse over my shoulder.

"See you in the morning," my best friend says, pulling me into a hug.

"Love you," I tell her freely, returning the gesture and holding on a little longer than normal.

She meets my gaze. "You'll get there, Oak. One day at a time, and before you know it, it'll be 'Nate Vaughn who?'"

I smile, even though I don't believe her. Something tells me, not in this world or any other, will there be a time I don't think of him. He's tattooed on my heart and embedded in my brain, and no amount of time will ever erase him.

I just need to learn to live with him always being there, even if it's just his memory.

chapter 11

NATE

IT'S BEEN EIGHT MONTHS SINCE my injury. Eight months of working through the pain to rehab my knee. Eight months of no longer knowing who I am. Eight months of missing her. Because I do. I miss her more than I ever would have thought I could. She was supposed to just be an arrangement, but she turned out to be so much more than that. I lost my career and my girl all at once, and I'm still struggling with both.

Technically she wasn't mine. However, I'd like to think that's where we were headed. That was against the rules we'd set in place. We were together for months in secret, and I got to be me. I got to be just Nate without the pressure of my career. Oaklyn just wanted my dick, not my money or my fame. I'd also like to think she wanted me.

No, I know she did.

I saw the look on her face when I pushed her away. It haunts me in my sleep.

Sitting back on the lounger on my parents' back deck, I close my eyes and let the morning rays of the hot July sun beat down on me. I can see her so clearly in my mind. I've thought about reaching out to her so many times, but I can't be that selfish. She has a life, and her career is just getting started. Hell, she's still training. I just don't see how we could make it work.

I'm doing well here. Still living with my parents, but my family has been essential in my recovery. They've put up with my mood swings, my pain, and everything that encompasses this journey of healing I've been on. I needed them, and they didn't hesitate to be there for me. There is a voice inside my head that tells me that Oaklyn would have done the same. I trust that voice, believe in it, believe in her, but that's a burden I could never have placed on her shoulders, especially since neither one of us was willing to admit that things were changing, that things *had* changed between us.

The back door opens and closes, which has me opening my eyes to see who's intruding on my quiet time. I smile when I see my uncle James take the lounger next to mine. "What's going on, old man?" I ask.

"Is that how you treat your elders?" he asks with a chuckle.

"Blame Dad." Uncle James and my dad are brothers, and from the stories they've told, they were hellions growing up.

He nods. "You are my brother's son."

"What's going on?" It's not unusual for him to stop by unannounced, but I'm pretty sure he's supposed to be working today.

"I was hoping I could ask you for a favor."

"Depends. Can it be done with a bum knee?"

"Nate." His tone is scolding. "You're walking great. Physical therapy is going well, I hear."

"Have you been checking up on me, Uncle J?"

"Can a man not worry about his nephew?"

Yeah, he's definitely up to something. "All right, now you're laying it on thick. What's this favor you're going on about?"

"I need you to come and talk to my guys."

Uncle James is the head coach for Purdue football. He was my coach and taught me so much about the game I love. The one that's no longer a part of my life. "Yeah, I don't know that I'm the best candidate. I can call one of the guys from the Storm and see if they can fly out?"

"I don't want someone else, Nate. I want you."

There's a twisting in my gut. I thought my time of people wanting me for anything in relation to football was over. "What do I possibly have to offer your players? How to get to the league, and then get injured and lose it all?"

"Have you lost it all? Do you not still have millions in the bank? Do you not still have endorsement deals for brands knocking down your door because they still love you? The fans still love you and look at you as inspiration for fighting back against your injury? Were you not the best quarterback in the league?"

"Past tense." My words are clipped. He knows I don't like talking about this shit.

"Stubborn," he grumbles.

"Real talk. Why me?" I refuse to be some pity case. I don't need him coming here talking about needing me when the true end game is to simply get me out of the house and back among the living. I don't want to be his charity case.

"Because, less than a year ago, you were the best quarterback in the league. These guys look up to you. It doesn't matter that you blew out your knee. You're Nate Vaughn. A visit from you, some feedback on performance will go a long way to boost morale."

"A has-been? Boosting morale? I think you're losing your touch, Uncle J." It's not that what he's saying doesn't make sense. I agree. When I was playing college ball, a visit from a player in the league would have made my entire year, but I'm no longer a player in the league. I'm officially retired from the game that consumed my life since I was five years old.

"Just humor me."

"He's right, you know." I look over to see my mom standing behind us.

"How long have you been standing there?" I ask.

"Long enough. Nate, you might not be in the league, but you've been there. You know the hard work and dedication it takes to get to that spot. You know the grind these young men are facing. In addition to that, you didn't leave the league on bad terms. You had an injury, something that every player faces. You could talk to them about the importance of taking care of your body and taking the needed time to heal from injuries." She holds up her hands. "Before you tell me that you took care of your body, I know. I'm not saying that you didn't, but you have the opportunity to make a difference in their lives. Think back to when you were in college if a player from the league in your situation were to visit. Would you feel cheated because he was no longer playing?"

"No," I begrudgingly admit.

My mom smiles and nods, liking my answer. "Humor the old man." She points at Uncle James. "Give his players something to talk about. Many of them won't make it to the league. Meeting you is their chance to meet one of the greats. You are one of the greats, Nathan Vaughn. Stop wallowing in what you've lost, and start living for what you have for each day that comes before you. Don't let life pass you by. It's terrible what happened to you, but you have the financial freedom to do anything you want. There are very few people in this world who can say that."

"Well said, Naomi." Uncle James holds up his hand for a high-five, making us all laugh.

"Fine. I'll come to one practice. One." The answering smile that my mother and uncle give me would have you thinking I gave them the antidote to cure world hunger.

"Great. I'll be out in the car." Uncle James smirks.

"What?" Panic starts to set in. Today? I thought they just meant sometime in the future.

"My team hits the field in an hour. No time like the present." He stands and walks back into the house. My mom laughs as she follows him inside.

"I've been played," I say to no one. With reluctance, I climb to my feet, something that does get a little easier each day, and head inside to go to practice with my uncle.

"Men, you looked good out there today," Uncle James says as his team is huddled around. "Does anyone have any questions or concerns?"

I hold my grin, but I love this about him. He's a no-bullshit kind of guy, and he wants any team issues to be discussed openly so they can be dealt with. Doesn't matter what it is, even if it's a decision he's made as a coach. He wants that shit aired out and forgotten before the next time their cleats hit the field.

"One question." A guy in the back raises his hand.

"Let's hear, Andrews."

"Uh, it's actually for Nate. I mean Mr. Vaughn," the guy corrects.

"What's up?" I ask him.

"The pressure of being in the league. How intense is it?"

That I was not expecting. "It's intense. The rookie season is the hardest. When you move from high school ball to college ball, there's a transition period that doubles in the league. The game is the same, but more intense, more grueling. You're up against the best players out there, and the competition is stiff."

"Any advice?" another asks.

"Keep a level head. Smile and wave to the cameras, and be good to your fans. Work hard, keep your body in top physical form, and… enjoy every fucking minute. You don't know when your last day to step out on that field will be. Some of you won't play past college, and that's okay. Do your best, have fun, enjoy your team, and savor the moments."

"Can we get your autograph?" someone shouts.

I pause. "You want my autograph? You know I'm retired, right?" My tone is teasing, but even I can hear the shock.

"You do know that you're *the* Nate Vaughn, right?" he fires back.

"Touché." I chuckle. "I'm happy to sign whatever you put in front of me." It's the truth. It's been a long time since I've been asked for my autograph. I know that has everything to do with my "don't fucking talk to me" demeanor, and the fact that I go home, go to therapy, and that's it. Outside of a quick stop at the gas station or convenience store, I've become a hermit.

I spend the next hour signing shoes, balls, T-shirts, hats, textbooks, you name it, I signed it. I enjoyed it. I feel like me for the first time in a really long time. By the smug look that Uncle James is giving me, he knows it. He's going to gloat about this for weeks, if not months.

"You made their day. Hell, their year most likely." Uncle James leads me into his office and motions for me to sit. "You're probably going to be trending or viral, or whatever it is they're calling it on social media these days."

"That's a pretty far stretch."

"The autographs were a nice touch, but I want to talk about practice."

"What about it?"

"The formations, the plays, the way you see the field. Nate, it's why you were the best. I'm not just blowing smoke up your ass because you're my nephew. You see the game, the field, with eyes unlike anyone I've ever met before. I need you on the sidelines with me."

"You feeling all right?" I ask him.

He steeples his hands and gives me a stern look. "I'm feeling great. It's you I'm concerned about. Are you having trouble hearing?"

I roll my eyes, and he laughs. "What do you mean that you need me on the sidelines with you?" My heart hammers in my chest. The possibility of being back on the field in any capacity is not something I've allowed myself to consider until today. I know that's what he's saying, but I need to hear the words one more time to let them actually sink in.

I love this game.

"I need an offensive coach. Miller's out. He gave notice of his retirement two weeks ago."

"I hadn't heard."

"It's not been announced."

"So, what? Do you want me to apply?"

"You already did." The look he gives me tells me that he's damn proud of himself.

"What?"

"Today, out there, that was your interview. You nailed it with flying colors."

"This is your choice? Do you get the final say in who gets the position? Aren't you worried that I'm your nephew and people will give you shit for it?"

"I'm not worried. You're Nate fucking Vaughn." He grins. "The choice is not entirely mine, no. However, those who need to offer their approval and place their signature on your contract were up in the booth today. They were watching. They knew I was letting you call the plays, and they want you." He turns his phone around for me to see a text message that simply says, *Sign Vaughn.*

"You're serious?" My eyes scan those two words over and over again.

"Come on, Nate, you know me better than that. I wouldn't kid about something like this. I know what this game means to you. I know what you lost, and I know what you are capable of. You can help me lead and guide this team."

Can I do that? Can I work as a coach? Sure, I know that many have mentioned that as something I could look into doing next, but to be honest, the last eight months have been spent rehabbing my knee, feeling sorry for myself, and missing Oaklyn. I know that I need to pick myself up and start to move on.

My grandma Vaughn always said that she was a firm believer that everything happens for a reason. I don't know what that reason is, but I do know that my uncle is throwing me a life preserver, and I want to grab onto it and never let go. The idea that I could still be closely involved in the game that I love, in the game that defines who I am? Getting back that identity has nervous energy roaring through my veins.

"I have rehab. I'm still going three times a week." I mentally go over my future appointments. I'll have to move a few of them, but it shouldn't be an issue.

Uncle James nods. "I know. We can try to work your appointments around the practice schedule. I'm sure they can be accommodating."

The excitement starts to build. "You'd be my boss," I remind him.

He sighs dramatically as he sits back in his chair and crosses his arms over his chest. "I know, but it's a sacrifice I'm willing to make for the sake of my team."

"Wiseass," I joke. "I feel as though I should tell you that I need to think about it."

"But?"

"But I don't need or want to do that. I know that this is an opportunity that I might never get again." I pause. "I put my house up for sale."

"You did?"

I nod. "Yeah, it should be listed today, according to the realtor."

"So, no more Nashville?"

I shake my head. "There's nothing there for me. I don't know that I could live there and be constantly reminded of what I lost."

My career.

My girl.

"So you're setting down roots here, in your hometown?"

Is that what I'm doing? Setting down roots? It took me a long ass time to realize that Nashville was no longer my home. I held on to my house for far too long. Part of me was holding onto the memories, holding onto Oaklyn, but after talking with my parents about it a few weeks ago, they're right. I'm wasting money on a house that I wasn't attached to. Not really. The only reason is because it's where I spent a good amount of my time with her, and holding onto it was foolish. My life is here, in Indiana, so yeah, I called the realtor and got the sale set in motion.

"Yeah, I guess I am."

"Well, you're going to need a job to pay your bills." He's laughing as he says it because we both know money isn't an issue for me.

"I'll do it."

He sits up in his chair. "I feel like I should record you saying that so you can't go back on your word," he teases.

"I'm in, Uncle J. Thank you for this opportunity. Thank you for being there for me and helping to push me to move forward.

I've just been going through the motions. Today was… probably the best day I've had since my injury."

He stands and offers me his hand. "Welcome to the team, Coach Vaughn."

I stand and place my hand in his, and it feels good. It feels right. This isn't where I saw my future, at least not this early in life, but I'm okay with that. I get to be involved with the game I love. Too bad I can't also get the girl.

"I'll have the front office get your contract ready and let you know when you can sign." He rattles off a schedule, and salary, which is more than I had anticipated that it would be. "I'll get you some Purdue coaching staff gear and drop it by your parents' place later this week."

"Perfect." I smile at him.

"Now, I'm starving. Your mom said she was making meatloaf for dinner. We can't be late." He grabs his keys from his desk and walks toward the door. I trail along behind him.

I'm going to be doing a lot more of that. Spending time in this office, in the locker room, on the field, and for the first time in months, I feel like me. I hope I can hold onto this feeling. I know that I'll never take a day on the sidelines for granted. If anyone understands how quickly dreams can be shattered and torn away from you, it's me.

chapter 12

Oaklyn

"Hey, Doc. Merry Christmas Eve."

"Merry Christmas Eve to you too," I reply before exiting the patient recovery room and heading for the nurses' station. "Mr. Cochran is feeling much better now that his nausea is under control," I announce to the charge nurse behind the counter.

"He's such a hoot. I was hoping he'd be able to discharge home for Christmas," the nurse, Adalyn, replies.

"Me too. Dr. Harrison says he'll move to a skilled care facility while receiving his antibiotic treatments." Plus, he won't have a knee for about six weeks and will require extensive medical care for a while. "In six weeks, they'll install his new knee, and he'll be good as new again."

Mr. Cochran came to the emergency department two days ago with extensive knee pain. At first, he thought it was your typical discomfort from the replacement surgery he had a few days prior. However, the pain continued to worsen, the surgical site swollen and hot to the touch. By the time he arrived to have it checked out, bacteria had spread to the implant, resulting in a joint infection.

Not what you want to have happen right before Christmas.

One minute you think you're going to be spending the holidays with your loved ones, and then next, you're battling a severe infection that requires hospitalization and surgery to remove the new knee they just installed a week prior. Then, more antibiotics to clear out the rest of the infection and hopefully reinstall a new knee again at a later date.

"You working tomorrow?" Anysa, another nurse, asks, dropping down onto one of the chairs beside Adalyn.

"I am," I tell them, finishing up my notes.

"You're working both?" Anysa asks, pity filling her dark eyes.

Shrugging, I reply, "I was scheduled for Christmas Day and volunteered for today so one of the others could take the night off to be with family. My parents live in Florida and were planning to come up for Christmas but pushed it back a few days."

They both give me a sad look. "You don't have anywhere else you could go? Friend? Boyfriend?" Anysa asks, a mischievous glint in her eyes.

"My friend Natalie will be with her family tomorrow, and while they always invite me over to their holiday celebrations, I don't mind putting in extra time here. I'd feel terrible if I was home doing absolutely nothing, when someone else is missing their kid's first Christmas or something."

"Yeah, but even you deserve a little time off. You work a ton," Adalyn says. I'm in week two of my orthopedic surgical rotation, and to be honest, I've been looking forward to this particular rotation for almost a year. Everyone knows I'm usually the first one to step up and pick up extra shifts, and that's definitely the case now. Not only is it educational, since I'm always learning and experiencing new things, but it keeps my mind busy.

Specifically, it keeps it away from a certain former pro football player, who still monopolizes way too much brain space, considering he's been gone over a year.

"I'll get two days off Tuesday and Thursday of this week," I tell them both, reaching for the next chart. "Plus, I'm off New Year's Eve and Day."

"Ohhh, big plans?" Anysa asks.

Flipping through some paperwork, I flash her a big smile as I answer, "Yeah, sleeping."

They both laugh and turn to the small television behind the desk. It's the first time I notice there's a football game on the screen. I watch a few plays, though the volume is down, and you can't hear what's being said. However, I can tell one of the teams is the Storm. I'd never forget those uniforms.

Or the way their team colors looked spread across Nate's chest and ass.

"Who's winning?" I ask casually.

"The Storm are up by seven," Adalyn replies, her eyes glued to the television.

I watch as the offense takes the field, the quarterback snapping on his helmet and kneeling in the middle of the huddle. My heart aches when I spot the number eight stepping out of the group and approach the line. It's a different player number leading the team, a painful reminder of what Nate lost last November.

"I'm going to check on the patient recovering from the ulna fracture surgery," I state, needing something to do instead of just standing here.

I take off down the hall in search for the room containing the four-year-old patient. He fell on the ice and snapped his arm yesterday. The bones shifted and displaced, resulting in a late-night surgery to repair the bone. He's handled everything post-op like a champ, and the goal is to send him home late tomorrow evening.

Knocking on the door, I poke my head inside. "How's my favorite patient?"

Damian Mitchell gives me the biggest, cheesiest grin I've ever seen. "I had ice cream!"

Chuckling, I move to the computer cart and boot it up, inputting my password to bring up his chart. "Did Nurse Anysa give it to you?" I ask, knowing everyone has a soft spot for the youngest patient we're seeing right now.

He nods, a hint of chocolate still smeared across his chin.

"How are you feeling?" I glance over his vitals from the previous round.

"'Kay. Santa comes tonight," he replies, the sadness unmistakable.

I glance at his mom, who looks incredibly exhausted, clearly having not slept much at all in the last twenty-four hours. "He does."

"But he won't know where I am!" he bellows, the excitement of his extra ice cream from earlier long gone. Now, he's a young boy who will be spending most, if not all, of his Christmas in the hospital.

"Are you kidding?" I ask, stepping around the computer cart and taking the empty seat beside his bed. "Santa knows everything. I bet he knows you're here. In fact, I bet he'll make a special trip here just to see you."

One of the hospital volunteers dresses up like Santa every year on Christmas Day and visits the patients at the hospital, especially those below the age of eighteen. I'll make sure to say something to the desk so they send the bearded man in the red coat this way when he arrives.

"He will?"

I nod. "He'll probably leave all of your presents at your house, though. That way, when you get home in a day or two, they'll be there, and you can open them with your brother and sister."

Damian beams up at me once more. "Okay!"

"Now, how's that arm feeling?"

"It hurts," he says, glancing down at his splinted arm. There's a lot of swelling on his little arm right now, so the orthopedic surgeon has it splinted and wrapped for seventy-two hours. He'll have a cast put on in the office on Wednesday.

"I bet it does, buddy, but remember, you're going to have a cool story to tell your classmates when you go back to preschool. You can tell them all about having surgery and getting to stay in the hospital for a few days," his mom says.

"Plus, they'll be able to sign your cast," I add.

"And Dara and Drake too!" he replies, referring to his sister and brother.

"Yes, Dara and Drake will be so excited to sign your cast," his mom agrees.

"Can I get you anything?" I ask his mom the moment his attention returns to the television.

"No, thank you. I'm hanging in there." Then she yawns big.

Chuckling, I say, "Hopefully we can get you home and into your own bed tomorrow night, but if not, definitely Tuesday. We have to make sure he has no reactions to the anesthesia, which I'm not seeing any signs of trouble, and that his pain is tolerable and his arm is on the right track."

"I understand. However long this takes," she states, her gaze moving to her youngest child. "I'm thankful my husband is off work and can stay home with the other two while I'm here with

Damian." She told me earlier he is a high school math teacher and off for holiday break.

"If you need anything, just push the call button."

"Thank you, Dr. Schmidt," she replies, offering a grateful smile as she moves to sit back down beside the hospital bed.

I ruffle Damian's hair before moving the computer cart out of the way and exiting the room. Light sounds of Christmas music and jingle bells filter into the hallway, making me smile. I make a mental note to send my parents a text later. I know the golf course Mom works at is hosting a Christmas Eve event, so it's unlikely she'll be available to take a call, but I want to let them know I'm thinking of them.

As I approach the nurses' station, there are a handful of nurses and assistants gathered around the television. I can't see what's going on, not that I'd really understand it anyway. All my football knowledge came within a three-month timespan while sleeping with Nate.

"Damn, that looks bad," someone says, grabbing my attention.

I worm my way into the mix and stare down at the screen. There's a Nashville player on the field, his ankle positioned at a terrible angle, clearly broken. The entire scene reminds me of the last major injury I saw happen like this, and my heart squeezes in my chest. The difference is, I'm pretty certain an ankle break is an injury you can come back from. With the proper therapy and time, a player can return to the game they love.

Major knee injuries — like what Nate endured — usually cannot.

"Do you think he's coming here?" one of the assistants asks.

"Probably. We're the closest hospital to the stadium," Adalyn replies, meeting my eyes.

"Remember when that basketball player came in a couple months back with the shattered ankle? That was gnarly," Anysa states, a bubble of anticipation evident in her voice.

"I remember how hot he was," one of the assistants, Emma, mutters, making the small group of women giggle.

"Definitely. Speaking of hot, too bad the Storm wasn't at home when Nate Vaughn tore his knee. That is one man I wouldn't mind seeing in a hospital gown," the other assistant, Maria, adds.

We all watch as they put the player on a stretcher and load him onto the cart. From there, they take off toward a tunnel, where I'm certain an ambulance is waiting. With an injury like that, it isn't necessary to go to the locker room to be checked out. Any physician or medical personnel knows that break will require surgery.

"Who's the player?" I ask, feeling bad I don't know many of Nate's former teammates, but once he stopped playing, I stopped watching.

"Jaxon Hudgins," Adalyn replies. "Tight end."

I nod, recalling the name. He was good friends with Nate. There were several times Nate would talk about their chemistry on the field. When he was in a bind, he said he could always count on Jaxon to get open and help make a play. Plus, I know they hung out together outside of work. There were several nights when I was working, and Jaxon would go to Nate's for pizza and to watch games.

For the next thirty minutes, there's a flurry of activity as we prep for the arrival of Jaxon. Dr. Harrison is the attending surgeon this evening and is waiting. He's already spoken to the head physician on staff with the Storm, and they know the break will require surgery. This won't be my first orthopedic surgery to assist on, but it is my first professional athlete.

Finally, the patient arrives and is brought straight up to the orthopedic surgical suite. The EMS wheel him into the first pre-op room and carefully transfer him to the bed we'll use to take him in for surgery.

Jaxon is... well, he's huge. His body fills the bed, despite having his shoulder pads removed prior to his arrival. His left cleat is still on, and the team doctor explains he didn't want to risk further injury by trying to remove the tight shoe. They strapped him to a board, wrapped the ankle and foot in ice, and took off for the hospital.

"We'll take care of it in the OR," Dr. Harrison assures the other physician. "Good evening, Mr. Hudgins. I'm Dr. Harrison."

"Hey, Doc," Jaxon says, his bright green eyes leveling on me. "I'll admit, I was kinda hoping she was my doc. She's much prettier," he adds, making everyone in the room chuckle.

"This is Dr. Schmidt. She's a second-year resident, and she'll be assisting me this evening. Can you tell me what happened?" he asks, turning to me and I can already read his unspoken request. I quickly pull up the notes section in the patient's chart and start typing.

"I'm sure you can catch the highlights online, Doc. I got tangled up with a defender while I was leaping to grab the ball and came down wrong on his foot," Jaxon says, wincing. I'm sure he's hurting greatly right now.

"We're going to do a few X-rays first so I can see the extent of the bone damage, but as you've probably heard already, surgery is likely needed to repair it," Dr. Harrison says.

"They told me. Whatever. Just do it right. I need to be back on the field next summer. We already killed our shot at the playoffs, so I don't have to worry about that this season."

"We'll get you fixed up and back on the field as soon as we can. You're in great hands," the doctor replies, turning to look at me. "Go ahead and complete the medical history part, and I'll order the X-rays. We'll get the portable unit up here quickly."

Nodding, I turn my attention to the man on the gurney. "Just a few questions."

"I have his medical chart," the team physician says, pulling a laptop from his bag. "Is there a place I can use to pull it up?"

"Yes, there's a small conference room at the end of this hall."

The team physician nods and excuses himself. I return my attention to the patient, who is watching me intently. "These questions are more about the last twenty-four hours, and I'll take another set of vitals."

"Do we know each other, Doc?" Jaxon asks, closing his eyes for a moment and resting his head back against the top of the elevated bed.

"No, I don't believe so, Mr. Hudgins," I reply, praying he can't hear the sudden acceleration of my heartbeat.

"You can call me Jax. I feel like I know you. Maybe you remind me of someone," he says softly.

"Perhaps," I reply casually, and I can't help but wonder if Nate ever talked about me to Jaxon. Natalie knew about our relationship, so is it possible Nate told his closest friend too?

He lifts his head and holds my gaze for several long seconds. "Ask me anything, Doc."

We run through a few medical questions regarding the severity of his pain, which isn't too bad right now, thanks to the morphine they gave him in the ambulance, how he was feeling prior to injury, and about any previous ankle injuries.

"Nothing prior, Doc. Been fortunate to have a solid career thus far."

I give him a small grin. "That's good."

"I've had some friends not fare as well. My closest friend had a career-ending injury last year. It's a painful reminder of what we endure every day and the risks we take to play a game. Football is the greatest sport ever, but it does a number on our bodies and minds."

It's suddenly warm in this room, and my throat is having trouble swallowing over the lump lodged. "Well, fortunately for you, you should be back on the field soon."

"Good. Nate wasn't so lucky, and he lost a hell of a lot more than just his career that day." He levels me with a look filled with sorrow and sympathy that makes me want to cry.

"Here we go," the technician says, entering the room with the portable X-ray machine.

I clear my throat and give the imaging employee a forced smile. "We're all set. I'll leave you to it," I reply, pushing the computer cart toward the doorway so I can finish charting in the hall.

"Hey, Doc?"

Spinning around, I give the patient my full attention.

"Nate lost everything he loved that day. He walked away from it all, even though he didn't want to. He did it because he thought it was best for him. *And you*. If you ask me, he made the wrong choice. He'll forever live with that regret."

Nodding, I blink multiple times to keep the tears at bay and exit the room. When I reach the hallway, I close my eyes and take several deep breaths, praying the pain in my chest subsides. There's no doubt in my mind now. Jaxon Hudgins knows exactly who I am, and for some reason, that makes the hurt even greater.

Nate told him about me.

Will it ever stop?

It's been thirteen months since he told me goodbye, and there are still days it feels like it happened yesterday. Days where it's too suffocating to breathe, the sadness too heavy to bear. Those are the days I force one foot in front of the other and refuse to sink into the abyss of heartache. Those are the days I live for my patients and my own career.

It's not easy loving the memory of a ghost.

And now what?

Even after hearing Jaxon's words, it doesn't bring Nate back to Nashville. He's still gone, living in another state and having sold his house here. He has no intention of coming back. So, despite the hurt and the fact our entire time together feels unfinished, he made his choice.

That choice doesn't include me.

NATE

I'T'S CHRISTMAS EVE, AND THE house is quiet. My parents had a party at a friend's place. They invited me to go, but I passed. Janelle is having Christmas with her friends, and Uncle James, well, I'm not sure what he's doing, but he's not here. I have the house all to myself, and it's glorious.

I love my family, but since moving back home to Indiana, they've been glued to my side, and it's nice to know that for at least a few hours, I get to just chill. I have my bag of chips and my ice-cold beer as I sit down to watch my boys, the Nashville Storm, play. It still hurts. I want to be out there on that field with them. However, since I accepted the position with Uncle James, the hurt has eased tremendously. I still have the game. Not in the way I had envisioned, but it's still a part of my life. I couldn't really ask for more.

The game comes back from the commercial break, and I watch as my replacement throws a perfect spiral. Jaxon jumps and goes up against a defender to catch the ball, and he does it with precision. However, he gets tangled up with the defender and lands hard on his ankle.

Sitting forward, I place my elbows on my knees as I stare at the screen. Jax is down and not getting up. The Storm team surrounds him, and flashbacks of that very scenario race through my mind. My knee aches just thinking about my own on-field injury. I watch as they load my best friend onto the cart and drive him back to the locker room. Quickly, I grab my phone and shoot off a text.

> **Me:** Fill me in, man.

I wait, holding my phone, willing him to respond. I know that they're taking a look at that ankle. From the replay, it's definitely broken. I'm certain he's in good hands, but I'm still anxious as I wait to hear from him. Guilt sets in. I haven't been to one of his games since I was injured. It was too much, too hard not to be out there with him. I need to man up and change that. Life moves on whether you are ready for it or not. It's several minutes before Jaxon finally replies.

> **Jaxon:** Ankle's fucked. Taking me to Heartland Community for further testing. The team doc thinks surgery.

> **Me:** Fuck. Do you need me on the next flight?

> **Jaxon:** Nah, I'm all good, man. Thanks. I'll keep you posted.

> **Me:** Let me know if you change your mind.

My head swarms with all that happened. Jaxon is hurt, and he's going to the hospital. Heartland Community is where Oaklyn is doing her residency. At least that's where she was when I left town. I can't help but wonder if Jaxon will see her while he's there.

Jax is the only person I ever told about Oaklyn. We were having beers one night at my place when she was working late, and I kept looking at my phone and checking the time. He called me out on it, and I confessed. As the months wore on, it was actually Jax who again pointed out I was being an idiot, telling me that what I had with Oaklyn was more than just a friends-with-benefits arrangement. It was those words that made me look deeper into what we were doing and how I felt about her.

It wasn't long after, I admitted only to myself that I was in love with her. It didn't matter. Jax could see right through me. He still does. With all our time together on and off the field, he knows me well. He knows that it wasn't just her heart I broke the day I left Nashville, but I broke my own as well.

I remain on the couch for the duration of the game, but I can't tell you a single play. The front door opens, and I hear my parents' chatter. "Hey, sweetheart." Mom smiles.

"How was the party?" I ask, standing from the couch and cleaning up my snacks.

"It was nice to catch up with everyone," she replies.

"How was the game?" Dad nods toward the television.

I turn and glance at the screen. The Storm lost by two touchdowns. "Brutal. Jax got hurt. Broken ankle."

Dad winces. "That's tough. How's he doing?"

"We texted. They were taking him to the hospital for further testing, but the team docs think he's going to need surgery."

"Oh, goodness," Mom says. "And this close to Christmas. Is his family close?"

"Yeah, he said his parents were in town for his game and the holidays."

"Well, that's good." Mom nods. "He's going to need his family."

I smile at her, knowing she's thinking about my injury and how I had to move home to live with them. "The house in Nashville sold," I tell them. We were able to sign papers electronically. "I think I'm going to start looking for my own place here."

"Oh, you don't have to do that. We have plenty of space," Mom speaks up.

"Naomi, he's a man. I'm sure moving back home with his parents long term wasn't his plan. He needs his space." Dad tosses me a wink that Mom can't see, and I give him a grateful nod.

"I'm cramping your style," I tell her. "I appreciate everything that you've done for me, but it's time for me to keep moving forward. I'm working again, and it's not like I can't afford to live on my own. I've just been… stuck, I guess." I wasn't planning on blurting that out, but it's time. I've been here for over a year, and I need to get my life back on track. I need to accept the things that I cannot change.

It's Christmas Day, and the house is quiet. A far cry from what it was like when Janelle and I were kids. Now that she and I are adults, we slept in, then made breakfast as a family before opening gifts.

Dinner was later, and Uncle James joined us. We all ate way too much, laughed, and caught up with each other, and it was a good day. A damn good day. Somehow telling my parents I was going to start looking for my own place here in Indiana lifted something from my shoulders. I hate what I've lost, but today was a perfect example of everything I still have to live for.

My parents are napping on the couch, and Janelle left at the same time Uncle James did. She said she was meeting up with friends, but I think she's seeing someone. I wanted to grill her. As her older brother, it's my job to protect her. Then my mind went to Oaklyn. I kept what we had under wraps from my family too. Janelle will tell us when she's ready.

In my room, I grab my phone from where it's been charging on the nightstand and see a text from Jaxon.

Jaxon: Happy Christmas

The text makes me laugh. He had surgery late last night, and it's my guess the painkillers are making him a little loopy. Instead of texting him back, I call him.

"You sure you don't want to keep me company?" he says.

I can tell he's not talking to me.

"Merry Christmas, beautiful." His voice sounds exactly as it does when he's picking up a woman. "Hey," he says, finally talking to me.

"Are you hitting on your nurses?" I laugh.

"Nah, the sexy-as-fuck resident. Long, dark brown hair, exotic hazel eyes, and smells like a fucking field of lavender with a hint of vanilla."

His description sounds like Oaklyn. *My* Oaklyn. He's there in the hospital. He said a resident. What. The. Fuck. I end the call, fumbling with my phone. If only the sports reporters could see me now. One of the best-known quarterbacks in the league can't even hold onto his fucking cell phone. I manage to pull up Jaxon's name and hit video call.

"You hung up on me."

"Just thought you'd want to see my smiling face. It is Christmas, after all. My gift to you," I tell him.

"Fuck off." He laughs. "How's the family?"

"Good. Yours?"

"Good. They just left about an hour ago."

"Let's see the digs," I say, trying my hardest to sound upbeat and nonchalant.

Jaxon smirks. He knows me well enough to know what I'm doing. "Just a boring old hospital room."

"No roommate?" I ask as he pans the phone around his room so that I can see.

"No. Thank fuck. That's a perk of playing for the Storm, I guess."

"They taking good care of you?"

"Oh, you know it. Sexy-as-fuck resident at my beck and call, and the nurses are F.I.N.E. fine," he says.

"This I gotta see," I say, hoping like hell that I'll get a glimpse. I've shown him pictures of Oaklyn. He knows what she looks like. He'd tell me if it was her, right? Do I really want to know? Do I want my girl to be there taking care of my best friend while I'm here, not able to see either of them?

My girl.

Except, she's not my girl anymore.

I made sure that was never a possibility when I pushed her away.

"It's just me," Jaxon says, giving me a cheesy grin into the camera. "How was your Christmas?"

We go on to make small talk about our days and just catch up with life. We shoot the shit for close to an hour without one single interruption. I want to ask him if it was her. Will he even remember what she looks like? Surely, he'd at least recognize her name, right? Oaklyn isn't very common.

"You done pretending?" Jaxon asks.

"What?"

"The reason you hung up on me and video-called. Are you done pretending why you did it?"

"I'm not pretending."

"Come on, man, level with me."

"Fuck," I mutter. "Fine. Was it her? Was it Oaklyn?"

Jaxon stares me down through the phone, and it annoys me. "It was her."

The air rushes from my lungs, and my heart begins to race. He was there with her. He got to see her and talk to her. He was close enough to touch her. "H-How is she?"

"I'm not telling you."

"What?" I sit up straight from where I was lying on the bed. "What do you mean you're not telling me?"

He has to tell me.

I need to know.

"I mean, I'm not telling you."

"What the fuck, Jax?"

"Listen, Nate. You made your choice. Me telling you how she's doing isn't going to change the choices you've made. You chose to walk away from her. That means, if you want to know how's she doing, use this little cellular device we're speaking on and call her. Ask her for yourself."

"I can't, man. You know I can't." She hates me. I'm sure of it. I was an ass that night. I didn't even give us the option to discuss long-distance. I didn't even entertain the idea of sticking around. I could have paid someone to take care of me, but I know Oaklyn would have insisted on running herself ragged to help me, and I didn't want that for her.

I wanted her to focus on her career. She's worked her ass off to get to where she is in life, and I was so fucking proud of her. I *am* fucking proud of her. My girl is a fucking doctor. That's important. I needed her to be able to focus on her dream, not on some washed-up football player who was too lost in himself to even admit to her that she had quickly become everything to him.

It's me.

I'm the washed-up football player.

"You can. You just won't. There's a difference. Do you think I haven't seen the way you've been moping around? You lost your career and your girl."

I should have known that if anyone would see through me, it would be Jax. "She was never really mine."

"If that's what you keep telling yourself, then you don't deserve her."

"Have you seen her other than today?"

"Yesterday," he admits.

"Come on, man. You've got to give me something." I'm desperate for any nugget of information he can give me.

"Knock, knock." I hear a female voice. "How are you feeling, Mr. Hudgins?" the voice asks. The phone gets placed down on the bed. I'm staring at the ceiling of Jax's hospital room. He could have hung up on me, but he's giving me this. I think because he knows it will torture me further.

That voice.

I would know it anywhere.

"Doc, we talked about this. It's Jax. How am I going to sweep you off your feet if you're all Mr. Hudgins this, Mr. Hudgins that? That's my father."

She laughs, and the sound twists my gut while shattering my heart. Fuck me. I've missed her. I knew I missed her. She's all I think about, but hearing her voice has me swallowing back my emotions.

"Pain level?" she asks.

"I'm good, Doc. Still doped up."

"Well, that's good. I'm just making rounds. I'm heading home in a little while and wanted to check. If you need something, just hit the call button. Dr. Morgan is the resident on tonight if you need anything."

"Merry Christmas, Doc."

"Merry Christmas, Jaxon Hudgins."

I hear footsteps, and then Jaxon picks the phone back up. "Sorry about that. The doc needed to talk to me."

"Jax," I growl.

"That, my friend, was your Christmas present from me."

"You want a thank-you?"

"It would be nice, yeah."

"You could have let me see her."

He shrugs. "You pushed her away, Nate. You made your choice, and now you have to live with it."

"I thought we were friends?"

His face sobers. "We are friends, Nate. I'm trying to get you to understand that you made a rash decision. You made choices that affected more than just you. You're miserable and refuse to do something about it, and before you start, don't tell me it's all about your injury and losing your career. We all go into this job knowing our days are numbered."

"She deserved better."

"Then it's best you didn't get to see her. Why put either of you through that? What would seeing her do? I let you hear her voice. I was hoping it might knock some sense into your stubborn ass and bring you back to Nashville."

"Indiana is my home. This is where I grew up."

"Maybe, but you made a life here. One you walked away from."

"I didn't have a choice." I raise my voice. "I didn't have a choice," I say softer this time. "I didn't know who I was without football. And she wasn't mine, not really, but I knew who she was at her core. A good person. A caretaker. She was already killing herself with the hours she was keeping with her residency, and I didn't want to add to that."

"I get it. I've heard the same story over and over again. What I don't understand is why you keep lying to yourself?"

"What do you mean?"

"You're in love with her. You loved her then, and you love her now."

"I know." The confession tastes bitter on my tongue. It's the first and only time I've admitted to loving her outside my own mind. We're both quiet. Jaxon stares off into the distance as if he's so disappointed in me that he can't even look at me.

"I'm getting out of here tomorrow," he finally says. "You want some company?"

He's letting me off the hook. This isn't like Jaxon to be all serious and introspective on life. I don't know if it's the injury or the meds he's on, but he's definitely given me some tough love on this phone call. Not that it's going to change anything other than the fact that I'm no longer afraid to admit that I fell in love with Oaklyn. What started as benefits turned into so much more, but the truth of the matter remains the same. I pushed her away, and I don't know if she will ever be able to forgive me for that. Hell, she might already be seeing someone. The thought has bile rising in my throat.

"I'm buying a place here." I offer him another confession. He gave me an olive branch on the subject change, and I'm taking it. "You could come stay in Indiana for a few weeks or however long. We have a great rehab team here."

"Maybe in a few weeks. Let me at least get into a boot or something before you have my ass flying to Indiana."

"Sounds good, man. Hey, that catch, it was fucking great, minus the landing."

"Fuck off." He laughs. "And of course it was great. I am Jaxon Hudgins, after all."

"I see your ego is still intact."

"The ladies love it," he jokes.

"I'm glad you're doing better. Thanks for... my gift."

He nods. "Merry Christmas, Nate. I'll hit you up in a few weeks, and you can show me all that your home state has to offer."

"Hopefully, I'll have my own place by then."

"Hey, your parents love me, and I'm sure Janelle misses me."

"No. Just no."

He laughs, the phone shaking in his hands. "You know I'm messing with you. Say hi to the fam."

I agree after telling him to do the same and end the call. I toss the phone on the bed next to me and drop back on the pillow.

Closing my eyes, I let the memories of Oaklyn filter through my mind. I know I fucked up. Pushing Oaklyn away will forever be my biggest regret in life.

chapter 14

Oaklyn

"DR. SCHMIDT, DO YOU HAVE a few minutes?"

I look up and find Dr. Muhammad standing in the doorway of the treatment room I just finished up in. The patient is gone, having received five stitches in his leg, thanks to catching it on a piece of metal at work and slicing through his jeans and skin. I'm wrapping up my notes in his chart and cleaning up the room when the knock sounds on the door.

"Yes, of course. I'll be right there."

He nods, turning down the hall that leads to the physician offices. My heart is beating a little faster as I exit the charting program I was logged into and close the lid on the laptop. I really hope there isn't an issue. Of all the departments, of all the places I've had the privilege to work and learn at, this has been my favorite and I've only been here a few weeks. After all, it's one of the top primary care clinics in the city, but it's more than that. A facility like this is exactly where I hope to land when my residency is up. To learn under these five physicians is a dream, and I hope I haven't done something to warrant them renegotiating the terms of my contract with this group. The plan is for me to work the remainder of my time here, and I hope that's still the case.

As I reach Dr. Muhammad's office, I rap my knuckles lightly on the open door and poke my head in. He looks up and smiles. "Come in, Oaklyn. Have a seat."

I do as instructed, hoping he can't see the nervous bounce of my legs as I position myself on the chair. "What can I do for you, Dr. Muhammad."

His smile is kind and doesn't show any indication of something bad coming my way within the next few moments. "The others and I had a meeting at lunch today," he starts, referring to the other four physicians who make up this medical practice. I know this because I saw it on their schedule and was told they do it once a month to discuss any practice or employee issues. "Your name came up several times."

"Oh?" I force myself not to fidget with my hands, holding them perfectly still on my lap.

"Yes. You're here for the final year of your residency, with the intention of going into general family medicine when you've completed your term. Is that still the case?"

I nod instantly. "It is."

He offers me a polite smile. "That's good. It takes the right person to go into medicine, and from what we've seen in just a few short weeks, you check all of the boxes. You're incredibly smart, empathetic, and willing to listen. The patients love you, and I'm not just talking about the ones you've seen here. The reports from the attending physicians at the hospital all have wonderful things to say about you, and we're honored to have you with us for the next year."

"Thank you, sir," I reply, unsure what more to say.

"So, the reason for this meeting is the other physicians and I have decided to strike while the iron is hot, so to speak. We want to offer you a three-year contract with Family Health and Wellness that would begin as soon as your residency is complete. At the end of that three years, we will discuss a long-term contract for you, with the possibility of buying into the practice. We know it's not easy for a new doctor, and the debt you incur from medical school can be staggering, so it's not something you have to agree to or even decide now. I just wanted to mention it to you as a possibility, especially with Dr. Rodgers looking at a potential retirement in three to four years' time."

When he stops talking, he chuckles, and I realize it's probably because I'm sitting here, stunned silent, with my jaw hanging wide open. "I don't know what to say," I whisper, my brain trying to catch up.

"Well, of course, our hope is you say yes, at least to the initial three-year contract. You're a tremendous asset to our practice, and we'd love to have you stay with us."

"Wow, thank you for the offer," I murmur, still a little stunned by what is transpiring.

"We understand if you need to think it over. It's a huge decision, Oaklyn, and we don't want you to *not* consider all angles. We've taken the liberty to offer you a compensation and benefits package that we feel is competitive with today's demand and the number of other facilities in the area with physician openings. The document should be in your secured employee portal now."

I nod in understanding. "I appreciate it. I'll be sure to take a look at the offer this evening when I get home."

"If you have any questions or concerns, please let any of us know. We're all in agreement to bring you on, Oaklyn. I just volunteered to do the honors of speaking with you."

"I don't really know what to say, Dr. Muhammad. Really. This is all a bit overwhelming," I reply with an awkward chuckle.

"I'm sure it is. I remember that last year of residency, when you're looking to find your place in this big medical world upon completion. All of us have been there, so please don't hesitate to reach out if you have any questions. And to be perfectly frank, I really hope you agree to stay on with us. You're a tremendous doctor and we'd be lucky to have you working with us every day."

I have to blink a few times to keep the onslaught of tears at bay. This is exactly what I've dreamed of since I started college. My eyes were focused on med school, knowing it would be challenging every step of the way. Yet, so far, despite the stress, the sleepless nights, and the constant fatigue, it has been the most rewarding thing I've done.

"I'll let you get back to it. I know you still have a few patients on the schedule this afternoon, correct?"

"Yes, sir."

"Well, take all the time you need to review and consider the offer. There is no pressure, Oaklyn," he says, standing up and offering me his hand.

I place mine inside his in a gentle shake. "Again, thank you, sir. I'm excited to see what you have to offer, and if I'm being perfectly candid, this is exactly the type of place I hope to land in when I've completed my residency."

"Happy to hear that," he replies.

With a grin I'm unable to hide, I step out of his office and walk toward my own alcove. It's not an office, but it's a private area they've given me to work away from the patient rooms. As soon as I take a seat, I pull my phone out of my jacket pocket and pull up Natalie's contact.

Me: Huge day today! Let's go to dinner.

Natalie: I take it margaritas will be involved?

Smiling, it feels good to send my reply, mostly because I haven't had nearly the flexibility in my schedule the previous two years that I've had so far in the beginning of my third year.

Me: Yep!

Natalie: I'll schedule the Uber. Six thirty give you enough time to get home and cleaned up from work?

Me: It does. See you then!

Natalie: Wear something sexy! We'll go to that little barbecue place off Honky Tonk Highway and dance to whatever band is performing.

My heart starts to race a little. How long has it been since I've let loose and gone out like this? A long time. Actually, I remember exactly when it was.

Seven months ago.

It was New Year's Eve, and I was off that day, as well as the next. Natalie convinced me to go out and hit the bars, and I'm glad I did. Despite waking up with a huge headache the next morning, I don't regret finally letting loose.

Mostly because Nate was consuming my every waking thought, and most of my sleeping ones too. After assisting with Jaxon's reconstructive ankle surgery, I continued to tend to his care the following day under the assistance of Dr. Harrison. I got to know Nate's friend, who is just as charismatic and funny as Nate. It took me exactly two seconds to understand why the two became friends in the first place.

By the time I returned to work after my day off, Jaxon was discharged home to recoup from his surgery, and that was the end of it. I haven't heard from him, not that I expected to. I was merely one of the physicians taking care of him post-op, and since that time at Christmas, there's no need for us to communicate.

Even if I had hoped to.

Not Jaxon, particularly, but for a couple of days, it felt like he was an extension of Nate, and I secretly hoped that extension would result in some sort of contact. That's why I finally tied one on for New Year's Eve. I fell face-first into another Nate-infused slump and used our night out as a way to evict him from my mind for good.

Dancing and tequila are magical like that.

It helped.

Until the next morning.

Since then, I've continued on with my life for the last seven months, trying not to give Nate a single thought. I wouldn't exactly call my plan a success, but if I keep telling it to myself often enough, it's bound to happen, right?

Now, I have plans to go out with my best friend again on this hot July Friday night. I can't wait to let loose.

"I'm so stuffed. I can't believe I ate that much," Natalie says, dropping her napkin on her empty plate and reaching for her drink.

"Me too, but I don't regret it," I reply, watching as the dance floor starts to fill up with patrons ready to enjoy tonight's live music.

"There're tons of guys here." She takes another look around the room at the cowboy hats, boots, and tight Wranglers. I've never been into the whole country boys craze, but I get the appeal. Those asses in tight jeans aren't something to balk about.

"You should have plenty to pick from tonight," I quip, slurping my fruity margarita through my straw.

She waggles her eyebrows at me suggestively. "Absolutely. And plenty left for you," she adds, giving me a pointed look.

I shrug, refusing to get into this conversation with her now. If I do, she'll insist I find a hot guy, let him lead me around the dance floor and grind against my ass, with the hope of getting invited back to his place at the end of the night for sweaty, naked mattress aerobics. In theory, the plan sounds great, especially since it's been a really long time since I've aerobicized. An embarrassingly long time, but we're not getting into that tonight.

We order new drinks and sit together for a few songs, people-watching. Finally, when the band starts playing a popular Luke Bryan song, she grabs my hand and drags me to the dance floor. I let the music wash over me, shaking my hips as the song instructs us to, and dance with my best friend. When the song ends, we stay out for the next one, and the following one after that.

Suddenly, I feel someone tap on my shoulder and I spin around, coming face-to-face with a person I wasn't expecting. "Doc!" Jaxon hollers over the music, pulling me into a hug before I can even process the gesture.

"Hey, you. How are you?" I ask, glancing down at his ankle, as if expecting to see a cast or something. Not that I should, considering his surgery was seven months ago.

He grins widely. "I'm great, thanks."

"How's the ankle?"

"Perfect. I've been cleared to play this season, thanks to you."

Warmth heats my cheeks at the compliment. "I don't know about that. I was just assisting."

"But you were part of the team, and I'm grateful. To show my appreciation, I'm going to buy you a drink," he insists.

"Oh, that's not necessary," I reply, noticing Natalie hovering right beside me, hanging on our every word. "This is my friend, Natalie."

"Natalie," he practically purrs as he draws her hand up to his mouth and places a kiss on her knuckles, making my best friend swoon. "Would you care to join me and a few friends for a drink?" he asks, his eyes focused completely on her.

"We would love to," she replies, letting him lead her off the dance floor and toward a sectioned-off area they use for VIPs. As they walk away, she asks, "So how do you know my friend, Oaklyn?"

Being left with no choice but to follow them, we walk into the small seating area and take the first table available. It's still noisy here, considering the restaurant and bar is small, but it's not as loud as on the dance floor. At least you can have conversations with your neighbors without having to yell.

Jaxon tells her all about his ankle surgery and my part in it without mentioning the other link between us, which I'm grateful for. "Ladies, pick your poison," he offers when the server arrives.

"Raspberry margarita for me," I order.

"Same," Natalie replies, turning her attention to Jaxon. "What brings you out tonight?"

"A few teammates decided to have dinner and a few drinks after a team workout. I'm starving," he says, grabbing the cardboard menu in the middle of the table. "Did you ladies eat?"

"We did before we started dancing. We're celebrating," she replies, giving me a wide smile.

"Celebrating? I love a good celebration. What's the occasion?" he asks, his eyes bouncing between Natalie and me.

"Oaklyn here got a job offer today at the clinic she's at," Natalie states proudly.

"No shit? That's great, Oaklyn," he boasts, taking his beer from the server when she returns. When Natalie and I each have our margaritas, he holds his bottle in the air. "To Oaklyn, the best damn doc in Nashville."

"To Oaklyn!" my best friend hollers, tapping her glass to mine and Jaxon's before taking a hearty drink from her glass.

"What'd we miss?"

I look up to find two large men approaching the table and taking the final two available chairs. "Ladies, these ugly bastards are Trace Whitman and Jefferson Kidding, teammates of mine. Fellas, this beautiful lady is one of the docs who fixed up my ankle, Oaklyn, and her friend, Natalie."

"You order food?" Jefferson asks Jaxon.

"Not yet."

"I'm starved. Order it all."

"All their food?" Natalie asks, her eyes wide with shock.

He just winks and places his hand on his belly. "I'm a big boy, darlin'. Takes lots of fuel to keep me going."

We spend the next two hours together, sitting in the VIP area, having drinks and talking. The server brought mountains of pork and deep-fried food, and I watched in complete fascination as Jaxon and his teammates devoured all of it. Of course, it reminds me of watching Nate eat, especially during the season. He could put away some serious quantities of food on a daily basis.

"Fuck," Jaxon grumbles, turning away from the entrance of the VIP section and shielding his face a bit.

"What?" Natalie asks, glancing around him to see who he was hiding from.

"Hey, guys," a deep voice booms as he joins our small group.

Looking up, I instantly recognize the man as the one I met last summer when I was eating lunch with Natalie. The big mountain man with the beard and a nice smile.

"Trevor," Jaxon says, looking at Natalie. "Care to dance?"

"You betcha," she states, glancing at me. "Watch my stuff?"

"Of course," I reassure her as she scoots out from behind the table and takes Jaxon's hand.

Trevor plops down in Jaxon's vacated chair and makes a grab at the small pieces of fries left on the platter in the middle as his eyes glance up and meet mine. "Holy shit, I know you."

I give him a polite smile. "Hello."

A wicked grin spreads across his full lips. "Oaklyn, right? I'd never forget a beautiful name or face."

"And you're Trevor," I reply.

He winks before waving down the server. "Miller Lite." Turning to me, he asks, "You need another drink, gorgeous?"

"No, thank you."

He turns to the other players at the table. "You ate all the food without me?"

"You snooze you lose," Trace states, his eyes watching a woman out on the dance floor. "Excuse me. I'm going in," he adds, taking a final drink of his beer and heading toward where the woman dances with a few friends.

"How have you been, Oaklyn?" Trevor asks, shifting in his seat so he's leaning toward me. I catch a whiff of his woodsy scent, and I admit, it causes my heart to skip a beat. He smells really nice.

"I've been well. You?"

"Fucking fantastic," he replies with a bit of cocky attitude.

I glance over at Jefferson, who has his face down in his phone, and realization sets in. "You play for the Storm?"

The grin he gives me is wide, proud, and a little on the sexy side. "Sure do, honey. Number seventy-three. The heart of the O-line and the beast on the left side."

I nod, as if understandin   g what he's saying. "That's impressive."

"What brings you out tonight? Your friend hookin' up with Hudgins?"

I glance out at the sea of people and easily find Jaxon and Natalie, thanks to his towering size. They're dancing and laughing, but it doesn't appear like foreplay. "No, I don't think so."

When I look back his way, he asks, "He hookin' up with you?"

My mouth opens immediately. "No."

Shrugging, he leans back against the wall and smiles once more. "Just checking. So what are you doing tomorrow night?"

"What?"

"Tomorrow night. Any plans?"

My mind is spinning. Is this guy hitting on me? Asking me out?

My question is answered when he continues, "I'd love to take you to dinner."

"Oh. I'm… well, I'm not sure."

"Seeing someone?" he asks, popping another small piece of french fry into his mouth.

"Not anymore."

"Ahh, break up. I get it. You know, they say the best way to get over a guy is to jump right in with another," he states with another wink and cocky grin.

Chuckling, I go for the easy letdown. "Sorry, I'm not ready."

He tsks and shakes his head. "Too bad. I think we'd be fire together, Oaklyn. But the good news for you, I'm in no hurry. I can wait."

My mouth falls open just a bit and I'm unable to find words to reply.

"I'll give you my number, darlin'. You give me a call when you're ready for that date. It's open-ended," he says, reaching for my phone. Once I pull up a blank contact, he taps in his information and hands it back with a smile. "There. Now you have my digits. Call me when you're ready for that date."

I slip my phone into my pocket, not really sure what to do with it. I'll probably end up deleting it later, but for now, I'll be nice and go along with it.

A few songs later, Natalie returns and yawns. "You ready?" I ask, already standing.

"Yes." She turns to look at Jaxon. "Thanks for the dances, cowboy."

"You're welcome." Then he turns to me and asks, "You two good?"

"Yep," I reassure him, already inputting my request for an Uber. "Car's on the way."

"Good. Stay inside until it arrives," he says, taking the seat I'm vacating.

"Thanks for inviting us to join you," I tell him.

"Anytime, Doc," he replies with a friendly smile.

Natalie takes my hand and guides us toward the front entrance. The car is pulling up just a few minutes later, and we're heading home for the night.

I think about Trevor, about his invitation. He was clearly asking for a date, and maybe I should have accepted. Perhaps this is exactly what I need to push me over the edge of forgetting all about Nate once and for all.

Something tells me it won't be that simple.

Nate Vaughn seems to be unforgettable.

chapter 15

NATE

IT'S A BYE WEEK, SO I'm spending the weekend holding down my couch. I moved into my condo back in the winter, and here I am, almost a year later, loving the solace it brings me. I spend a lot of time alone, much to my mother's displeasure, but that's just where I am right now in my life. I'm not depressed, but I also don't feel like being the always-on life of the party that I had to be when I was the quarterback for the Storm.

I get to be me. I get to be just Nate, and I'm good with that. Sure, I miss my career, but the fame, I'm not all that torn up about losing that. The only other thing I miss from my past life isn't a thing. She's a living, breathing person.

Oaklyn.

Before I can let my mind wander, my phone rings. Glancing at the screen, I see Joel's name. He's pretty much the only person

I've been hanging out with. He was my physical therapist and kicked my ass on the daily. We became friends. We're not as close as Jaxon and I, but we get together for a beer from time to time.

"Hello," I greet him before the call can go to voice mail.

"What's up?"

"Holding down the couch," I tell him with a laugh. "No game today," I add to make myself seem a little less pathetic. He probably could have guessed exactly what I was doing.

"I figured as much. Listen, I need a favor."

"Should I be worried?" I ask my friend. "You never call for a favor." It's true. Joel is one of those friends who doesn't care about your bank balance. He's just a good guy all around, and he's never once asked me for a favor.

"I'm very selective on my favor asking. That makes it harder for the ask-ee to say no."

"Is askee even a word?" I'm shaking my head, a smile pulling at my lips.

"It is now. Anyway, about that favor."

"Hit me," I tell him.

Joel is a pretty even-keeled kind of guy. We hit it off when he told me about his shoulder injury in college. He was a baseball player, and his injury ended his career before it even got started. After that, knowing he'd worn my shoes, or a pair similar in size, we became fast friends, even when he tortured me in therapy.

"So Chance has a fight this weekend."

"Okay. Do you want to watch it on my big screen? Sure, bring some beer. I'll order us a couple of pizzas and some wings." Chance is his younger brother, who has made a name for himself on the MMA circuit. He's one of the best in his weight class. If not *the* best.

"Yeah, I was thinking you'd go with me to watch him fight."

It takes me a minute to compute what he's saying. "The fight's in Vegas, right? Tonight?"

"Yep."

"You know we can't just jump in the car and drive there and get there on time, right?" I'm fucking with him.

"That's why I booked us both a flight."

"When?"

"Wheels up at two. We have reserved seats for the fight down in front, so that gives us plenty of time to check into our hotel, which I have already booked, and get to the arena."

"And if I say no?" I won't. We've talked about going to see Chance fight for a while now, and we've just never made it happen.

"You won't," he replies with confidence.

"Why such short notice?"

"Chance's team had extra tickets they forgot to tell him about. He called me twenty minutes ago."

"You managed to book flights and a hotel and call me in twenty minutes, all on your own? Aww, Joely, you're all grown up," I tease.

"Fuck off. I'll be there in thirty to pick your ass up. Be ready."

"Yes, sir." Ending the call, I toss my phone onto the couch next to me and head to my room to pack. I don't need much, just a change of clothes, my phone charger, and toiletries. I shove everything I'll need into a backpack and make my way back to the living room to wait on Joel.

"Damn," I mutter as we take our seats. "Front row, little bro has some pull," I tell Joel as he takes the seat next to mine.

"Yeah, he's killing it. If he wins this fight, the next will be a title fight for his weight class."

"Nice."

"Nate Vaughn?"

I turn toward the voice to find a man in a suit smiling widely. "Big fan, my man. I'm Roger Bayless." He offers me his hand. "Manager to a few of the guys fighting tonight."

"Nice to meet you," I say politely.

"Who are you here to see?" he asks me.

"All of them, but we're with the Chance Granger camp."

"Hell of a fighter." He nods.

"This is his brother, Joel." I introduce the two, and the three of us make small talk until the first fight starts.

Two fights in, and the cameraman finally realizes I'm in the crowd. The camera pans toward us, and I smile and wave. Joel and Roger do as well. However, they're not the only ones. I feel hands land on my shoulder and boobs next to my cheek. I pretend like it's no big deal when in reality, it's a very big fucking deal.

A few years ago, I might have played it up for the cameras that a woman was throwing herself at me, but now that I know what it's like to be with a woman who doesn't give a fuck about my status or bank balance, I can't seem to find it in me to engage.

The cameraman moves on, and I lean forward to get away from her. "How about we have some fun tonight?" she coos, pressing her tits against my back.

"Not tonight." My voice is loud enough that she can hear me. I don't even bother to turn and look at her. I don't care what she looks like.

She's not Oaklyn.

It's at this moment that I realize I have a problem, one I'm not sure how to solve. It's been years since I've laid eyes on her, since I've kissed her or felt the softness of her skin, but that doesn't keep me from aching for her. No other woman holds my interest, and if I'm being honest, I'm not sure one ever will.

I'm starting to realize that Oaklyn Schmidt was the love of my life, and I tossed her away. I hate myself for doing so, but even though I miss her like a fucking limb, I know I made the right choice for her. That's what love is about, right? You put the one you love first, and that's all that I was trying to do. I didn't know that I'd still be hung up on her over two years later.

"Oh, come on. What happens in Vegas stays in Vegas." She laughs. The sound is high-pitched and fake as fuck.

"Guys' night," I tell her, still not bothering to turn and look at her.

Her hands begin to rub my shoulders. At the same time, Joel elbows me and gives me a subtle nod. We're back on the jumbotron. Apparently, the cameraman can't find anyone more interesting for airtime. I smile and wave as the woman leans forward and presses a kiss to my cheek. I grit my teeth until my face leaves the huge screen before turning to look at her.

"Not interested." My tone is clipped, and the fury I feel is obvious.

"You don't have to be an asshole," she spits.

"No, you're right. I don't like to be, but no means no." I feel like I'm reciting the words from an old after-school special, but that's the most polite thing I can come up with at the moment. She doesn't want me. She doesn't want Nate. She wants Nate Vaughn, the quarterback, and yeah, there's a big fucking difference between the two.

"Asshole," she scoffs as she settles back into her seat.

I can feel Joel's stare, but I keep my eyes on the cage as the next fight starts. The fight is short-lived, and a tap-out happens at the end of the first round.

"Chance is up next," Joel tells me. He's looking down at his phone.

"Glad we're finally doing this," I tell him. "And these seats, let me know if I owe him anything."

"Nah, his camp has extra for fighters' families," he tells me.

"Well, thanks for this. It was nice to get out of the house."

"You sure about that?" He raises his eyebrows in question.

"Why wouldn't I be?"

He nods behind us, and I roll my eyes.

"She's not going to ruin my night."

"She could have helped make it a little better," he jokes.

"I can ask her if she's into you," I offer.

Joel tosses his head back in laughter. "I think I'm all set."

"Dodged a bullet," I mutter, but the way he bobs his head tells me that he heard me.

A few hours later, we're at a steakhouse on the strip. It's just the two of us, as Chance had contractual obligations with his sponsors and the media. He won his fight, and everyone is buzzing about the title fight that is rumored to be next. We're going to meet up with him a little later.

"Here you are. I'll be back with some refills," our waitress says, dropping off our sizzling plates of steaks before she dashes off again.

"So, who is she?" Joel asks as he slices off a piece of bread from our shared loaf on the table, slathers it in cinnamon butter, and pops it into his mouth.

"She who? Our waitress?" I ask, cutting off my own piece of bread.

"The girl."

"What girl?" I think the hunger has gotten to him. We didn't have time to eat once we landed. We dropped our stuff in our suite and headed straight to the fights.

"The one who has you saying no to a sure thing."

I swallow my bread and take a long pull of my draft beer before answering him. "Maybe I'm not into sure things. What about that?" It's a lame comeback, and we both know it.

"Try again."

"I'm not sure what you want me to say."

"Tell me about her."

I pretend to be way too interested in my steak as I use my knife to carve out a bite and pop it into my mouth. Joel smirks and does the same.

"I can wait you out," he says once he's finished chewing. "We are staying in the same suite, and I'm sitting next to you on our flight home."

"You're not going to let this go, are you?"

"Nope." He grins, shoving another bite of steak into his mouth.

"She's someone I had a thing with before my injury. We were just supposed to be benefits, but I knew as time went on, we were way more than that. At least, it felt that way to me."

"So what happened?"

I take a long pull of my beer and sit back in my seat. "What happened was I got injured. She's a doctor. She had just started her residency, and her schedule was insane." I pause, debating on how much to tell him and decide to just go for it all. What do I have to lose? I've already lost her.

"She's one of those people who is a natural-born caretaker. Thoughtful and giving, and I knew without a doubt that she would work her ass off to help take care of me."

"You didn't want her to?"

"No. I mean, at the time, I was a mess of emotions. I knew my career was over. I knew I was facing months of intense therapy, and I knew she would have done whatever it took to stay by my side, putting herself and her career last and possibly on hold. That's just who she was."

She was always offering me massages and making sure I was eating during the season. Sure, I did the same for her, but to me, it was different. I'd never met a woman who cared about the man I am. Her kindness and the heart she wore on her sleeve touched me in ways even I didn't understand at the time.

"So, you what? Told her to get lost?" Joel asks.

I expel a heavy sigh. "I told her I was moving back home to Indiana. I explained how we were just having fun and with me moving, our time together was over."

"Ouch." He winces as if my words sliced through him. His expression is almost exactly the same one that Oaklyn had that day on my couch. "You fucked up."

"Yeah," I admit.

"So, all this time, she's still in your head."

"She's right here." I tap my hand over my chest. "I knew I cared about her. I was torn up myself with pushing her away, but it wasn't until I had to live without her that I truly understood the gravity of my actions."

"And why haven't you called her?"

"I live in Indiana now."

"Why?"

I take another bite of my steak and give myself time to form an answer. "I needed the help getting back and forth to therapy."

"I get that." He nods. "I understand it, but why did you leave your life in Nashville behind you?"

"Are you sure your name isn't Phil? Doctor, maybe?" I say, deflecting, knowing damn well he's not going to let me get away with it. It's one of the reasons we're friends. He's not afraid to call me on my bullshit.

"Just answer the question, wiseass. I'm a therapist, after all." He gives me a wide grin, and I roll my eyes.

"I don't know. I guess, at first, it was because it reminded me too much of what I'd lost. The longer I was home, the longer it seemed as if my life in Nashville was firmly in my rearview mirror. I sold my house, bought my condo, and here we are."

Joel nods and takes a few more bites of his steak. I do the same, relieved that his line of questioning seems to be over, but I should have known better. He wipes at his mouth, drops his napkin onto the table, and steeples his hands, staring me in the eye.

"Let me get this straight. You had the girl. *The* girl. You had her, didn't tell her you knew she was *the* girl, got injured, pushed her away, breaking her heart and yours, I'm sure, and moved home. You got better. Fought me all through your rehab and sold your place there to buy one at home, and none of that is what you really wanted."

"My family is there."

"So you're telling me those guys on your team weren't your family? That *she* wasn't your family?"

"Are you trying to twist the knife in my chest?" I ask.

"Come on, Nate. You're running from her."

"My job is there."

"Oh, you mean the job you don't need? And don't tell me for a second that you couldn't reach out to the Storm or any news outlet and not be hired on the spot."

"Coaching puts me close to the game."

"You can't coach in Nashville? Do they not have colleges?"

I don't answer him because what could I possibly say to that? He's right. We both know he's right. If I'm being honest with myself, I'm scared to reach out to her. She could be with someone new, or hell, married by now. I don't deserve her, no matter how badly I wish that were not the case.

"Look, Nate, you only get one life to live. One. You have to do what makes you happy. If it's her, then fight for her. Tell her you made a mistake, grovel, woo, and buy out every florist in a fifty-mile radius. You do what you have to do to be happy. You're existing in Indiana. You're not living."

Before I can reply, not that I would know how to reply, my phone rings. I check it and see my Uncle James calling. He knows we're here. I sent pictures to our family group chat. "It's my uncle. I need to make sure nothing's wrong." Joel nods as I lift the phone to my ear. "Hey, everything okay?" I ask.

"Everything's great. I know you're busy, but I just heard a rumor that I wanted to pass on to you."

"O—kay."

"Michael Cunningham is announcing his early retirement. His wife is ill."

"Coach Cunningham?" My heart drops. The head coach of the Storm and his wife were always good to me. She's one of the sweetest ladies you will ever meet.

"Yeah. Nothing has been announced yet, but I have a pretty solid source."

"Who?" I can't help but ask.

"Michael himself."

"Right." I swallow hard. "I'll reach out to him next week and see if there is anything that I can do."

"He asked me to have you call him."

I nod even though he can't see me. "Of course I will. Thanks for calling to let me know."

"Safe flight. That was one hell of a fight."

"It was even better live," I assure him.

"I bet it was with those seats. Call me when you get back."

Ending that call, I relay to Joel what's going on. "I told you, Nate. Life is too short."

I nod because he's right. I've been going through the motions. I know I fucked up, but I also know I don't have the right to ask her to take me back. In her eyes, she was a fun time for me. How do I make her see that she is more than that? How do I explain that she's still, after all this time, the only woman I want?

Oaklyn

"Dr. Schmidt, I'm working through the field of insurance companies to get your credentials started for June first," Jessica Borgers states as I pass through the front office at the clinic.

"Great, Jessica. I know it's a lot of tedious work on your part, and I appreciate it so much," I reply, offering her a grateful smile, even though it feels a little forced at the moment. I woke up feeling a bit under the weather this morning, and I'm waiting on the dose of medicine I just took to kick in.

"That's my job," she replies with a chuckle. Even though I've only been here for eight months, I know Jessica is the heart of this clinic. She's the office manager and does an incredible amount of work behind the scenes. Not to mention, filling in when needed at the front counter and helping man the phones.

I've seen her even clean when needed and assist with patient care when we're in a bind.

"And you do such a beautiful job at it," I tell her, waving as I continue through the office and head toward the small hallway where the physician offices reside. I'm still in the small alcove area, but I don't mind. It suits me just fine.

I'm one step closer to finishing. The cold January carried over to a chilly February, but I'm not letting it bother me. I'm in the home stretch. Despite the dreary bitterness outside, with each day that passes, I'm almost there.

After a few days last July of weighing the pros and cons of working for Family Health and Wellness, I accepted their offer, and things are starting to fall into place. I'm sitting in the small alcove still, but the five physicians assured me they'll have a formal place for me come June first.

The day my contract officially begins.

A loud sneeze halts the joy I've been basking in. My head is starting to swim, feeling like it's going to explode at any moment from the pressure. I snatch a tissue from the pocket of my physician's coat, grateful to have shoved a handful in there when I arrived at work. What started off as a small headache and a bit of sinus pressure when I woke this morning is quickly transforming into something much more inconvenient as the day starts to progress. It's not even noon, and I'm starting to worry I may not be able to make it through the day.

"Are you feeling all right?"

I look up and find Dr. Gomez standing in front of my small work area, a worried look on her face. "I think I'm coming down with something," I tell her, tossing my Kleenex into the trash and pumping some sanitizer into my hand.

"There's that terrible sinus infection going around, which I'm sure you're aware of," she says, leaning against the wall. "Plus, we've seen an influx of cases of influenza A and strep."

"I don't have a fever," I assure her. I wouldn't be working if I did.

"Not yet," she replies with a chuckle. "Symptoms?" She steps forward and runs her hand along my glands.

"An increase of weakness, headache, stuffy nose, and now that I think of it, my throat isn't feeling so hot."

She gives me a smile. "Take an influenza test, as well as one for strep, and take the rest of the afternoon off."

My eyes go wide. In all the time I've been working in medicine, I've never had anything other than a basic common cold. "I can't be sick. I have patients."

The older physician just laughs. "Spoken like a true doctor. You've heard the saying we make the worst patients, right?"

I groan, then wish I hadn't. My throat is dry and sore, feeling a bit like I've swallowed gravel. "I never get sick. I *hate* getting sick."

She nods and holds up her hand. "Wait right here." Within a minute, she's back with the swabs needed to test me for both influenza and strep. I sit still, grumbling as she uses the first swab to secure fluids from the back of my throat—fun, by the way—and then uses the second to swipe the inside of my nose—also, loads of fun.

"Now I see why everyone freaks out when we come into the room with those darn swabs," I mutter, reaching for my bottle of water and taking a long drink.

"I'll go run these, but either way, you should take the afternoon off. Actually, I insist. We'll cover your patients, Oaklyn. All five of us are working, so between the group, we've got you covered. We'll play tomorrow by ear, okay?"

I nod, not really having anything else to say. Even if the tests come back negative, I'm still not well enough to see patients. The proper thing for me to do is to go home and rest. Hopefully, a little sleep will have me feeling as good as new in the morning, and I won't have to worry about creating more work for the office ladies by moving my appointments.

"Stay put. I'll let you know when the results are in," Dr. Gomez says before heading off to complete the tests.

"This sucks," I grumble, taking another drink.

The longer I sit here, the worse I start to feel. My eyelids grow increasingly heavy, and the prospect of a nap is looking more imminent. I also wonder if the heating system is malfunctioning, since all of a sudden, it feels ten degrees colder in here.

"Hey, Oaklyn," Vivian says as she steps around the corner and points a thermometer at my forehead. "Doc Gomez says you're sick and going home." I don't confirm, because I'm certain she can tell. Vivian takes my vitals, while I sit still, wishing I were at home and in bed.

"Temperature's 100.6 and your pulse is elevated."

"That's because Dr. Gomez just shoved a Q-tip up my nose to my brain," I state, making her giggle.

"You should try being the one who has to administer those tests. Between those and vaccinations, us nurses are the most hated people in the clinic," she replies with a cheeky grin.

"All right, the results are in. Positive for both influenza A and strep, my friend," Dr. Gomez announces. "Looks like you're off for a few days."

"No," I grumble, hating the thought of being stuck at home instead of working.

"'Fraid so. I'll have Viv send in a prescription. Amoxicillin okay for you?"

"It's fine," I grumble, reaching into my bottom cabinet for my purse.

"I'll send it in right now to the hospital pharmacy," Vivian says, offering me a look of pity. "Feel better, Oaklyn."

When she walks away, Dr. Gomez gives me a stern look. "It's Wednesday. Take the rest of the week off to recoup." I go to open my mouth to argue, but she holds up her hand. "No, I'm serious. We'll be fine, Oaklyn. It's two and a half days. I'm sure you'll be good as new on Monday."

Sighing, I slip my purse over my shoulder and stand up. "Thank you, Dr. Gomez. And, I'm sorry."

Her eyebrows pull together in confusion. "For what? You're a physician. We're not immune to the illnesses we're surrounded by. It happens to all of us. Get some rest, and you'll be good as new in no time."

"Thanks," I mumble, wishing there were a way to teleport myself directly into my bedroom. Something tells me this drive over to the hospital to get my prescription and then home isn't going to be fun. Good thing home is only a few short blocks away.

"If you need anything, give us a call. And don't worry about saying anything to the office. I'll go up there now and have them work on the schedule."

I sigh, hating to create extra work for everyone else. The office staff have to rearrange the appointments and the doctors will have to see extra ones this afternoon in my absence.

Stupid germs and viruses.

I make my way out of the building, wrapping my winter coat around me a little tighter. As soon as I'm in my car, I fire it up and crank on the heat before reaching for my phone and firing off a text to Natalie.

> **Me:** I'm sick. They sent me home.
>
> **Natalie:** Oh no! What can I do? Need anything?
>
> **Me:** No, I'm gonna stop at the hospital and grab a script and go home and crash.
>
> **Natalie:** I'll bring you chicken noodle soup for dinner from that café we like by the stadium.

Me: You're the bestest estest ever. Ever.

Natalie: Duh. *insert winky face*

Natalie: Drive safely.

Me: Will

I don't even have the energy to give her more words. I drop my phone onto the passenger seat and slowly back out of the parking spot. The drive toward the hospital is at a turtle pace, but eventually, I make it. I park in one of the designated pharmacy parking spots and almost forget my keys in the ignition as I climb out.

Of course, as soon as I get inside the small public pharmacy located inside the hospital, I can tell there's going to be a wait. I'm about ten people deep in the line, and it takes everything I have not to just leave. This is when I wish I had a person. Yes, I know Natalie would buzz over here as soon as possible to grab my prescription, but that's not her responsibility.

If only Nate were here.

No. No, Oaklyn, we're not going there. I'm not Nate's responsibility either. He made that abundantly clear over two years ago when he had his accident. He left Nashville so others could care for him.

Not. Me.

Finally, I get to the front of the line and retrieve my antibiotic. I need to get out of here as quickly as possible and back to my apartment. Being sick is messing with my head. I go for long periods without thinking about him, and then all of a sudden, he's all I see. I hear his voice. I smell his cologne. It's so fucked up, and quite inconvenient to be stuck in a past life like this.

I need to evict him for good.

Maybe I should look into hypnosis?

Climbing into my car, I toss the white bag containing my drugs onto the seat beside my phone. Well, thank God no one broke into my vehicle and swiped that. Clearly, I'm not thinking straight. As I start my car, I sneeze hard, my head throbbing, and my throat feeling like I swallowed shards of glass.

I reverse from my parking spot and drive the few blocks to my building. I don't even remember letting myself in the gate or pulling into my designated space, but suddenly, I'm in the elevator and moving up to my floor. It's a short ride and as soon as the door opens, I'm practically falling out of the car and stumbling to my apartment. I can only imagine how I look. Probably like a drunk girl, tripping and weaving to her apartment at three in the morning after a night of drinking.

It takes me several tries, but I eventually get my key into the knob and the lock released. I drop my purse on the floor, kick the door closed with my foot, and slip off my coat, depositing it somewhere along the way. I make my way to the kitchen. Even though I'd much rather go straight to bed, I know I need to get the first dose of antibiotics in my system, stat. Then I can pass out and wake up in three days.

I pop open the pill bottle, pull out the proper dosage, and grab a bottle of water from the fridge. A bark of a cough comes out of nowhere, causing my head to pound even more and my entire body to ache. I ignore the pain and pop the pill in my mouth, swallowing a small amount of water to wash it down. Finally, I head for my bedroom. Sleep is imminent.

And so fucking welcome.

I fall onto the mattress without so much as removing a scrap of my work attire or shoes, even though I should. Shoes are filthy, but I just don't have it in me. My eyes are closed before my head hits the pillow, and I fall into the deepest sleep of my life.

Thankfully.

What the hell is that noise?

I open a single eye and stare up at my ceiling. My brain is slow to compute, but is that… a vacuum?

Turning on my side, I glance at my alarm clock, surprised to find it's after eight at night. I slept like a comatose patient for a huge chunk of the day. My throat is still sore, but the pounding in my head doesn't seem as bad as it was earlier.

I force myself to sit up, knowing I need to take another dose of antibiotic, some Tylenol, and drink a little water. If I'm not careful, I'll find myself dehydrated, and that's the last thing I want. I know all too well how fast an individual can get dehydrated, especially when they're sick. That's exactly why I throw my legs over the edge of my bed, despite the achiness of my body, and slowly stand.

Plus, I really need to find out where that vacuuming is coming from.

Just as I start to shuffle toward my closed door, it opens, startling me. "Mother of all things holy," I practically scream, hand pressing over my racing heart. "What are you doing here?" I ask my best friend.

"Making sure you're not dead!" she declares. "You haven't drunk that water."

"What water?" I ask.

"The water on the nightstand, silly. There's also some cold and flu meds and Tylenol. I wasn't sure which you'd want to take."

I glance over at the table, and sure enough, there's a bottle of water and the meds sitting right beside my alarm clock. How I missed them is beyond me. "Thanks," I grumble, retrieving the items she left for me. "I need to take my antibiotic too."

"I can get it," she replies.

"No, I want to stretch my legs for a minute and take a shower," I say, following her out of my room.

"Well, come drink some Gatorade. I picked up a few bottles, and that soup is in the fridge. I can heat it up," she tells me, walking from the bedroom. When I join her in the kitchen, she says, "I am glad you're alive. I was starting to wonder there for a minute. I tried waking you up two or three times, and you didn't stir."

"I still don't feel very human. I'm not sure food is on the menu."

"Start with the Gatorade," she insists, grabbing a bottle from the fridge and handing it over. She then goes to the counter and takes my next dose of antibiotics from the bottle. "You really made a mess when you got home. I picked up your purse and coat off the floor, and your meds were spilled all over the counter. I'm pretty sure I found them all. Oh, and you didn't lock your door. Good thing this building is secure. You could have been robbed and wouldn't have known until hours later."

I close my eyes and shake my head. I know I was a little out of it when I got home, but I didn't realize I hadn't locked the door. She doesn't say anything else as I sip my Gatorade. I'm not a huge fan of the stuff, but my body definitely needs the electrolytes, and I'm so thirsty, the weird taste doesn't seem to bother me much.

Glancing around, I spot the vacuum in the middle of my living room and the dusting cloth on the coffee table. "What are you doing?"

"Cleaning," she replies, opening up the fridge again. "You want this soup?"

"Not yet."

"Well, when you wouldn't wake up, I decided to hang around a bit in case you stopped breathing so I could call 911. I also picked up a few things and did the like five dirty dishes in the sink, and from there, it turned into me cleaning your apartment. By the way, you're out of Clorox wipes in the bathroom."

I nod, even though I probably won't remember tomorrow.

"You're the absolute bestest friend a girl could ask for, Nat. Really." I close my eyes for a moment and take a deep breath, my mind still a little fuzzy. "I'm going to take a shower. I feel nasty."

"You still have a low-grade fever. Or at least you did when I used that infrared thermometer on your forehead. By the way, you snore when you're sick."

"Thanks for letting me know," I grumble, exiting the kitchen and passing through the living room. As I shuffle in the direction of the hallway, my eyes catch on the television, and it makes me pause. "Are you watching sports?"

She shrugs. "My phone said there was huge news regarding the Storm coming, so I turned it on as background noise to see if I could catch the announcement."

Just then, the two gentlemen on the screen grab our attention. *"Huge news coming out of Nashville today, where the Storm announced the formal retirement of head football coach, Michael Cunningham."*

"Sources tell us Coach Cunningham will be focusing on family and has stepped away immediately from the team he's coached the last twelve seasons," the second guy states.

"The search for his replacement is underway. We're told they've already compiled a list of potential head coach candidates and interviews will begin right away. Although preseason doesn't begin for several months, the Storm will waste no time in securing the man or woman who will helm their organization."

"Experts in the sports world are already buzzing about prospective coaches, including Siarra Fredricks, the first female offensive coordinator in the league, as well as Nate Vaughn, former Storm quarterback. We'll see how this transition plays out for the Storm. More after this."

I blink at the screen, clearly hallucinating.

No way is there a chance Nate's coming back to Nashville. He's in Indiana, doing who knows what.

This virus is doing a number on the few functioning brain cells I have right now. It's causing me to conjure up Nate, even when he's not here, nor is he going to be. This is the fever talking. That's the only reason I'm hearing his name on the television.

I decide to bypass the shower for now. I'll take one next time I get up. As I climb back into bed, I immediately close my eyes, the sickness pulling me into the cloudy abyss once more. Only this time, it's the face of a gorgeous quarterback I see behind my eyelids, and despite trying not to, it's his memory that carries me off to sleep once again.

It's Nate who fills my dreams.

NATE

"You should throw your name in the hat," Uncle James says.

We're sitting outside on my back deck, having a beer. We've been talking about the team and the changes we want to incorporate. That's why he's here. At least, that's what he led me to believe. I now know the true reason he wanted to stop by my place tonight.

"I'm a retired quarterback. What do I know about coaching?"

"Are you not the offensive coordinator? Does that not put you in the position of assistant coach to one of the best college teams out there right now?"

"That's college."

"It's football, Nate. If you know anything, you know the game. You see the field with a vision few do. It's like you can visualize the plays before they happen. That's talent, nephew."

"I'm not qualified."

"The hell you're not. You have a degree in sports medicine. You've played the game since you were five, not only at a grueling collegiate level but in the pros. We both know you'd still be out there on that field dominating the game had you not been injured. Your stats still list you as the best in the league, and you've been out of the game for a few years now."

I open my mouth to debate him, but I can't. He's right about all of it. However, I never imagined this was the route my life would take. I've made peace with where I am. I hate the way my career ended, but I can't change it. I miss the game, miss the Storm and my teammates, but most of all, I miss my girl. If I have any regrets, it's walking away from her.

"You love the Storm." My uncle James pushes forward in his quest for me to toss my name into the mix for the new head coach position.

"I do."

"You love the game."

"I do."

"You love Nashville."

"Yeah," I agree. "It's a great city." What I don't say is that I envisioned that's where my life would be. Retiring from the Storm and staying in the city I'd built my life around.

"So?"

I think about Oaklyn. Moving back to Nashville would give me the excuse I need to see her again. Fear grips me from the inside out as I think about her being married, maybe even having a kid by now. She should be finishing up her residency soon, and I wish that I could tell her how fucking proud I am of her.

The thought of her in my arms again has something surging inside me. Something that feels an awful lot like hope. It's been two and half years, and she's still all I can think about. I don't even look at other women. I'll never be able to move on from her unless I try. Sure, I'm risking seeing her happy with someone who's not me, but maybe that's what I need to see in order for my heart to understand that she's no longer mine. However, if there is a slim chance that she's single— "I'll do it." The words fall from my lips before I have the chance to stop them.

"Hell, yes!" Uncle James stands and pulls me from my chair, wrapping me in a hug. "My nephew is a head coach for the football league," he boasts.

"Let's not go getting ahead of ourselves, old man."

He chuckles. "They've called me every day for the past two weeks. They want you, Nate. From the eagerness coming from the Storm camp, my guess is that the job is yours, nephew."

"Tell me what I need to do," I tell him.

"I'll take care of it." He pulls his phone out of his pocket as his fingers start flying across the screen.

I should be paying more attention to what he's doing and saying, who he's texting, but all I can think about is Oaklyn. If this goes through, if I get this job, then I'll be moving back to Nashville. I'm not much of a praying man, but I send up a silent request to let her be single. Then I send up another, just in case.

Please let her be mine.

The last month has been a whirlwind. When I told Uncle James I was interested in the position of head coach for the Storm, I never anticipated I'd get called in the next day. I packed a bag immediately and drove to Nashville.

The drive there gave me not only time to think but time to hope. I told myself that if I got the job, it was a sign. A sign that I needed to reach out to Oaklyn and, at the very least, offer her an apology and an explanation. She deserves more than that, and fuck, I'd fight like hell every single day to be what she needs—what she deserves if given a chance.

I can still remember the way that my heart raced as I passed the city limit sign. It had nothing to do with the job I was about to interview for and everything to do with the woman who unknowingly stole my heart and still lives in that town.

Now, here I am, just four weeks later, pulling into my parents' driveway for the farewell dinner my mother insisted on making. I leave first thing in the morning for Nashville. I'll be starting the following day as the new head coach for the Nashville Storm.

Turning off my car, I make my way inside. The aromas of home hit me, and I get a little choked up. I love my family, and I'll miss them, but this is an opportunity of a lifetime. Not only that, I need to see her. I need to know if there's a chance for me to repair all the damage I've caused with Oaklyn.

"I made Grandma's chicken and dumplings recipe," Mom says, pulling me into a hug.

"Smells great." I return her hug, holding on just a little longer than normal.

"It's ready. Let's eat."

With my arm slung over her shoulder, we make our way to the kitchen, where my dad and Uncle James are already making their plates. "What's this?" I ask. "Shouldn't you be waiting on the guest of honor?" I joke.

"Son, I love you, but I've been smelling this meal all damn day. My stomach is pissed at me. It had to be done," Dad explains, taking a huge bite of one of Mom's homemade rolls.

"What he said." Uncle James grins before he, too, shoves a roll into his mouth.

"Dig in." Mom hands me a plate, and like the good son that I am, I do as I'm told.

"I'm stuffed," I say a little while later, pushing my plate away from me. I had two huge helpings, and if there was room in my belly, I would have gone back for a third. "I'm going to miss your cooking," I tell my mother.

"Oh, I see. My only son moves away after being home for years, and the only sentiment I get is that he's going to miss my cooking." She pretends to wipe a tear from her eye, making us all laugh. Dad puts his arm around her shoulders and pulls her close, placing a kiss on her temple.

Is it bad that I'm jealous of my parents?

Not really. I love the way that they love one another, and to be honest, I never really thought much about that before now. Before I lost everything. I grew up watching them be loving and affectionate toward one another and toward me. It's just how I was raised.

When I reached college, I learned quickly that women would pretend to be into me because they knew I was going places, or at least they assumed I was. I was their meal ticket, and I didn't want any part of that. I wanted love like my parents, but I wasn't in any hurry to find it. Football was my life. When I made it to the league, the fake interest expanded, and I became even more detached from it all. I didn't even attempt a relationship.

Not until one night I'd had enough and found myself sitting alone in an old bar on the edge of town. That night changed my life. I remember my dad used to ask me when I was going to settle down, and I'd always say there was plenty of time for that, that I wasn't looking. His reply every single time was *"You usually find most treasures in life when you're not looking."*

I haven't thought about that in a long damn time, but as I sit here around my family's dining room table, I realize Dad was right. I wasn't looking when I found my treasure. I wasn't thinking when I lost her, but I'm both looking and thinking now, and I hope like hell I can win her back.

"You know I love you," I tell her. "All of you. I know it wasn't easy to live with me these past few years. Thank you for picking me back up and kicking some motivation into my stubborn ass." I laugh.

"You were motivated," Dad replies. "The dedication you showed during rehab was unprecedented."

"It was everything else that you lacked," Uncle James chimes in.

"Thank you for giving me a chance. For pulling me out of my funk," I tell him.

He nods. "That's what family is for."

"Speaking of, I'm not selling my condo."

"You're not?" Mom's eyes light up.

I shake my head. "I need somewhere to stay when I come to visit so I'm not cramping your style."

"Never," my parents say at the same time.

"This will always be your home, Nate," Mom says softly.

"I know that. It's going to be nice to know I can come home whenever and have my own place to stay."

"Yeah, because when you start having me some grandbabies, those trips are going to need to be more often." Mom laughs.

"I'm not even dating anyone." It's my canned response, but in my mind, the only person I can see having my babies is Oaklyn.

"Well, maybe you can work on that once you're settled in Nashville, yeah?" Dad asks.

I toss my head back in laughter, hiding the pain that slices through me when I consider that the woman who I want to carry my babies might not be available. She could be the mother of some other man's kids, and that tears a hole in my heart at the thought.

"I'll see what I can do," I tell my dad.

He nods and winks, and the conversation turns to where I'll be living and when I'm going to start looking for a home base in Nashville. I answer their questions, but what I don't tell them are my plans once I get into town. I arrive in town tomorrow, which is Sunday. I report bright and early Monday, and then the weekend, well, I'm going to reach out to her. I don't know if she's changed her number. I've been too afraid to try, but next weekend, one week from today, that's going to change. It's going to be a crazy busy week, and when I call her, I want to be available whenever she is. If she is, I'll meet her anywhere, or she can come to me. She needs to see that this time, she comes first.

Pulling into the parking lot of the stadium, a million memories hit me all at once. I love this organization, and it's humbling to know that they've chosen me to lead them. I'm thankful for my deep-tinted windows that hide my grin as I park in the reserved spot for the head coach.

Nate Vaughn, Head Coach of the Nashville Storm.

No matter how many times I say that over and over in my head, it doesn't seem real. My name might not be on the sign, but in a few hours, it's going to be all over the news and social media. The press conference is scheduled for noon today. I don't know if Oaklyn is working, but I hope, wherever she is, she hears that I'm back in town.

Pulling in a long, slow deep breath, I exhale the same way before grabbing my keys and my phone and heading inside. I stop at security and see Michael Cunningham waiting for me. "Coach," I greet him. He was my coach and will never be anything but in my mind.

"Coach." He grins.

"What are you doing here?"

"You didn't think I was just going to throw you to the wolves, did you? I told them I'd stick around, bring you up to speed with where we are so that you are better equipped with the team and decisions that will need to be made after training camp and the start of preseason."

"Thank you." I nod. I truly am grateful. Michael was a huge advocate for me taking over for him, and he will forever have my gratitude for that.

"Come on. Let me show you to your office." He nods, and I follow him to the elevator as we take it to the administration level of the stadium. We stop outside what used to be his office. The nameplate now says Nate Vaughn and I'm not gonna lie. I get a little choked up seeing that.

"Hits different, huh?" he asks.

"Yeah," I croak. "Wasn't expecting that."

"After you." He motions for me to push open the office door, and I do. The walls are bare except for the team logo. "It's ready for you. I cleaned out everything that was mine, and I tried to organize it as best as I could. We all know that's not my strong suit." He chuckles.

We spend the next few hours going over where everything is in his office and the current roster, as well as the strengths and weaknesses of the team. Before I know it, there's a knock at the door, and we're led to the conference room down the hall.

I barely remember a single thing about the press conference. It's been a minute since I've been in the spotlight, but it all comes back to me. I thank the Storm and the city of Nashville for their strong welcome, and I promise to do the best that I can to follow in Coach Cunningham's footsteps. I nod and smile like I'm supposed to, but always in the back of my mind, I'm thinking about her.

Is she watching?

Has she heard the news?

Today, and every day since I pushed her away, Oaklyn is on my mind. However, we're in the same city now. She doesn't have to give up her dream for me, and even though I meant well, I know that I was a jackass. I just hope that I can convince her how sorry I am. I hope I'm not too late, that there's still a chance for us after these years apart.

I finish out the day in my office. It takes me a few hours to fill out paperwork for health insurance and benefits. I signed my contract last week, but today, this is all normal new-hire stuff. When it asks for next of kin, my hand shakes. I want so badly to write her name on that line.

I'm losing it.

Being in the same city as her has my thoughts swirling and memories crashing back like a tidal wave onto the shore. How could I have been so blind? The man I am today could kick the ass of the man I was then. At the time, I thought I was doing the right thing. I only wanted to do right by her. Present-day me sees the act for what it was.

Fear.

Fear of the unknown, fear of being a burden, fear of her making the choice to walk away.

This time, I won't let fear rule me.

This time, it's my heart that's doing the talking.

Finally, I finish all the paperwork and drop it off to human resources on my way out. I take the long way home, driving past her old place. Does she still live there? Does her best friend still reside there too? Does she still think about me? Does she miss me?

So many thoughts. So many lingering questions. I'm counting down to Saturday. The day I call her for the first time in years. I really hope she hasn't changed her number. I hope she answers, and I hope like hell that one day soon, I'll be able to call her mine.

chapter 18

Oaklyn

"Well, well, if it isn't the beautiful doctor."

I turn around and find Trevor standing behind me, a wide grin on his face. "Hello," I say, giving him a small smile of my own. "How are you?" I holler over the loud music, shifting on my stool.

"Fucking great now that I've run into you," he says, squeezing between mine and the seat beside me, leaning on the bar. "What brings you here tonight? Hot date?" he asks, waggling his eyebrows.

"Oh, no, no. I'm waiting for my friend, Natalie. She's on her way."

"Well, come hang out at my table over in the VIP overlook. At least you can wait in style," he says, already placing his hand around my upper arm to escort me toward the reserved seating area.

"I should probably wait here," I tell him, glancing around the crowded bar. "We agreed to meet at the bar."

"She'll find ya," he insists, bright pearly whites on full display. "Or send her a message and let her know where ya are, darlin'."

I'm hesitant, and I'm not certain why. The couple times I've been around Trevor, he's always been polite. A little flirty, but I think that comes with the territory of professional athlete. You can tell he's cocky, arrogant, and used to women fawning over him. That's evident by the number of women suddenly flocking to where I sit, all trying to get his attention.

He winks at a group, making them giggle, and levels his flirty gaze back at me. "Whatcha say, Doc? You wanna come keep me company while you wait?"

Figuring it wouldn't hurt, I grab my drink off the bar and stand. Even though it's still early, there's already a crowd in the popular bar owned by a famous country singer. But hell, aren't all bars in Nashville owned by musicians? This one I've never been to. Popular tourist traps aren't my thing. I prefer the quieter bars with small crowds compared to this chaos, but here I am, right smack dab in the middle of Blake Shelton's bar during a heavy tourist season.

Trevor places his hand on my back and guides me through the crowd. Several people stop to catch his attention, but he just smiles or gives them a nod as we pass on by. We reach the stairs, and as I try to put a little distance between myself and Trevor, he keeps his body close to mine with his hand on my hip. As soon as we reach his booth, I slide inside, keeping myself on the opposite side from where he sits.

Grinning at me from across the table, he says, "Blake's supposed to be here later and play. That's why the place is already packed."

"Ahh," I say, taking a small sip of the fruity concoction I ordered from the bar. I pull out my phone and fire off a message to Natalie.

Me:	Bar is already packed. I'm up in VIP with that Trevor guy who plays for the Storm.
Natalie:	My Uber is stuck in terrible traffic. I could probably walk there faster. I'll be a while yet. Will find you when I get inside.
Me:	I hope you can get in. I wouldn't be surprised if they've already reached capacity.
Natalie:	Don't you worry about me. That guy Felix I've been seeing is a bouncer. He'll get me in.
Me:	K. Hurry.

I shift in my seat, setting my phone on the tabletop. Trevor is watching me with what I'm certain is desire in his eyes. He's asked me out, offered me that open-ended invitation to have dinner with him, but has never pushed. The way he's looking at me lets me know he's still very much interested, would probably walk right out of the bar with me if I suggested it.

Unfortunately for him, I'm not. He seems like a perfectly nice man, but I'm just not attracted to him. Not like that, and to be honest, it sucks. I wish I could throw caution to the wind, say the hell with it, and go out with him.

I wish I weren't being held hostage by the memory of a man from my past.

Yet, here we are.

"All good?" he asks, nodding toward my phone.

"Yep. I just let my friend know where I was."

Trevor nods and takes a pull from his beer bottle. His eyes are locked on mine the entire time, making me a touch uncomfortable. I've had people stare at me before, but never for this length of time. I really hope Natalie hurries up.

"So, are any of your teammates here?" I ask.

"Not yet. Probably later, though. You know many of them?" he asks, catching the attention of a server as she passes. "Two shots of Patron, love." He winks, and the way she blushes and bites her bottom lip is an indication they've probably slept together. Especially when his eyes drop down to her short skirt as if he's visualizing more than just what she might be wearing underneath it.

"Just Jax," I reply, drawing his eyes away from the server he's eye-fucking.

"You were his doc, right?"

I nod, even though technically I was just a resident and not the attending. I was able to be an active part of the surgery, but Dr. Harrison took the lead and gave all the instruction. Not that Trevor really cares or needs to know all of that.

Suddenly, he slides around the crescent-shaped booth and is right next to me. He brushes my hair off my forehead and cups my cheek in his big hand. "You're a very beautiful woman."

My throat is dry and my breathing is coming in short little pants. "Thank you."

He grins, gliding his big, meaty thumb over my bottom lip. His eyes zero in on where he touches me, and I can tell he's thinking about kissing me. Suddenly, I pull back, wanting to put a little distance between us. I didn't come up here to make out with him. Is that what he's expecting?

"Umm, excuse me. I need to use the restroom," I say, scooting back and practically stumbling out of the bench seat.

Trevor looks confused for a moment before offering me another wide grin. "No problem. There's one just down that hall there," he says, pointing to my left where a handful of people come and go.

I grab my phone, plaster on a fake smile, and make my way toward the bathroom. There's a small line, but fortunately, it doesn't take me long to get inside one of the stalls. As soon as I do, I enter my phone's code and pull up my text message app.

Me: I think Trevor was about to kiss me.

Natalie: Shut up, really? That's great!

Me: Why does it feel wrong?

My heart hammers in my chest while I wait for her reply. The crazy part of it is, as good-looking as Trevor is, I don't want him to kiss me. The thought makes my stomach clench, and not in a good way. He seems perfectly nice, but he's just not who I want to kiss.

How fucked up is that?

The only man I want kissing me left two and a half years ago. Yet, he's still an active part of my life, as if he's truly here.

My God, how long will this longing for him go on? When will I finally be free of his memory?

Natalie: Because you're still stuck on the man we're not naming. There's nothing wrong with kissing someone, Oaklyn. If you think that man is sitting at his home, pining over a woman he hasn't seen in more than two years, you're sadly mistaken.

I blink hard as tears fill my eyes. She's right. I know she is, but I can't seem to get my heart to catch up with my brain. Even after all this time, I still feel stuck.

Me: I know.

Natalie: I'm still trapped in traffic. There appears to be a bad accident, and no one knows how to maneuver around it.

Me: I think I'm going to go home.

Natalie: No! We're supposed to be celebrating! You're almost finished with your residency and will begin your first official gig as a doctor soon. This was our night to party!

I let out a sigh in frustration.

Me: Yes, but you're not even here. You're stuck in an Uber somewhere.

Natalie: True. This sucks. I'm sorry.

Me: It's fine. We can plan another night soon.

Natalie: I'm holding you to that.

Me: Of course you are. I might even let you talk me into coming back to a bar like this. But maybe not this one. This place is madness with people.

Natalie: Where are you?

Me: Hiding in the bathroom.

Natalie: Jeez, Oak. Call a ride and go home. Text me when you get there.

Me: You too.

Natalie: I've already told the driver to take me back in the other direction. I'll let you know when I finally get there.

Me: Be safe.

Natalie: You too. *insert kissy face emoji*

I take a deep breath, slip my phone into my wristlet, and step out of the stall. The lady at the front of the line gives me an annoyed look, as if she knew I wasn't actually peeing in there, and scrambles around me to close the door. I stop at a sink to wash my hands before exiting the room, anxious to get home.

The plan is to find Trevor, thank him for inviting me to join him, but politely excusing myself to go. I move around two women waiting near the bathroom door, but don't make it any farther. I'm pulled backward and pressed against the wall, a large body caging me in place.

"I was starting to wonder if you slipped away," Trevor whispers, leaning into my much-smaller frame. His erection presses into my stomach as unwelcome as rain at an outdoor wedding.

"Long line in the bathroom," I tell him, turning my head so my lips are off to the side. "I need to get going, though."

"I thought you were waiting for your friend." He grips my hip, his fingers angling downward over the globe of my ass.

"She was stuck in traffic, so we decided to meet at her place. She's expecting me."

He hums and leans in closer. His mouth glides across my neck. "I thought we were having fun this evening."

I clear my throat and try to pull away from his lips. "I appreciate you inviting me to sit at your table, but I really need to go."

He pauses and meets my gaze. "So that's it?"

"Yes," I whisper, my throat Sahara dry.

"So you're just a cock tease?"

My eyes widen. "What? I didn't tease you."

"No? You were practically begging for my cock when we were downstairs."

You could probably pick my jaw up off the floor right now. "Excuse me? I never once said anything to lead you on."

He snorts in disgust. "Do you know how many women come to my table? I could have had anyone in this bar, and I picked you. And this is how you repay me?"

"You're disgusting," I counter, pushing back against his chest to create space between us. He doesn't move. Trevor has me at a big advantage here, both in weight and height.

"Whatever, bitch," he mutters, taking a step back. He turns to his left and finds two women there. They're wearing skimpy little dresses and too-tall heels that look hard to walk in. He walks their way and smiles. "Ladies, care to join me this evening?" he asks, throwing his arms around their shoulders and walking away, leading them to his table.

I sigh a deep breath, my entire body filling with relief. Without even a look to where he sits with the blonde bimbos, I move quickly through the crowd and head for the stairs. My feet carry me as fast as they'll go, bobbing and weaving through the masses, trying not to push my way through. When I finally hit the sidewalk outside, my chest feels a little looser than before.

My hands shake as I pull my phone out of my wristlet. Tears swim in my eyes again, but I refuse to let them fall. One asshole is not going to cause me to have a total meltdown in the middle of Broadway. I'll wait until I'm home—alone—before I let the tears fall.

Pulling up Natalie's name, I click Call right away. I know I need to organize a car, but I need to hear my best friend's voice first. I take a few steps away from the crowd outside the bar, distancing myself from the higher noise level in search of a space to talk.

It rings once.

Twice.

"Oaklyn?"

My heart seizes in my chest at the sound of his voice.

"Nate?" I whisper, pulling my phone away from my head to check the screen.

Oh. My. God.

I called Nate, not Natalie.

"Oaklyn? Is that you?"

I close my eyes, letting the deep timbre of his words wash over me.

"Oaklyn, you're starting to scare me. Are you all right?" There's definite worry in his question as he tries to get me to talk to him.

"I… uh… I didn't mean to call you," I say quietly, the erratic beat of my heart probably louder than the words I speak.

"Okay," he says calmly. "But that doesn't answer my question. Are you okay?"

I blink several times. "I—I… I don't know."

"Where are you?" he asks, an urgency coming across the line.

"I'm on Broadway. In front of Ole Red," I tell him, realizing I'm already about half a block away from the bar. I stop walking and move out of the way for the people passing by.

"And Natalie? Is she with you?"

"No," I reply softly. "She's stuck in traffic."

"I'm three blocks away, Oaklyn. I'm coming to get you."

"That's not necessary," I say, my brain finally starting to catch up a little. "I'll schedule a ride."

"Don't be ridiculous. I'm two blocks away now. I'm almost there," he tells me calmly.

Something about his collected demeanor has me breathing a little slower and relaxing a bit more. "I'm near the Candy Kitchen," I say, stopping directly in front of the small business.

"I'm approaching from your left, passing Ole Red now. Do you see me? I'm the black SUV," he says.

Stepping forward to the edge of the sidewalk, I spot a new blacked-out Range Rover slowing down and stopping directly in front of me. He rolls the passenger window down, and my heart just stops.

"Get in," he gently instructs.

I glance back toward Ole Red. Definitely not going back there. I pull open the door and climb inside the SUV without giving it a second thought. I'm fastening my seat belt as he presses down on the gas pedal, causing us to surge forward.

We make it two blocks before either of us speaks. "Are you all right, Oaklyn?"

Exhaling, I nod. "Yeah. I am."

"Okay."

We drive a few more blocks before I glance around at the plush interior. "An SUV? What happened to that fancy sports car?"

He smiles, causing warmth to spread through my entire body. "I had to give it back to the dealership after my injury. Too hard to get in and out of it with a bum knee anyway, so when I was finally able to drive again, I went and ordered this. She's a pretty lady, isn't she?" he asks, running his hand along the black console.

"It's all black," I state unnecessarily.

"It is," he agrees. "I like her."

I glance at the man sitting behind the wheel, looking as comfortable in the SUV as he did in that small sports car he used to drive. His dark hair is a little longer on the top than it used to be and he has a few wrinkles framing his hypnotic dark eyes. His build is still fit and his skin tan, and all I can think of is how familiar he looks.

Yet so very different all the same.

"Oaklyn?"

"Hmm?" I ask when I realize he's talking to me.

"I asked where you live now."

"Oh, uh, at the same apartment."

His eyes flare just a bit, but he keeps his eyes on the road ahead of us.

"Is something wrong?" I ask, shifting in my seat and wishing I could see his face fully.

"No, nothing's wrong. I just, well, I thought you would have moved by now. I drove past there earlier in the week and wondered if you were still there."

He drove by my house?

Intentionally?

As we near my neighborhood, I blurt, "I didn't mean to call you. I thought I was calling Natalie. I must have hit Nate by accident."

He slowly nods, not saying a word as he nears my apartment. Pulling into the drive and stopping in front of the security box, he puts the SUV in park and grabs his wallet from the cupholder. "Oaklyn, you did call me, and I consider that a sign."

Before I can say a word, he pulls a card from his wallet and holds it up. "Did you change my visitor's security clearance?"

I shake my head, shocked he still has my visitor's card in his wallet. "No."

He rolls down the window and scans the card through the device.

"You still have my card?"

Glancing my way, he grins. "Watch and learn, baby."

Once the gate opens, he drives through, winding his way into the lot where my designated parking spots are positioned. As if he was here just the other day, he pulls into the spot beside my vehicle and stops, turning off the ignition and facing me.

"We need to talk."

"Talk?" I ask, my mind spinning.

"Yes, talk. You need to tell me what happened back there."

"Why are you here?" I blurt, completely ignoring what he was saying.

Nate grins softly. "I have so much to tell you. Can we go inside? To talk?"

"Talk," I say, repeating that word once more. It wasn't that long ago when *talking* was the last thing on our minds when we were together.

He climbs out of the driver's seat and comes around to where I sit. When he opens the door, he extends his hand. I stare at it for a few seconds before reaching out and placing my own within his. My mind is swimming, spinning in multiple directions. What in the world is he doing here? Despite accidentally calling him, the fact he was mere blocks away when I phoned is a little hard to process. And now he wants to go to my apartment? To talk?

This has bad idea written all over it.

Yet, I know there's no other real option right now.

As I stand up, I confirm, "Talk."

Nate nods, holding onto my hand. "Yes, Oaklyn. We need to talk. Can I come inside?"

"Yes," I find myself replying, my heart trying to beat right out of my chest.

We walk toward the entrance of my building.

Me and Nate.

Together.

For the first time in years.

And I don't hate it.

Not even a little.

NATE

I KEEP HER HAND LOCKED in mine as I follow Oaklyn into her building and onto the elevator. She steps to one side while I take the opposite. There are a few feet between us, but it feels like miles. The miles that I created when I pushed her away.

My palms are sweaty, and my heart is hammering inside my chest. I've imagined this moment so many times, but it never started like this. It never started with a random phone call that wasn't meant for me. Regardless of how we got here, I'm with my girl, and I know it's going to fucking kill me to leave her tonight.

Hope wells in my chest, but so does the anxiety. Hope, because she still lives here, and she's letting me come up so we can talk. That means she lives alone, right? Surely, if she was married or dating someone, she wouldn't have agreed. My eyes drop to her hands.

No ring.

Anxiety bubbles for a few reasons. First of all, I'm here with her because she called me thinking she was calling her best friend. I could hear in the tone of her voice she was upset. She looked distraught when I picked her up, and that's not okay with me. She was there at that bar all on her own, and if someone hurt her, laid a hand on her, I don't know what I'll do. The rage that boils inside me at the thought is scary even to me.

Another reason I'm anxious is because seeing her again validates why there has been no one else for me since the moment I pushed her away. I know deep in my soul that Oaklyn is the only woman I will ever love. Can I show her that? Can I convince her that we should be together and that I fucked up? That pushing her away was not only the biggest mistake but also the biggest regret of my life.

Will she believe me when I tell her I love her? It's more than just the emotion. She's in my veins, her hands are wrapped around my heart, and I know without a shadow of a doubt that's how it will always be.

I'll always be hers.

When the elevator doors slide open, I wait for her to step out before following along like the lovesick sap that I am for her. I wait patiently. My hands are still fisted at my sides while she unlocks her apartment. She steps inside and motions for me to do the same. I know it sounds crazy, but as soon as the door closes behind us, I feel as though I've taken my first full breath in over two years.

"Can I get you something to drink?" Her voice is soft and uncertain.

"No, baby, I'm okay right now." Her eyes widen at the term of endearment. "Can we sit?"

"Sure." She kicks off her shoes and curls her legs beneath her on the couch.

I take the seat next to her, turning so we're facing one another. I study her features. Fuck me. I didn't understand how much I missed her until the moment I saw her name on my phone earlier tonight. I knew I missed her, but this, being here with her, sitting beside her… I never want to leave.

"I have so much to say. I don't know where to start," I confess. I reach for her hand but quickly pull back. I don't have the right to touch her. Not until she hears me out. We sit in silence while I process my thoughts, all while the urge to feel her skin against mine is too strong. Reaching out again, I take her hand in mine, lacing our fingers together. "I miss you."

The look on her face tells me I've shocked her. "I'm a big girl, Nate. You don't have to give me all the pretty words to make this less awkward." She drops her gaze to her lap as if she can't bear to look at me.

"I know that. I do, and I'm not just spewing pretty words to make this less awkward. I miss the fuck out of you, Oaklyn. I didn't want to be a burden to you, so I pushed you away." I pause and lift the hand that's not gripping her to cradle her soft cheek. The freedom of finally confessing to her is a huge weight off my shoulders.

"I know your heart, baby. I knew you would sacrifice yourself for me. I knew you would have worked yourself to the bone to help take care of me. I didn't want that for you. You were just starting your residency, and you needed to focus on yourself and your career. I'd already lost mine."

I watch as she closes her eyes and takes a deep breath. I would give anything to know what she's thinking. I know I fucked up. I know I have to prove to her she's the only one for me. What I don't know is if she's going to let me.

"Say something," I whisper.

Slowly, her eyes blink open, and they're shimmering with tears. "That was my choice to make. Besides, we were just friends with benefits, right?" She pulls her hand from mine and crosses her arms over her chest.

"That's what we said we were, yes."

"That's what I was to you. I was a convenient way for you to get your dick wet."

I'm already shaking my head. "No. No, you were everything. You're still everything."

She scoffs. "You really expect me to believe that, Nate? It's been years. Years!" she exclaims. "Years and not one attempt to contact me. I've been here in this apartment the entire time. You knew my residency was at the hospital. You knew my best friend's name. There were ways. Hell, you still had my fucking number in your phone. When you answered, you said my name. You. Said. My. Name." She sucks in a ragged breath. "Now, here you sit, expecting me to believe you missed me? Nice try, quarterback."

"I'm not a quarterback, not anymore." She gives me an exasperated look, so I keep going. "I took a new job. With the Storm. I'm the new head coach." Something flashes in her eyes, a sparkle that I've missed like fucking crazy, but she masks it quickly.

"My mistake. Nice try, Coach," she says, rolling her big hazel eyes.

"I'm here to stay. I don't know how long I'll hold this position, but I'm not leaving Nashville. Not without you."

"Nate—" she starts, but I hold my hand up to stop her.

"I thought you were better off without me. Not a single fucking day has passed where I didn't think about you."

"Right," she says, dragging out the word. "The next thing you're going to tell me is you've not dated anyone else since me."

"I haven't."

"Don't lie to me, Nate. I deserve better than that."

"You do," I agree. "That's why I'm not lying to you. I have not touched a woman since you. I've never lied to you. I'm guilty of not knowing my own heart and pushing you away, but I never once lied to you. You're it for me."

Her lips part in shock, but she quickly schools her features. "You really expect me to believe that?"

"It's the truth. I lived with my parents until last year, and then the only person I hung out with was my family, or Joel, who was my physical therapist. He's a good guy. You'd like him."

"I can't do this with you right now," she says. Her shoulders fall, and it's as if all the fight has drained from her body.

"What upset you tonight? I could hear it in your voice."

"Nothing. I was just ready to go home. Nat was stuck in traffic on the other side of town, and I was letting her know we could reschedule another night."

She's lying. "Now, tell me the real reason."

"I don't owe you anything," she tells me. Her tone is soft, and her voice is shaky. She's deflecting because she doesn't want to talk about it.

"You don't owe me anything, but I owe you my truth, and I hope that one day I'll earn your trust." I take a deep breath and lay it all out for her. "I missed the fuck out of you, Oaklyn. The only reason I took this job is because I knew that Nashville was where you were. I wanted to see you. I wasn't sure if you had moved on. Hell, for all I knew, you could have been married by now. I hoped like hell that you weren't, and here we are." I take her hand in mine once again, this time bringing it to my lips and pressing a kiss to her palm. "I want you. I've always wanted you."

"As long as no one knew we were together." There is hurt in her tone, and it crushes me. It wasn't about hiding her as much as keeping what we had out of the media.

"No. I mean, yes, that's how it started, but, babe, by the time my injury rolled around, you were all I could think about. I wanted you with me all the time. We spent every night I was not traveling together. Even nights when you worked late. There was never a time, not a single fucking moment from the night I laid eyes on you, that I didn't want you."

"Do you understand why this is hard for me, Nate? The entire time we were together, we were never really together unless it was at your place or mine. We never went on a date, and we were in a closet relationship. Now here you are after pushing me away, telling me you've wanted me all along? Am I dreaming right now? I know what we had. I was good with how things were, but here you are telling me that it was more, that you want more after more than two and a half years apart."

"We started out in the closet. I didn't want the media to hound me about you or you about me. We started out just hooking up, but it became more for me. You were more to me than just getting my dick wet."

"You never said a word." Her voice cracks.

"Because I was in denial. I didn't understand what I was feeling. I didn't realize until the moment you walked out of my door for the last time that you were everything. Days, weeks, months, and years passed by, and that feeling never wavered. I fucked up. I let my fears push away the best thing that ever happened to me."

"We could have made it work," she says softly.

"We still can."

Her eyes bore into mine. "Has too much time passed?" If I'm not mistaken, there's hope in her voice. She's afraid to believe that I'm real, that I want her. Want us for a lifetime.

"No." I shake my head because just saying the word isn't enough. "No. I fucked up, but I'm going to show you what you mean to me. I'm going to make sure the entire fucking world knows you're why I'm here. You are my reason for being back in this city. If you decide your career is going to take you elsewhere, then I'll resign and follow you."

"Nate, that's… a bold statement."

I place my hands on her cheeks. "Isn't it obvious?" I ask her, my voice soft.

"What?" she whispers.

"How much I love you." She sucks in a ragged breath. "I love you, Oaklyn. Every fucking day has been nothing but thoughts of you, and I know it's my fault. I know I ended things, but I truly didn't want to be your burden."

"You could have never been a burden to me, Nate." She swallows hard, forcing back her emotions.

"I see that now. Then, I had so many emotions going through me I just reacted. I regret it, and I'm here now, and I'm going to make it right."

"How do you plan to do that?" she asks. I can tell she's starting to thaw a little. I can only hope I'm getting through to her.

"Watch and learn, baby. Watch and learn." I smirk, and she shakes her head, and if I'm not mistaken, there is a slight tilt of her lip. A barely there hint of a smile, but I'll fucking take it.

"Now, tell me, what happened that had you so shaken up?" I take a risk by sitting back on the couch and pulling her onto my lap. She doesn't resist, and I take that as a win.

"Just a mouthy, entitled asshole not wanting to take no for an answer."

I take a minute to get my anger under control. The last thing I need to do is go all raging Hulk and scare her or piss her off. "Did he touch you?" My anger is barely contained, and you can tell from the tone of my voice. My words are gruff, full of grit and concern for her. Although I tried to mask my anger, I did a shit job of it.

"No. He kind of caged me in, but he didn't hurt me. Just had too many beers and thought he was God's gift to women."

"Do you know him?"

"Yeah."

"Are you going to tell me who he was?"

"No."

"No?"

"He's high profile here in Nashville. I've run into him a few times over the past couple of years. He's always asking me out, and I always politely decline. Tonight, he asked me to sit with him and his buddies in the VIP section while I waited for Natalie. My gut said I shouldn't, but I let him talk me into it. I knew immediately, just from the way he was looking at me, that it was a bad idea. I excused myself to the restroom, and he cornered me as soon as I came out."

I tighten my hold on her. "I'm gonna need a name, babe."

"I handled it. I left. He didn't hurt me. I needed to call Nat. I need to hear her voice. I was upset. It was dark, and I hit your name instead of hers."

"You kept my number."

She shrugs. "I didn't plan to use it." She squirms in my lap. She might not have planned to use it, but she didn't want to lose that connection, and I'm so damn thankful it was me she called tonight.

"It was fate. Not that I wasn't already planning on coming for you."

"What do you mean? Coming for me?"

"I had a plan. A grand plan. Tomorrow morning, I was going to show up outside of your door and knock. I hoped like hell that you were going to be home and I wouldn't find someone here with you."

"Why not call?"

"I wasn't sure if you would pick up, and that's not a chance I was willing to take. So, yeah, fate stepped in, and here we are."

"This has been a weird day."

I laugh softly and place a featherlight kiss on her shoulder. "It's been the best day. Well, I could have done without some asshole scaring you, but everything else, it was good. This" — I give her a gentle squeeze — "is good."

"It's getting late," she says, and she tries to move off my lap. Of course, I don't release her.

"When can I see you again?"

"I still work a lot. I'm wrapping up my residency."

"We'll make it work. You tell me, and I'll take care of the rest."

"You walked away from me once, pushed me away, and I'm scared you'll do it again."

"I won't," I say with conviction. "I'll prove it to you. I'm not afraid of hard work, Oaklyn. You know this about me. I'll never stop. Every fucking day for the rest of my life, I'll bust my ass to show you that you are the most important person in my life."

"Coming from a man I haven't seen in two and a half years."

"Coming from a man who knows he fucked up. A man who knows you own every single piece of his heart. A man that would do anything to make sure not a day goes by that you don't know how much you mean to him."

She relaxes into me. "Big shoes to fill, Coach." Her tone is lighter, and it feels as though we've turned a corner tonight.

"I told you, baby. Watch and learn."

"Still cocky as ever."

"I'm confident in my love for you. I'm confident there is no one else on this earth I could feel this way about."

She sucks in a ragged breath. I watch as she opens her mouth, then closes it before finally replying, "You should go."

This time when she tries to move from her place on my lap, I let her. She settles back onto the cushion next to me.

"I assume, since you were going out tonight, that you're off tomorrow?"

"Yeah, I work a clinic schedule mostly, which means no weekends unless I pick up shifts at the hospital for the remainder of my residency."

"I'll let you sleep in, but I'll be here around nine to take you to breakfast."

"Nate." She sighs.

"Let me show you, Oaklyn. I know I hurt you. I hurt both of us, and I know I have a lot to make up for. Let me."

"You've been gone for a couple of years, but as soon as you step out onto the streets of Nashville, people are going to recognize you. Especially with your new position."

"You're right. There is nothing that I can do about that. The recognition and the fame come with the job. I'm sorry you're going to be thrust into the spotlight, but, baby, I'm all in this time around. Hell, I was all in the last time. I was just too fucking caught up in denial. I couldn't see the forest for the trees. I'm seeing clearly now. In fact, things have never been clearer."

"Rumors are going to start."

"What rumors?"

"About me. About us."

"Baby, they're not rumors if they're true. I want you. I want all of you, and I want the entire fucking world to know it."

"Nate. You've been gone a long time. We're different people now." She's trying to protect her heart, but she'll soon realize that it's my job to protect every piece of her.

"No, we're not. Sure, we've changed, but my heart still recognizes yours. However, if you're not ready, I'll give you a little time to adjust. We're still having breakfast. I'll still be here at nine. I'll bring breakfast."

"You don't have to do that."

"I want to. Please let me." I'm not opposed to begging for morsels of her time. Whatever it takes to make this right. To make her see that she's mine.

"Make it ten." There is a slow tilt of her lips, and it takes everything I have not to lean in and kiss her.

I smile. "Ten it is." I stand from the couch, lean over, and place a kiss on her forehead. "Lock up behind me." I move to the door and stand, waiting for her to come to me. She rolls those beautiful eyes of hers again, and my smile grows. Once she's close, I snake an arm around her waist and pull her into a hug.

"I love you. I'll see you tomorrow." I don't give her a chance to say it back. Instead, I open the door and stroll out of her apartment, feeling like the king of the fucking world.

I'm getting my girl back.

Permanently.

Oaklyn

Nate: Good morning, beautiful. See you at ten.

I CAN'T HELP BUT SMILE as I read the message on my screen for the umpteenth time.

Is this real?

It feels more like a dream, honestly. I've imagined Nate coming back so many times over the last two and a half years, but I never actually expected it to transpire. And I never thought our first communication after years apart would happen the way it did.

It's fate, silly girl.

It's not fate.

It's happenstance.

I didn't mean to call him, that's for sure. If I were going to pick up the phone and call his number, it wouldn't be when I was on the verge of tears and having a mini freak-out on the streets of Nashville. I pictured our first meeting after all this time to be a bit more glamorous, like where I'm wearing something super sexy and look amazing, and maybe with fewer tears. Not that I was dressed poorly last night, but the basic skinny jeans and light blue short-sleeved sweater wasn't anything fancy.

At least I wasn't in scrubs.

I think back to all the times I was wearing just that, and he didn't seem to mind. Of course, that was when we were basically just fucking and those scrubs were coming off pretty quickly. But at some point, it changed into something more. I felt it, but did he really too? He says he did but was just too afraid to own it.

So what now?

I wish I had the answers. If anything, since I accidentally called him last night, the waters seem incredibly murky. I don't like not knowing what's out there, swimming around me. In medical school and throughout my residency, I never knew exactly what the next day would bring, but there was always a plan. A strategy for achieving what was laid before me. An opportunity to learn and grow.

Now, I have no idea what that is, and it's bothering me.

A lot.

I called him on his bullshit about dating, and he adamantly denied it. That I don't get. He's Nate freaking Vaughn. Women threw themselves at him. I've seen the articles and the photos from his time in the league. Hell, I even saw a few from when he was in college at Purdue. Was he really telling me he hasn't dated one woman since he left Nashville?

Yes, I realize I could say the same thing. I haven't dated, but because I felt stuck. Trapped in his memory with no way out. So I focused on my work to the best of my ability and ignored the ache in my heart. The idea was to keep doing so until it finally stopped hurting. Now that plan is blown to hell, thanks to his sudden appearance in my life.

Numbly, I climb out of bed and head for the shower. If I'm going to face Nate Vaughn again after two and a half years, I'm doing it freshly showered. And perhaps well caffeinated. As I strip out of my tank top and sleep shorts, I wonder if I'll have time to run down to the coffee shop on the corner. I should be considered part owner at this point. It definitely has helped keep me going throughout my residency.

I could also ask Nate to stop by and grab me something. He is bringing breakfast, after all. What's a few extra minutes for a large caramel latte with extra whip? No, I'm not asking him to bring me coffee. That doesn't seem appropriate, considering he's not my boyfriend.

I spend a few extra minutes in the shower, washing my hair twice and shaving my legs. I don't know why, other than it boosts my confidence. I have no intentions of letting Nate discover just how smooth my skin is or how fruity my hair smells. We'll sit a respectable distance apart from each other for this shared meal, and all hands will be kept to themselves.

Yeah. Keep telling yourself that.

I leave my wet hair down to dry naturally and add just a touch of makeup to my eyes to make them pop. Once I'm presentable without looking like I'm trying to impress him, I head to my closet to find something to wear. I settle on a pair of black capri leggings and an old fitted T-shirt with my college logo on the front. I'm definitely not going for style here. This morning is all about comfort for me, in an attempt to keep an even footing and a level head. Finally, it's time to search for coffee.

Before I make it to my kitchen, however, there's a knock on my door. I'm not expecting Nate for another fifteen minutes, so it must be Natalie. I haven't told her about last night yet, mostly because I haven't had the time. Last night, by the time Nate left, it was late, and I needed a little time to process. Lord knows there's plenty for us to talk about since I talked to her last.

I'm still trying to process his sudden appearance in my life again. It's confusing, especially with his sudden insistence to prove to me how much I mean to him. Not because I don't feel the same, but simply because I'm overwhelmed. I want to jump straight into his arms, to bask in the warmth and comfort they provide, but I'm scared. Last time I was with him, he tossed me away out of fear. Yes, I can understand his reasons to an extent, but it still doesn't change the fact I was hurt.

I don't bother with the peephole and throw open the lock. When I pull on the door, I'm surprised to see Nate at my doorstep. He holds up a coffee cup and says, "Caffeine."

My eyes narrow as I reach for the cup. "Did you bug my house or something?"

"What?" he asks with a chuckle.

"How'd you know?" I ask, bringing the cup to my mouth and taking that magical first sip.

Nate leans in and kisses my cheek. "Because I know you, Oaklyn. And I knew you'd want one of those fancy caramel drinks you used to live off that first part of your residency. I figured if I grabbed one for you early enough, I'd get here before you ran down to the corner shop," he says.

I gape at him as he passes by me, entering my apartment like he's done it a million times before.

"How'd you sleep?" he asks after I close and lock the door and follow him into my kitchen.

"Fine," I tell him, even though it's not exactly the truth. I couldn't fall asleep for the longest time last night, and when I finally did, it was pretty fitful.

He watches me, those dark eyes tracking my every move. "Hmm," he says, setting a paper sack on the table and pulling out the contents.

"What does that mean? 'Hmm'?"

"It just means *hmm*. I was trying to gauge if I believe you or not."

"How'd you sleep?" I ask, turning the question from me and pointing it directly back at him.

"Like a baby," he says, boasting a wide smile that lights up his entire face.

Ugh, stupid heart getting all mushy and skipping a beat when he does that.

"Hmm," I reply, turning my attention to the containers of food on the table.

"Aren't you gonna ask me why?" He opens the first container, revealing fluffy pancakes and small cups of syrup.

"Why what?" I ask, my stomach growling as the aromas hit my nose.

"Why I slept so well," he says, popping open the second container, which is full of crispy bacon and sausage links.

I reach up and wipe my mouth, fearful I'm drooling, and turn to grab two bottles of water from my fridge. "Okay, I'll bite. Why did you sleep so well, Nate?"

He grins smugly, opening the third and final container. Inside, it's heaped with biscuits and gravy. My mouth waters. "I slept so well because I finally have you back in my life and am going to do whatever it takes to keep you there. Sit."

I blink a few times before his words really register. I drop down onto the seat unceremoniously and stare blankly at what he's brought. He places a plate in front of me and starts piling on the food. He scoops up a biscuit with gravy onto each plate, then adds some sausage and bacon. He tops it off with a pancake and slides one of the small cups of syrup toward me.

"Eat, Oaklyn."

I do as instructed, sipping my coffee and taking bites of my breakfast, all while keeping an eye on the man sitting across from me. He's watching me intently, too, as if we're both afraid the other might vanish if we glance away for even a second.

"How's work?" he asks, breaking the silence.

I let out a sigh of relief, grateful he's talking about something else. My world has been spinning since last night, and work makes me feel like I have both feet on the ground. "Good. I'm finishing my residency at a family clinic and will be starting full time with them on June first," I state proudly.

His smile is breathtaking. "That's awesome, Oaklyn. I'm so fucking proud of you. You're almost there. Two weeks?"

I nod, unable to hide my own grin. "Yeah. Two weeks left and it's official."

"You're gonna make a kick-ass doctor."

My eyebrows pull together in question. "How do you know that?"

He meets my gaze, setting his fork down on his plate. "Because I know you. I know your heart. You are the most caring, empathetic, and respectable individual I've ever known, and being a doctor is in your blood. One of the first things that caught my attention when I met you was how your face lit up like a Christmas tree as you talked about med school and how you wanted to be a physician because of Natalie's asthma. I knew from that moment you were special and would change the world, one diagnosis and patient at a time."

My cheeks feel hot as I look back at him. "When you met me, it was for sex."

He pulls a face and grabs his fork once more, stabbing a piece of sausage and taking a bite. "It may have started as something casual, but it was anything but. I made a mistake, Oaklyn. I shouldn't have pushed you away, but I can't change it now. All I can do is learn from my mistake and make amends. I plan to do just that."

"How?" My heart starts to gallop in my chest with something that feels a lot like hope. It's wild to want something so badly, yet still being so terrified to grab onto it.

Nate gives me that cocky grin I remember. The one he'd flash me right before he took the field or made a big play. "I'm going to woo you."

A snort of laughter flies from my mouth as my heart flutters in my chest. "Woo me? Is this the nineteen fifties?"

"I'm going to show you exactly how I feel about you. I'm going to date you. And no, we're not going to have sex."

What? No sex?

Why does that thought make me incredibly sad?

And a little uncomfortable, because sitting here with Nate, listening to the deep timbre of his voice again, is causing all sorts of tingling between my legs. This no-sex thing isn't going to help relieve the ache, that's for sure.

The corner of his mouth curls up. "I like where your mind has gone. I'm not saying no sex ever. I'm saying it won't happen until you realize I'm all in. I'm going to woo you, and when you finally see how much I love you, then we'll take it to the next level. Until then, I'm keeping the horse in the barn," he says, standing up and taking our empty plates to the trash.

"Nate?" I turn in my chair to face him, while he leans against the counter. He's wearing athletic shorts and a Storm T-shirt, looking as edible today as he did the night I met him. "I'm not trying to make this difficult on you. I'm just a little… confused."

He pushes off the counter and stalks my way. Bending down, he places his lips to my own in a chaste kiss. "Make me work for it, baby. That's the only way I know how to win. To put in the time, to focus on the goal, to fight."

"What's your goal?" I ask, my throat suddenly dry and my tongue heavy.

He kisses me once more but doesn't deepen it the way my body craves. "You. You're the end goal, Oaklyn." He stands up to his full height and grabs his water bottle, tossing it in the trash as well. "I'll lock up behind me."

"Where are you going?" I ask, a hint of panic in my voice as I jump from my chair.

"I'm going to my new place to do some more unpacking. One of these days, I'll show it to you."

"You have a house?"

He nods, keeping his hands at his sides, even though I really wish he'd reach for me. "It's not too far from my previous place. This one's even closer to the stadium. The owners moved out almost four months ago now, and it's sat empty since. When I made an offer, they agreed to let me take possession right away, renting it until the paperwork for the sale all goes through."

"That's nice," I tell him lamely.

"It's a great place." His eyes burn with something that looks a lot like longing mixed with truth. "It'd be the perfect place to start a family."

My mouth drops open.

Is he saying what I think he's saying?

"We're not there yet, Oaklyn. I know that, but a man can dream, right? Like I said, I've got goals, baby."

Shaking my head, I reply, "This is all so overwhelming." My mind is struggling to catch up with my heart. That pesky organ is all in, ready to commit, but my mind is still a little hesitant. My brain wants to make sure we're doing the right thing by taking small steps forward.

It's been years since I've felt like I wasn't stuck in limbo, and it feels nice.

"I know. That's why I'm leaving, even though I don't want to, but I know you need time. I won't crowd you, but I am pursuing you."

"Wooing me, right?" I ask, grinning up at him and feeling a bit lighter than I did earlier. My heart is… well, happy. That's the only way to describe it.

He places a kiss on my forehead. "You got it, baby. Watch and learn." Then he turns and walks out the door. I don't follow him, even though I really want to. Instead, I stand in my kitchen and listen as the door closes, most certainly locked behind him.

"Oaklyn, you have a delivery," our medical receptionist, Samantha, announces, stepping into my alcove.

I look up, unable to see the young woman because of the massive bouquet of flowers in her hands. "What in the…?"

"These just arrived for you. They're gorgeous," she whispers, placing the huge vase on my desk and stepping back. "Who are they from?"

My heartbeat skips in my chest. I know exactly who they're from. There's only one man who would send something so mammoth and flashy as red roses and white lilies. And I'm not talking a dozen roses either. There must be four dozen red roses in this vase. "Umm…"

"Fine, fine, keep your secrets, but eventually it'll come out," Samantha states with a grin as she turns and walks away.

I find the small white envelope and grab the card from within. Butterflies take flight in my stomach as I read the handwritten note.

> *My dearest Oaklyn,*
> *A rose for every time I thought about you last night, and that doesn't include my dreams, which you starred in. Hope you're having a great day. Can't wait to see you again.*
> *Love,*
> *Nate*

I read the card a second time before digging my phone out of the pocket of my jacket and pull up his name in my message app.

> **Me**: I just received the most stunning bouquet of flowers.

The bubbles appear almost instantly.

> **Nate:** From someone I know?

I'm smiling as I type out my reply.

> **Me**: Probably not. Just some football coach who used to throw balls for a living.

> **Nate:** He sounds like my kinda guy.

Mine too.

> **Me**: Thank you. They really are beautiful, but now I have to explain why I'm receiving a gigantic bouquet at work.

> **Nate:** Tell them you're being wooed by a handsome man who thinks you're the greatest thing since the league introduced the illegal contact rule in 1978, restricting contact beyond 5 yards downfield for receivers.

A bark of laughter flies from my lips.

> **Me**: That sounds like a big deal.

> **Nate:** Oh, it is.

> **Nate:** Anyway, you're welcome. I'm glad you like them.

"Dr. Schmidt, your next patient is in room four," one of the nurses says just down the hall.

"Thanks, I'll be right there."

Me:	I need to go. My next patient is ready for me.
Nate:	Go save the world. And have dinner with me later.

I shake my head and type out my reply.

Me:	At my place or yours?
Nate:	Neither. I'll pick you up at seven. Dress casual.
Nate:	I told you I wasn't hiding us.
Me:	I'll be ready.
Nate:	See you soon, baby. Have a good day.
Me:	You too. And thanks again for the flowers. I love them.
Nate:	And I love you. I'm going to prove it to you, Oaklyn. One day at a time.

My breath hitches in my throat as I read and then reread his message. He's said it a few times since he picked me up on the street last weekend, drove me home, and confessed his feelings. Since then, we've taken it at a fairly slow pace, communicating mostly through text or phone calls. Tonight will be the first time we've shared a meal since he showed up with breakfast.

And a public one at that.

A mixture of anticipation and nervousness spreads through my chest, but now isn't the time to let it get the best of me. I can freak out about what I'll wear, where he'll take me, who'll see us, and how Nate will react under the incredibly watchful public eye later.

Now, I have patients to see.

I slip my phone back into my pocket, inhale the sweet, floral fragrance filling my alcove, and head to do my job.

Everything else will have to wait.

NATE

WE'RE JUST WEEKS AWAY FROM training camp starting, and the press has been hounding our PR department for an interview. I hate that shit, but I know it's part of my job. It's the downfall of the position, but nothing I can't handle.

I have to be in the media room in fifteen minutes, plenty of time to text my girl. It's been a few weeks since we reconnected, and I'm doing exactly what I told her I was going to do. I'm wooing her. Flowers, dinner, coffee, lunch, and anything else I can think of that will put a smile on her beautiful face.

We're still taking it slow. Slow, as in, I kiss the hell out of her, but nothing more. I need her to understand that I'm in this for her, not for the sex. That's how we started, but that's sure as fuck not how we're ending. No, fuck that. We're not ending. That's not how this is going to play out. She's mine. I'm hers. We have forever, and that's just how it's going to be. I know she wants me. I can see it in her eyes, but there is something else there as well. Fear of being hurt, of being rejected. That's on me. I'll spend the rest of our lives together making up for that mistake.

It's one I'll never make again.

Me: How's your day, baby?

She finished her residency, and today is her "official" first day of her contract. She took a couple of weeks off, which the practice insisted on, and was well deserved after all her hard work. The physicians she's working with who own the practice are good people in my book. They're looking out for her. They've all been there—that's what they told her—and even though she was excited to get started establishing her own patients, she needed the break.

I wish we could have gone somewhere, but I couldn't get away. I wanted to say fuck it, claim a family emergency and go anyway, but Oaklyn insisted all she wanted to do was be lazy. She smiled when she said it, and she truly looked happy. She just wanted time to just be, so that's exactly what we did. We've hung out at her place or mine and did a lot of snuggling and kissing. So much kissing I feel like a teenager all over again, but it was time we both needed. We needed to reconnect emotionally. We've always been good at the physical.

Oaklyn: So far, so good. I'm seeing acutely ill patients just like I did before, but some new patients to the practice, and I'm their primary care provider. It's surreal, Nate. After all this time, the hard work, and late sleepless nights, I'm finally doing it.

Me: I'm so damn proud of you, baby. You've been doing it all along.

Oaklyn: I know, but it feels different. Better.

Me:	Don't forget I'm taking you out tonight.
Oaklyn:	I remember. Still no hints?
Me:	Nope.
Oaklyn:	I used to like you.

She follows her text with a winking emoji, and I laugh out loud. I'm wearing her down, and we both know it. She loves me too. I can feel it in her touch, in her kiss, in her eyes when she looks at me. I broke her heart and mine, and I knew it was going to take time to put all the pieces back together.

Me:	I love you.
Oaklyn:	See you at seven?
Me:	I'll be there.

Sliding my phone back into my pocket, I stand and make my way to the media room. It's time to get this interview over with so I can get on with my day. My incentive is Oaklyn at the end of the day. At the end of every day.

Taking my seat behind the table, with a sea of reporters ready to aim questions my way and just as many photographers here to record and snap pictures of the moment, is surreal. I never thought I would be back here, working as part of the Storm organization, but life has a funny way of working out.

The interview starts, and the questions wage on about the team roster, the training camp that's coming up, as well as how I feel we're going to do this season.

"We have a great team and a solid organization. I've worked with a lot of these guys and played side by side with them on the field. I hope that chemistry shows through from the sidelines as well as it did on the field."

"Nate, how does it feel to be back in Nashville?" a female reporter asks.

"Great." I smile at her. "I've always loved this city, and it feels like coming home."

"Was that what drove you to apply for the head coach position? The city?"

"Do you want an honest answer?" I chuckle. She nods, and I grin. "I love this city. I love the Storm organization. They both feel as though they're a part of me. However, that's not what brought me back to Nashville, not entirely. My girl lives here, and that's ultimately what brought me home."

"You're dating? Is this new?" Question after question is fired off. I count to twenty in my head before nodding and leaning toward the mic to answer.

"I'm dating. It's serious. It's not new. We've known each other for years, dated a few years ago, and lost touch, but we're back. I'm back, and I couldn't be happier." I smile at the camera and wink. I know this clip is going to be played over and over, and I can't wait for Oaklyn to see it.

"Can we get a name?" someone calls out.

It's on the tip of my tongue to announce it to the world, but then that would ruin my plans for this evening. "You'll find out soon enough," I tell them. Thankfully, the head of the PR department turns the interview back to football. I answer a few more questions, thank them all for their support, and hightail it back to my office. Just a few more hours and the world will know who owns my heart.

Rapping my knuckles on her door, I shove my hands in my pockets. I can't wait until she moves in with me. In my head, I have us much further along in this relationship than where we are, but that's my end game. I want Oaklyn so entwined in my life that it's no longer my own. It's ours.

She pulls open the door, and I suck in a breath. "You're beautiful," I tell her. I take a small step and lean in to kiss her cheek.

She's wearing a short black dress that hits midthigh and shows off her incredible figure. Her hair is in soft curls hanging down her back, and I want nothing more than to strip that dress off her and grip those silky strands as I pump my cock in and out of her. Fuck me, I need to focus. Resisting gets harder every single day.

"Thank you." A slight blush coats her cheeks. "You want to come in?"

"I do." I nod, but my feet stay planted. "But I can't. You look—yeah, it's best I wait out here."

"Nate." She breathes my name, and it reminds me of how she used to do the same thing when I was inside her. My cock thickens, and I will it to behave. This is her special night. The night we celebrate her success and the night I tell the world that she owns me. All of me.

"Get what you need, baby. I'll be right here." She nods and turns back to grab whatever it is she needs for the night out on the town. However, when she returns to the door, she's holding her purse in one hand and a small overnight bag in the other.

I swallow hard. "Let me take that for you." I take her bag with one hand and reach for her with the other. She sidesteps me, pulling her door closed, making sure that it's locked behind us. I slide my arm around her waist and lead her to the car I hired for us this evening.

"Nate? Is that ours?" she asks once she sees the stretch limo.

"It is. I wanted to give you all my attention, and I can't do that if I'm also driving."

"It's just dinner."

"It's never just anything where you're concerned. It's everything. Time with you is important to me. My life is about to get crazy, and I need as much time with you as I can get before that happens."

Pulling the door open, I wait for her to get settled before I slide in next to her, placing her bag on the seat in front of us.

"Come here." I hold up my arm, and she slides next to me, letting me hold her. "How was the rest of your day?"

"Good. But this is the best part."

I press my lips to her temple and breathe her in. "The night is just getting started, baby." We make small talk during the short drive to our destination. "We're here," I tell her when the limo pulls up outside the Redneck Riviera.

"I've never been here." Her eyes sparkle, and that's just something else that I love about this woman.

She doesn't care about my career or how much money I have in the bank. I could have taken her through a drive-thru, and she would have been perfectly content. My heart hammers in my chest as I lean in and softly press a kiss to her lips. "I love you." I've lost count of how many times I've said the words. She's yet to say them back, but that's okay. I know she feels it. We'll get there, but in the meantime, I'll never pass up a chance to tell her what she means to me.

"Ready?" I ask.

She smiles and nods, and I push open the door. As soon as I do, the photographers jump out of the woodwork, just like I knew they would. I didn't hide the fact I rented the private room for tonight, and word travels fast in this town.

I pull Oaklyn to my chest, my arm wrapped around her waist as I wave to the camera, flashing them my Nate Vaughn signature grin.

"Nate, is this her?"

"Nate, is this the reason you're back in Nashville?"

"Nate, can we get a name?"

Question after question is fired at me, but I ignore them all and look down at the love of my life. She's smiling up at me, and she bites down on her bottom lip. She's worried about how I'm going to react. That's on me. A few years ago, I would have blown them off, telling them we were just friends. I'm not that man anymore. I lost everything, my career and my girl, and that puts a man's priorities into perspective.

"Nate." She tries to take a small step away from me, but I hold her in close. I dip my head so that my lips are next to her ear.

"You remember when I said I would show you what you mean to me?" She nods. "Watch and learn, baby."

My voice is strong, loud so they can hear me. "This is her," I say, and Oaklyn scrunches her brow in confusion but quickly masks it. "She is the biggest reason I'm back in Nashville, and her name is Oaklyn." My girl gasps, and a smile takes over her face. I lean in close and lay my heart out on the line. "I love you. You are my everything, and I didn't give them your last name because I'm hoping one day soon it will match mine." With that, I kiss her. Just a soft press of my lips to hers. I know she wouldn't want an outlandish display.

Resting my forehead against hers, I let the photographers have their fill. There is no one who will see a video or picture of this moment and not know she's my entire world. Her hands grip my shirt while mine rest on the small of her back, holding her as close to me as I possibly can.

This is what it's all about.

Not the fame, not the fortune, nothing matters but her. I'd walk away from all of it if it meant a lifetime with her.

"Nate?" I pull back and give her my full attention. Her hazel eyes shimmer with tears, but she's smiling. "You mean that?"

"Every word, Oaklyn." She bobs her head, and it's time to get her inside. The reporters have more than enough material to send to the masses. By tomorrow morning, hell, maybe by the time we leave here tonight, the world will know she's mine and, more importantly, that I'm hers.

I wave to the reporters and guide her inside. Once in the door, we head to the stairs. I rented out the third floor and the entire rooftop for tonight. As soon as we push open the door to the roof, cheers ring out, and Oaklyn freezes. Her mouth falls open before she turns to look at me.

"Nate? What is this?"

"This is us celebrating you, baby. You're a fucking doctor, Oaklyn. You busted your ass, and we're celebrating."

"You did this?"

"Of course I did. You are the most important person in my life, Oaklyn. I want to celebrate you. We all do." I nod to the crowd. "I had some help. I had to recruit Natalie because I don't know many of your friends. I know we hid from the world before, but, baby, we're never hiding again."

She nods and glances around the room. She gasps and buries her head in my chest. "Nate?"

"Yeah, baby." I run my hands up and down her back.

"Is that your parents?" she asks.

I'm not surprised she recognized them. I have pictures of them all over my house. "Yeah. Yours too."

"What?" She lifts her head. She only has eyes for me.

"I wanted you to meet mine, and I wanted to meet yours. They're going to be family someday."

She swallows hard, and I see it. The moment she finally accepts that this is more. That we are the real deal. Her overnight bag was a pretty good indication that she was starting to come around, but I see it in the depths of those hazel eyes.

She's mine.

I'm hers.

"I love you, Nate Vaughn. I love you with my whole heart." She pauses as a single tear slides over her cheek. I capture it with my thumb, giving her all the time she needs to articulate whatever it is she's trying to find the words to say. "My heart was broken," she replies softly. "Nate, I can't do that again."

"Never." I crush her in a hug. "Never, Oaklyn. You hear me, baby? You are my fucking heart. I will spend every day of the rest of our lives showing you that. I want you. All of you."

She nods, and I kiss her forehead. "You ready to celebrate being a kick-ass doctor?" I ask her, lifting the mood.

She stands up straight, blinks away her tears, and smiles so big it could light up all of Broadway. "Yes."

"Come on, let's go say hi to our parents." I lead her to where our parents are now standing together. Both our mothers have tears in their eyes and smiles on their faces, and our dads, they're smiling, too, as I shake both their hands. Introductions are made, and we chat for a few before we step away to say hello to all the other guests. I say "we" because she's not leaving my side. Not now. Not ever. I hate that I have to leave her for away games and training camp. It's going to suck, and she can't just drop what she's doing to come with me. She's a doctor and is literally saving lives. I've already got some ideas up my sleeve to show her that she's on my mind, no matter where I am.

We can do this.

The alternative is losing her, and that will never happen. I'll resign before we get to that point. Oaklyn is my future, and nothing is going to change that.

We spend the next few hours talking, laughing, eating, and drinking, and just enjoying our closest friends and family. We stay until the final guest has hugged us goodbye before I lead her back down to the limo that's waiting to take us home.

"My place?" I ask.

She nods. I pull her onto my lap and hold her close while she rests her head on my shoulder. "When you're ready, I want it to be your house too. I'm not pressuring you," I'm quick to add. "I just want you to know where my head is at. In case you still don't know, it's on forever. You and me forever."

"That's a big step."

I nod. "Is it the house? We could move if you want?"

"What? No, I love the house. You know I do."

"Good. We can hire a decorator, and you can do whatever you want to it."

"Nate—" She lifts her head and places her hands on my cheeks. "I just want you."

"I'm yours."

"And I'm yours."

"So, you're moving in?" I ask her.

Her soft, beautiful laugh fills the back of the limo. "I'm spending the night. We'll take it one day at a time."

"I'm not going to stop asking."

She chuckles, kissing my cheek. "I love you."

"I love you too."

chapter 22

Oaklyn

TODAY THE STORM IS ROUNDING out their first week of training camp. The facility is packed to the gills with fans of all ages, all watching the players practice and vying for their attention or an autograph.

I'm here on this busy Saturday with Natalie, seated not too far from the Storm's bench at the fifty-yard line, and taking in the sights and sounds at my very first training camp. Nate is on the field, working with his starting quarterback, demonstrating a few moves and offering encouraging words of wisdom. He looks completely at ease, just like the leader he was when he was on the field.

"I've never been to training camp," Natalie says, her eyes glued to the field.

"Nate mentioned it would be busy, but I wasn't expecting this," I state, glancing around the field, sidelines, and stands.

"It's Saturday, so I'm sure that has something to do with why there are so many people here. Plus, this town loves football," she agrees. "Hey, Nate's looking this way."

My eyes return to the field, where the man himself is standing, staring up at me. When he waves, a small smile spreads across his handsome face, and my heart does that weird pitter-pat series of beats that makes it hard to breathe sometimes. I hold up my hand, waving back. A handful of people around us turn to see who he's acknowledging. Even though we went *very* public with our relationship, it's still weird to be under the microscope, so to speak.

"That's her? She's nothing special," a woman sitting two rows in front of us says very loudly to her friend. "Her hair is gross. I bet she gets the dye from Wal-Mart."

"Did you see the shirt she's wearing? Like, who goes out and buys a shirt like that?" the friend adds with a snicker. "A desperate woman who wants to be seen."

"Ignore them," Natalie mutters. "Clearly they're just jealous."

I nod, but my heart is still beating a million miles a minute. It's not like I didn't expect to see this side of "fame." No, I'm not famous, but when you date someone in the public eye, your life is always under the microscope. Even when you're not the one in the spotlight, that scrutiny carries over to you.

"Seriously, like, why is she here? Why are some women so desperate for attention?" the first one says, clearly wanting the attention she claims I'm after.

"Be careful, ladies. Your bitterness and jealousy are showing," Natalie finally says, unable to bite her tongue any longer.

They both turn around, decked out in their best cleat-chasing digs. Skimpy little tank tops with the Storm logo on the front. Fake boobs that require their own zip code barely contained by the material. Obviously, they're here to catch the attention of a player, considering they've only discussed the players' appearances and assets and not their stats on the field.

"Jealous? Of *her*?" the second one says, a humorless cackle spilling from her red lips.

"Yep," Natalie replies, earning her comment a dual eye roll from the Triple D twins.

"What. Ever."

I almost laugh at the *Clueless* reference, especially coming from bleached-blonde Barbie number one.

As if sensing my discomfort all the way over here, Nate turns, removes his sunglasses, and meets my gaze. I give him a small smile, hoping he can't see the turmoil brewing in my head, but as expected, Nate is too attuned to me. He places his hands on his hips, says something to the coach standing beside him, and heads my way.

"Oh my God, he's coming over here," Barbie number two says to her friend. This time, I do smile, especially because they both sit up straight in their seats and take a few seconds to fluff their hair.

I almost laugh.

Hard.

When he reaches the roped-off area, he waves me down. I'm only six or seven rows up, and the best part is, I get to walk right by the bitchy twins on my way down. I give the one closest to me a gentle tap with my leg as I pass, smiling to myself when she mutters another expletive.

"Good afternoon, baby," he says when I approach the rope. "What's wrong?"

"Nothing," I assure him, pasting a smile on my lips.

His eyes narrow just a bit. "Try again," he instructs, reaching for my hands and linking our fingers together.

"It's nothing, really. Just a couple of mean girls who think their good looks give them the right to put others down," I reply.

He looks over my shoulder, his dark eyes narrowing. "The two blondes who probably don't even know what team they're here to see?"

Smiling, I nod. "They're the ones."

His lip curls up in disgust. "You know there was a time when I was first in the league where something like that might have caught my eye, but I haven't been into the big, fake arm candy in a long damn time."

"It's okay. They're pretty. I know it."

He shakes his head. "No, they're not pretty, because the ugliness on the inside takes away from their external looks. Nasty and pettiness isn't a good look," he says, giving me his full attention. "Besides, I only have eyes for one woman, and she's a hell of a lot prettier than those women. She's beautiful, inside and out, and I'm so fucking lucky to have her by my side."

Then, he leans forward, kissing me as if we're not standing in front of hundreds of people. His tongue coaxes my mouth open, sliding easily against mine. It's the kind of kiss that's a prelude to something more, something dirty.

"Get a room!" someone yells, making everyone around us laugh.

"Do you think I have time?"

"No," I reply, laughing. I step back and take a gentle swipe at his arm. My face is flaming red, I'm sure, after being kissed like that in front of a huge crowd of people.

He tsks. "Too bad. Are you having a good time?"

I nod. "There's still so much I don't know about what's happening," I confess, wishing I were a little more knowledgeable about the game he loves so much.

"This is just a glorified practice, baby. Lots of conditioning and training before we start running through plays and game scenarios. But the fans love being a part of this. Even during the week, camp is packed with them."

"That's cool that they get to be a part of this with you all," I say, just as a whistle on the field blows.

"I gotta go, baby. You staying until the end?"

Nodding, I reply, "We plan on it. We're going to hit up that hot dog vendor near the entrance."

"Good call. Their dogs are the best. See you after camp," he says, releasing his hands and bringing them to my face. He threads his fingers into my hair and kisses me soundly. "Don't ever for one second doubt how much I want *you*, Dr. Oaklyn Schmidt. There has never been anyone but you since you stumbled off that stool in that dive bar on the edge of town, and there never will be. I love you."

I open my mouth to tell him how much I want to take our relationship to the next level, but it gets stuck in my throat. Not because I don't want to tell him I'm ready to take him up on his offer to move in and be his forever, but simply because I want to tell him in private. Later tonight, when we're alone. Not surrounded by hundreds of people while he's about to take the field again for more practice. It'll be when I can show him how much he means to me with my body.

A shiver sweeps through my limbs.

"Later, you'll tell me what you were just thinking about to put that look on your face." He leans forward, placing his lips against mine one final time. "See you soon."

"Okay."

He takes two steps back before saying, "Oh, and, Oaklyn?" When I meet his hungry gaze, he offers me that trademark smirk of confidence and sex appeal I've come to expect from him. He places his fingers on his lips and holds two digits up in the air.

My body is suddenly alive once more.

Alive in a way it hasn't been since he left Nashville and took my heart with him.

Yes, it's definitely time to confess how badly I want him. Tonight, I'll show him.

A lot of the players are mingling with fans, signing autographs and taking pictures. I'm way over to the side, waiting for Nate, who's surrounded by members of the media. He's been giving interviews since the conclusion of camp, and may be busy for a while yet, if the line growing near him is any indication.

"I have a client with a security breach on their site," Natalie says, tapping away on her phone. "Shit, they accessed her store and banking information."

"Oh, no. If you need to go, go. I'll wait for Nate."

"You're welcome to go with me, but I really need to go try to get her site back," she replies, shaking her head. Natalie works from home as a website designer. She's incredibly talented and is booked out six months for new designs. She also maintains them for several clients, and as far as I know, she's never had a security issue like this before.

"Yes, go. I'm sure he'll be fine with it. I'm probably going to his place tonight anyway."

Natalie gives me a knowing smirk and waggles her eyebrows. "I'm sure you are."

"See you later," I tell her as she turns to walk away, throwing me a wave as she goes.

I stay off in the distance, checking email on my phone and replying to a request for a consultation through the patient portal. My eyes are on the device, and I don't hear anyone approach until a shadow falls over the screen. It's immediately followed by the stench of body odor, and I'm certain it's not Nate. Even when he's sweaty, he doesn't smell like he's expunging garlicky food and possibly a touch of liquor from the night before.

"Oaklyn."

I take a step back, putting a bit more space between myself and Trevor. "Hello." I keep my tone even, my voice pointed. "May I help you?"

He turns his large frame so he's facing the field, clearly not planning on going anywhere. "So, you're fucking the coach again, huh?"

The hairs on the back of my neck stand up. "That's none of your business."

"Funny, it wasn't that long ago, you were hanging all over me. I never pegged you for a cleat chaser."

His stupid comment doesn't warrant a response, mostly because it's the furthest from the truth. I never hung all over him, nor will I ever. When I realized he was hoping for a hookup, I bowed out politely. He just didn't like the fact I wasn't interested.

"Nothing more to say? I guess the truth hurts."

"You have no idea what you're talking about," I state, taking a step to the side, away from Trevor.

"So you're not a cleat chaser? Just after the money? You bang Nate while he was our QB and now you're right back to throwing your feet in the air when he returns."

The breath stills in my lungs. "What'd you say?" My voice is barely above a whisper.

"You two thought you were hiding it, but you did a shitty job."

I turn to face the big, hairy man standing beside me, realization setting in. "You knew who I was when you approached me that day in the coffee shop with Natalie."

He snorts. "Of course I did. I saw you two together at the hospital a few times. There was this particularly bendy nurse I was banging when the mood struck, and I used to meet her in the parking lot during her break. Funny thing, finding Nate Vaughn's fancy fucking sports car they gave him to drive because everyone thought he was the shit parked in a vacant section of the lot. There's only one reason a man parks way the hell back there. He's getting tail."

Bile rises in my throat. I take another step away, trying to put as much distance between him and me as possible.

"Now look at you. Spreading your legs to get some of that money."

"Oaklyn."

I turn to my left and find Nate approaching, an unreadable look on his face. "Hey," I say, pasting a grin on mine and hoping he can't read the discomfort.

Nate's gaze zeros in on Trevor. "Thomas. Whatcha doing over here?" he asks the big man.

"Saw Oaklyn and came to say hello."

Nate's gaze bounces between the two of us. "I wasn't aware you knew each other."

Before I can open my mouth, Trevor waves his hand. "Yeah, met her one night at a bar with Jax. She was his doc."

Nate nods. "She was." When he looks my way, his face softens a bit.

"Well, I'll let you two get going. I'll see you Monday at camp, Coach," Trevor says, turning friendly eyes my way. "Nice seeing you again, Doc. Enjoy your evenin', Coach."

"You too," Nate says, watching the player walk away. When he's out of earshot, I hear him add, "I hate that guy." He turns his full attention my way and glances around. "Where's Natalie?"

"Work emergency. I was hoping I could catch a ride with you," I reply, shaking off the confrontation with Trevor. I'm not going to let that jerk ruin what I'm trying to build with Nate.

I'm rewarded with a wide grin. "I would love to give you a… *ride.*"

A bark of laughter slips from my lips at his innuendo. "So dirty," I quip.

"I gotta run to my office first. Wanna come with me?"

"Is that code for something naughty?" I find myself asking as we turn to head for the building where the offices are housed.

He slips his hand in mine. "It definitely can be. I've had this particularly dirty fantasy ever since I saw the desk."

We walk together, Nate greeting a few people we pass, and make our way up one floor and down a long corridor of offices. Stopping in front of the door with his name, a buzz of anticipation sweeps through me. Nate releases the lock and pushes the door open, allowing me to enter first.

The room is spacious, with minimal personalization. The walls are adorned with framed portraits of former players and game highlights. I walk the perimeter and look at them all. When I've made it around one half of the room, I stop in front of the wall of windows. The office overlooks the field, and I observe the grounds crew cleaning up from today's camp.

"What do you think?"

I turn and give him a smile. "It suits you."

"The office I'll use throughout the season is over at the stadium. I prefer to be there, with the team, than here. Coach Cunningham was the same way when I played for him."

"Understandable," I tell him, walking over to the desk and taking a seat in his chair. The first thing I notice are a few stacks of folders, all the contents hidden behind the front cover. Not that I'd know what I'm looking at, but I can tell he's taken care of keeping documents from the general view.

"Let me grab the stuff I need to review for Monday, and we'll be ready to go." A look crosses his face as he gathers the top couple of folders, sealing them in a satchel bag.

"What's the matter?"

"Hmm?"

"Something's wrong."

"Uh," he replies, glancing down at his bag. "My first employment issue. Another team has offered us a deal on a top-notch kicker in place of one of our players."

"And you don't want to lose him?" I ask, getting up from his chair and positioning myself in front of him on his desk.

"It's not that. Personally, I hate the fucker, but I have to put my feelings aside for the good of the organization."

Nodding, I totally get what he's saying. My job isn't exactly black and white either. There are lots of gray areas, and at times, I, too, have to put personal differences aside for the sake of a patient.

When he has his things bagged up or locked in a drawer, he turns and extends his hand in my direction. "Ready to go home?"

I arch an eyebrow upward. "You're taking me home?" I tease.

"Fuck no, I'm not. You're going to my house, Oaklyn. If I have my way about it, you'll always be at my place," he states, bringing my hand to his mouth and placing a kiss on my knuckles. Desire swirls through my veins, anticipation of what's to come in the forefront of my mind.

Nate Vaughn may not know it, but tonight, I'm going to make his wish a reality. It's time to put all the past where it belongs so we can move forward with our future. And if the last month or so has taught me anything, it's that I want one with him.

I'm all in.

NATE

"I'm stuffed," Oaklyn says as she places her half-empty sweet-and-sour chicken container on the coffee table.

"You barely ate half of it," I say, peering into the box.

"I had two egg rolls too," she reminds me.

"They were so good." I shovel in the last bite of my own sweet-and-sour chicken. It's her favorite and has quickly become mine as well. "I'll clean up. Why don't you go upstairs and get ready for bed?"

"I can help."

"Nope. Go. I'll be up in a minute. I just need to toss the trash and store the leftovers in the fridge." I press a quick kiss to her lips and start gathering everything to take to the kitchen. It takes me five minutes tops to clean up, make sure the house is locked up, and turn out all the lights before heading to our room. Okay, it's my room, but it's going to be ours soon enough. At least, I hope that it is.

As I step into the bedroom, the dim light from the nightstand offers a glow. That glow is shining like a fucking beacon on my girl. Oaklyn is on top of the covers in nothing but her birthday suit. I give myself time to let my eyes roam over every inch of her. We've fooled around since being back together, but it's been too damn long since I've seen all of her laid out like this for my eyes to feast on.

"Whatcha doing, baby?" I ask as I take slow, measured steps farther into the bedroom. My cock is straining against my zipper, but I don't make a move to relieve it just yet. I'll deal with the discomfort until I know where her head is at. We've yet to have sex since getting back together. It's been a test of my willpower, but I wanted her to know that this time we're different.

"Waiting on you."

"I can see that. You got something on your mind, Oak?" I ask, my voice gravelly with desire. My eyes roam over every inch of her. I want to memorize this moment. The one where she gives herself to me, the one where I know for certain we are both in this all the way. If this night is going where I think it's going, that's what this means.

"You."

I swallow hard. "Me?"

"I miss you."

"I'm right here."

"I miss your hands on my body. I miss the way you used to kiss every inch of me. The way you made sure that I was... taken care of." She licks her lips. "I need you, Nate." Her voice is soft, but that does nothing to detract from the seriousness of this moment.

This is us.

We're finally back on track and better than ever. At least, I think that's what her being naked on our bed means.

The strain of my cock against my zipper is too much. I quickly discard my shorts and boxer briefs. I need relief, and even if it comes from my own hand, it's happening. Seeing her like this is the only solution to ease the steel rod between my thighs.

"Shirt too." She grins, and I do as I'm told.

Tossing the shirt to the pile of clothes on the floor, I spread my legs and grip my cock. I take my time with long strokes from root to tip, trying like hell to quell some of this ache. "What now?" I ask, my voice gruff.

"As much as I like watching you, I need you." She palms her tits, and I groan at the sight.

"I need you too." The confession falls freely into the air between us, thickening it with so much desire, you could cut it with a knife.

"Come lie with me." She pats the bed next to her.

Not needing to be told twice, I go to her side of the bed and snuggle in next to her. Wrapping my arms around her, I hold her naked body to mine. She giggles at first contact, then moans when my hard cock presses against her belly.

"When you left, I was crushed. My heart was shattered into a million tiny pieces, and I was angry at you for pushing me away, for not wanting me. However, I was angry at myself as well. I knew we weren't supposed to be serious, but I let myself fall for you anyway."

"I fell for you too, baby. I was just too blind to see it, and then I was injured, and—there is no excuse good enough. I'll never forgive myself for doing that to you. To us."

"I forgive you. It's partly my fault. You didn't know I was in love with you then."

"I didn't know I was in love with you either. I knew it hurt like hell to push you away, and then bam, a little time without you, and I knew there would be no one else for me."

"There really hasn't been anyone?"

I rest my palm against her cheek. "No. No dates, no hookups, and no kisses. I couldn't think about anyone but you."

"Me either."

"I think I know how you want this night to end, and believe me, I want it, too, but I need you to tell me that you understand that we are it. You're mine. I'm yours, and the future is ours. I lost you once, and I know that was on me, but, Oaklyn, I can't live through that again. I can't imagine my life without you in it."

"I'm in love with you."

I smile. "And?"

"I'm yours, Nate. Only yours. Have been since that night in the bar."

The words that I've been dying to hear fill the room, and my heart hammers in my chest. She's mine. I mean, I knew we were back together, but I was still proving myself. This tonight, our quiet confessions, they've sealed our fate. "Move in with me."

A slow smile tugs at her lips. "Okay."

"Baby, I—Wait. What did you just say?"

Her smile is blinding. "I said okay. I already planned to tell you that if you really think we're ready, I'll move in. My lease is up next month."

"Don't renew." My mind races in time with the thunderous beat of my heart. "Live here. Make this our home."

"That's a big step, Coach Vaughn."

"Not the biggest we'll take, Dr. Schmidt." I pause when something hits me. "When we get married, will you change your name? Will you be Dr. Vaughn?"

"You want to get married?" There's awe mixed with uncertainty in her voice.

"To you. I want to get married to you."

"What else do you want?"

"Babies. You by my side."

Her eyes shimmer with tears. "Really?"

"Of course. We have lots of bedrooms to fill."

"How many bedrooms exactly?" she asks, biting down on her bottom lip.

"We have seven total."

"Six babies?"

"We can add on if we need to," I tell her. I'm only half joking, but she playfully swats my chest.

"Nate!"

"I want as many as you want to give me. I know your career is important to you, and mine is a little unorthodox with travel, but we can do it, Oaklyn. I know we can."

She nods. "Let's start with me moving in."

"Deal. Now, about that last name?" I ask, kissing the tip of her nose.

"I want to take my husband's last name. There will be a lot of paperwork involved, but when I get married, that's something I want to do."

"Me. My last name. I'm going to be your husband. Oaklyn Vaughn, Dr. Oaklyn Vaughn that has a nice ring to it."

"Nate?"

"Yeah, baby?"

"Kiss me."

"Yes, ma'am." The time for talking is over. Our future is set. We know where we're heading, and we're both driving in the same direction. I might be driving a little faster, but I know Oaklyn, and she's right behind me. One day soon, she'll be right beside me.

I put everything I am into this kiss. I want her to be able to taste, to feel how much I love her. My hands roam all over her body, my palm stopping to grip her hip. I'm so lost in her I don't realize her hands on my chest and she's pushing me to my back until I'm already falling backward on the mattress. She straddles my hips, and her wet pussy settles over my cock.

"What's this?" I ask, tucking her hair behind her ear that falls, hiding her face. I want to see all of her.

"This is me taking what I want."

"Tell me what you need."

"Just you, Nate. I've only ever needed you." With that, she reaches between us, grips my cock, and rises on her knees, slowly sinking down until I'm fully seated inside her. I moan as my hands grip her hips. It's taking everything I have not to take over, but I'm letting her have this. I'm hers. She can do whatever she wants.

She lifts and settles back down again, and that's when I realize something's missing. "Baby, condom." It's not that I want to wear one, but I'll always protect her. She'll always come first, and even though she's the last person I've been with, I still issue the reminder.

"I'm on the pill."

She was back then, too, but we never took the risk. "I'm ready to start our family when you are, Oaklyn."

"You mean that, don't you?" She tilts her head to the side, and my cock twitches inside her, causing her to swivel her hips.

"Yes."

"Let's try to do this in order, Coach." She smiles, and I swear that smile reaches inside my chest and squeezes my heart.

"Timeline?" I ask, lifting my hips, and she falls forward. Her palms rest on my pecs as she stares down at me. I run my fingers up and down her back, waiting for her to reply.

"Let's see how living together goes."

"I already know how it's going to go." I flip her over, causing her to laugh and dig her nails into my shoulders. "It's going to end with me fucking you every night in our bed and waking up to do it all over again. Then we're going to get married and have lots of babies. Soon," I add, just so she understands where I'm at.

She hitches her legs around my waist and locks her feet at my ass. "I love you. I love talking about our future, but right now, I need the old Nate to show up. The one who fucked me like he owned me."

I pull out of her and slowly slide back in. "You don't want me to make love to you?" I ask. I give her another slow stroke that I know is torturing both of us.

"There will never not be love, Nate, but it's been too long. Way too damn long, and I need you to make me—"

She doesn't finish the sentence. Her words are cut off by my hard stroke, and I don't let up this time. Over and over again, I give her exactly what she's asking for, what we both need. Each thrust of my hips is rigid. I feel as though I'm losing control. I'm being too rough, but when I start to slow, she growls. My girl growls and shoots me an angry glare.

"Don't you dare stop, Nate Vaughn. Please." She arches her back as I gain momentum. "Yes. Yes," she cries, her eyes rolling back in her head.

"Look at me, baby."

Her eyelids pop open, and the look she gives me steals the air from my lungs. Everything I feel for her is staring back at me in those big hazel eyes. Love, lust, hunger, desire, faith, hope, happiness, and so much more.

I see our future.

The tingling starts at the base of my spine. If you would have told me a few years ago that thinking about being married and my wife being swollen with our baby inside her would turn me on, I would have laughed in your face and told you to fuck off.

However, today, that does it for me, and I know it's the woman beneath me who I have to thank for that.

Gripping the backs of her thighs, I push her legs forward as I thrust harder. "Touch yourself. Rub that clit, beautiful."

Her hand slips between us, and she moans at the first contact. I thrust faster, chasing my release, hoping she gets to hers in time. "I want to feel your pussy milking my cock, Oaklyn. Make that pussy sing for me."

"Oh, God," she breathes. Her pussy clamps down on my cock as her release tears through her.

I try to hold on, but it feels too fucking good, and it's been too fucking long. Her pussy is tight and wet, and I can't control it as I call out her name—only ever her name from here on out—as my orgasm barrels through me. I release inside her, filling her with everything I have, and the thought that maybe her birth control could fail filters through my mind.

Could I be that lucky?

Now that I've got my girl back, I want it all. It's a race to the finish line to tie her to me in every single way possible.

Living with me.

Married to me.

Babies with me.

I can see it all. It's a clear picture in my mind. My cock twitches, where it's still buried balls deep inside her. "I love you." I kiss her softly. Those three words don't seem like enough to explain the depth of what she means to me, but they're the best I've got.

Her palms rest on my cheeks, and she smiles up at me. It's sleepy and sated. Her skin is flushed, her hair has that obvious just-fucked messiness about it, her chest is rapidly rising and falling from the exertion of her release, and she's never looked more beautiful.

"Come on, you. Let's get cleaned up." Slowly, I pull out, and sex without a condom is messy, but it feels too damn good to worry about that. I climb off the bed, offering her my hand. She stands and scrunches her nose. "What's wrong?" I'm worried I hurt her until she darts off to the bathroom.

"It's running down my thighs!" she calls back.

I chuckle as I follow her into the bathroom, where she already has the water running. "We could take a bath," I offer.

"Maybe next time. Right now, I just want to get cleaned up." She covers a yawn. "You wore me out."

I nod and step under the spray, offering her my hand to join me. "We need a good night's rest anyway."

"Why? Do we have plans tomorrow?" I can see her running what we might possibly have to do through her mind.

"We have to start packing you up. You only have a month."

She smiles, wrapping her arms around me, and I hug her back. "Nate, that's thirty whole days."

"That's too long. We're going to make this happen tomorrow. I can call a couple of guys on the team, and I know Jax will come and help."

"No. We don't need that. We'll start packing the essentials, my clothes, and things I need all the time, and then we can decide what to do with my furniture, and I can put what we don't need here in storage or donate it."

"Donate. We can call someone to come pick it up."

"Deal."

Regardless of both of us being exhausted, we take our time showering one another before falling naked and sated into bed. I wrap my arms around her and close my eyes. I remember so many nights when my arms would ache to hold her. I was certain I never would again. Now that I have her back in my life, I know with absolute certainty that this is where she will always be.

Never again will anything come before her. Oaklyn is what's important in my life. Oaklyn and the life we're building. I smile into the darkness of the bedroom when I think about the engagement ring that will be ready to be picked up from the jewelers next week.

Dr. Oaklyn Vaughn is going to be more than just a name that sounds good. It's going to be our reality. I can't wait to make this woman my wife.

chapter 24

Oaklyn

"I'M EXHAUSTED," I SAY THROUGH a yawn. "Ready for bed?"

We spent most of the day today at my apartment, packing up the essentials I wanted to bring over here. We made another stack of things that will be brought over in the coming weeks, and one for the stuff I'm donating. We agreed to put my bedroom suite into one of the many spare bedrooms at the house, even though he already has a room set up for his parents. This way, we'll have a second room for his uncle or sister when they come too.

After we sorted a big part of my belongings, we had dinner with Natalie. She's super bummed I'm moving out but was okay with it once I told her she can be my plus one to upcoming games. I'm certain she only agreed because of the tight football pants, but whatever. As long as she goes with me, who cares about the reason?

Now, we're on the couch, watching *10 Things I Hate About You*. Well, I'm watching it. Nate's reviewing the paperwork he brought home yesterday from training camp. I know it involves a trade, and since this is his first one to be involved in, he wants to make sure it's the right move.

Nate looks down at me, a smile on his handsome face. "Almost." He still looks a little concerned, but I try not to read too much into it. I'm sure the heaviness and finality of this is weighing heavily on him. He glances at the TV. "Your movie isn't over yet."

"No, but I've seen it a thousand times. I know the hero ends up with the girl," I tell him, sitting up from my position. I've had my head on his lap for the majority of the movie, while he reads and focuses on work.

"Hmm, sounds like my kinda movie."

I can't help but scrunch up my nose. "Seriously? There's no gun violence, explosions, or big fight scenes."

"You said the hero gets the girl. That's my favorite kind," he says with a wink.

I can't help but chuckle. "A little cheesy, Coach Vaughn, but I definitely appreciate the effort." Again, I yawn. "Are you about done?"

He sighs and rubs his fingers to his temples. "I suppose. I've read these documents a hundred times already and the facts remain. The trade is solid and a good move for the organization."

I turn toward him and cross my legs. "So, what's the problem then?"

"The player, well, I'm not a fan. I've been able to put my personal differences aside, because it's my job now. I have to look at it objectively, and I've struggled to do that. He's the reason I was injured. He missed a tackle, and I'm certain he did it on purpose. I don't know why, other than ego. The man's got one the size of Texas. We played against each other in college, me at Purdue and him at University of Illinois, and he was always gunnin' for me. Then I found out some girl I went out with a few times actually broke up with him for me. He's just… I don't know. Not a good dude."

"So, this trade sounds like a good thing," I reason.

"I think it is, for two reasons. One, he's an asshole and I don't want him in the organization anymore, and two, we'd be trading him for a veteran kicker, which we desperately need. The one we have now is very green. We have an opportunity to get this guy for the remaining two years of his contract, and then he wants to retire. We can use his expertise to take the new guy under his wing and teach him, hopefully, to help get him where he needs to be to be a successful starting kicker for a professional football team."

"It sounds like you've made your decision," I say softly, reaching for the hand that isn't holding the papers and lacing our fingers together.

"That's the thing. It's not really my decision. At least not totally. Phillip, the team owner, and his son, Rogan, who's the VP, basically already sealed the deal," he tells me, the worry lines around his eyes prominent once more.

Needing to get closer, I crawl onto his lap, setting the paperwork down on the end table, and straddle his thighs. His hands instantly wrap around my hips before sliding down and gripping my ass. His cock starts to get hard immediately. "Do you know what I think?"

"No, but I'm damn interested in finding out more," he says, flexing his hips upward and rubbing his erection against my clit.

"I think you're doing what's best for the team. Sometimes, the decisions we make are the right ones and sometimes they're wrong. All you can do is weigh all the pros and cons and choose the one that makes the most sense. Does this trade make sense?"

"Yes," he replies, without hesitation.

"Then, I'm certain you're basing your decision on facts and not letting your personal opinion sway your decision."

He smiles softly and leans forward, placing his lips to my own. "You're amazing, Dr. Schmidt."

Giggling, I rock my hips, earning a deep growl from him. "I am, aren't I?"

He slaps me on the ass before rubbing his hand over it to ease the sting. "I have to meet with Rogan and Phillip in the morning before camp to make sure we're all in agreeance. Then, I'll have to tell the player at the end of practice."

"You're the best coach. Do you wanna know why?"

"Because I have a whistle?"

A bubble of laughter slides from my mouth. "Well, no. I was going to say because you care."

"And because I have a whistle."

"Okay, and because you have a whistle."

We stare at each other for several long seconds before a wolfish grin breaks out across his lips. "Wanna give my whistle a blow?"

I watch the clock, slowly pacing my small office. Mondays are always the busiest day at the clinic, mostly because everyone who was sick over the weekend is trying to get an appointment today.

I received a text from Nate earlier today, after his meeting with the team owner and vice president, and he said it went well. I could also tell he was stressed about their decision and has likely been worrying himself into a tizzy all day.

Camp is about to be released for the day, and I know he has about thirty minutes between the end of practice and when the player is scheduled to arrive at his office. At the end of each day, the players all visit with members of the media and fans, and while Nate would usually do the same, he told me he asked to be excluded from today's post-camp activities so he could prepare for his meeting.

My last patient has gone, and I check the clock once more. If I hurry, I can make it to the practice field to see him. A naughty grin spreads across my face, and while I'd usually use this time to catch up on patient charting, I know what I need to do.

I grab my purse from my desk drawer and head for the exit. I make sure my office door is locked before quickly moving toward the rear entrance of the clinic. Once I reach my vehicle, I slip inside, toss my purse onto the passenger seat, and press the button for the ignition. Within seconds, I'm backing from my parking spot and driving the short distance to where Nate is.

As soon as I pull in, I find a parking spot, grab the visitor's badge Nate gave me, and jump out. Fortunately at this point, the lot is less crowded than it was on Saturday, and I'm able to get through the lot fairly quickly. Once I reach the gated entrance, I hold up my badge and hand over my purse to be checked.

"You're all set, ma'am."

"Thank you. I'm looking for Coach Vaughn. He should be done with camp and perhaps in his office. Is it all right if I head that way?"

The pleasant man at the gate nods. "Of course. Head up this walkway to the first double door on your right. A man named Jerry will be there. I'll radio him and let him know you're on your way. He'll make sure you get up to the coach's office."

"Thank you, Roland," I reply after checking the name on the badge hanging on his uniform. "You've been a huge help."

"No problem, ma'am. See you around," he states with a grin before turning his attention to fans leaving the practice stadium.

I follow the walkway as instructed, finding the double doors about halfway down. A man is waiting, smiling as I approach. "I'm Jerry. You must be Dr. Schmidt."

"I am," I reply. "Thank you for helping me find Coach Vaughn's office, Jerry."

"It's no problem at all," the older man says. "Right this way. I'll have you up there in no time."

We pass through the doorway, and as soon as I'm inside — in the air-conditioning, mind you — he leads me down the familiar hallway toward the stairs. Except, he presses a button and calls an elevator instead of moving for the staircase. I want to tell him I don't have time to waste, but the elevator arrives only a couple of seconds later. Once we're inside, it whisks us up one floor and deposits us near Nate's office.

"He's the second door on the left, ma'am," he says, stepping off the elevator but going no farther.

"Thank you, again, Jerry. You've been very helpful."

With a nod, he slips back onto the elevator before the doors close, leaving me alone in the hallway. I take two steps forward but pause when I realize I'm not exactly wearing something sexy for what I plan to do. Comfortable dress shoes, black slacks, a light-blue dress shirt, and my physician's coat doesn't scream seduction, that's for sure.

Oh, well.

Something tells me Nate won't mind.

I walk toward his door, which is open only a few inches, and rap my knuckles on the frame. "Come in," he instructs, his voice deep and firm.

A shiver sweeps through my veins.

Pushing the door open, I step inside his office, catching him by surprise. "Oaklyn? What are you doing here? Is everything all right?" he asks quickly, standing up from his chair.

Before he can walk around the desk to meet me, I throw the lock on his door and approach where he stands. He's wearing black athletic shorts and a team T-shirt that fits him perfectly. My mouth waters as I take in the way the material stretches tautly around his upper arms and hugs his chest.

My man's a walking wet dream.

"Everything's fine," I insist, stopping when I'm standing directly in front of him. Then, before I can chicken out, I drop to my knees and wrap my hands around the waistband of his shorts.

"Jesus, Oak, what are you doing?"

"Helping," I state, pulling them down in one swift movement before turning my focus to his boxer briefs.

"Helping with what?" he asks, humor lacing his question.

"Helping to relieve some of the stress you've been under. You have a big meeting coming up in a few minutes, right?"

Wide eyes cast my way, and he nods as he gazes down at me.

"Then let me help."

Nate doesn't say a word as I take his hardened cock in my hand and give it a gentle squeeze. "You're already hard," I murmur, snaking my tongue out and licking the precum oozing from the tip.

"I seem to have that reaction anytime you're near," he states, his words a little tighter than before.

"Hmm," I hum before opening my mouth and wrapping my lips around his cock.

"Fucking hell, baby." He groans as I suck him in deeper, slowly working my wet mouth down his length as far as I can go.

My left hand reaches between his legs, cupping and caressing his balls, while my right strokes his cock. Nate reaches down and grabs my hair, pulling it to the side to keep it from falling in my face. I start to pick up speed, twisting with my wet hand and sliding his cock between my pursed lips. His cock gets even harder as he grunts and thrusts into my mouth, chasing the release I'm promising.

"I'm getting close, baby. If you don't want me to come down your throat, tell me now."

I meet his fiery gaze, pausing only long enough to say, "I want it down my throat."

"Fuck," he groans, closing his eyes as the sensations take over.

I gently squeeze his balls, massaging them with my palm, as I tighten my hold on his cock. Ignoring the numbness in my arms, I center all my focus on him, making sure he has the best damn blow job in the history of blowies.

"Coming, baby," he informs, right before I hear the groan and feel the first string of warm cum hits the back of my throat. I swallow it down and every ounce that follows, using my tongue, lips, and hands to draw out every drop he possesses.

"My God, that was fucking amazing," he whispers, his entire body relaxing.

I pull my mouth from his dick and grin up at him, licking my lips as I say, "You taste fucking amazing."

His eyes darken, and he's moving before I can process the act. He unsnaps my dress slacks and has them and my panties down in one swift movement. Nate lifts me onto his desk and crawls between my legs. Considering I'm still wearing shoes and my pants are around my ankles, it's a tight fit for him, but when I spread my knees apart, there's just enough room for his broad shoulders to fit.

"What are you doing?" I whisper.

"Returning the favor," he retorts, running his tongue from the bottom to the top of my pussy.

"Oh, God," I whisper. "But you have a meeting."

"In six minutes, baby. I can make you come in six minutes."

"But," I start, but he cuts me off by sucking my clit into his mouth.

"No talking, Oaklyn. I need you to come on my desk right now, so hold on, baby. This is going to be a quick one."

His mouth descends, latching onto my clit and drawing it into his warm, wet mouth. Stars burst behind my eyelids as the sensations sweep through my veins. His tongue dives into my pussy, fucking me hard and fast. I thread my fingers into his hair, holding on for dear life as he manages to get a hand between us. He swipes his thumb over my clit while thrusting his tongue in and out. I'm already close, and we've been at it less than a minute.

"I want to taste your cum on my lips, baby. Five minutes. You better hurry."

And then he's right back at it, driving me wild with his talented mouth and fingers, switching them up after another minute. He slides two fingers inside me, curling them upward, looking for that magical spot deep inside. When he licks my clit and draws it into his mouth, I know my release is close. All I need is…

He pumps his fingers and glides them over my G-spot, sending me straight into orbit. I fly high, riding wave after wave of my orgasm, crying out his name and wishing it would never end.

"Fuck, I could watch you come every morning and night and never get tired of it."

"You know, at some point, you'll have to give me a rest," I quip, not really wanting that at all. Nate is incredibly giving when it comes to our lovemaking, and even when I'm not feeling it, he manages to get me completely worked up and ready in a matter of minutes.

He tsks, pulling his head out from the triangle made with my legs and helping me stand on the floor. "You can rest when you're dead, my love," he states with a proud smile on his face, his lips still glistening with my juices.

"You keep that up and I'll be dead in no time," I say, reaching down and pulling up my panties and slacks.

"Can't have that, now, can we?" he asks, righting his own underwear and shorts. There's no missing the fact his cock is already hard again. He notices where my eyes are focused, and adds, "We'll save that one for when I get home."

Smiling, I go up on my tiptoes and press my mouth to his. "I'll hold you to it."

"Done."

When I pull back, I glance at his appearance. "You look like you just got head, Nate. Your hair's all wild and you have this dopey grin on your face that screams orgasm."

"And you look like a woman who just had her man's mouth on her pussy, sucking her juices and eating her out until she was screaming."

"Oh, God," I groan, running my hand through my hair and hoping it's not as unruly as his. "Did I scream?" I ask, appalled by the notion.

He laughs. "Only a little. No one's on this floor right now, so you're good."

He walks me to the door and kisses me soundly. I can taste myself on his lips. "Next time, I'll make it last longer than five minutes."

"The speedy version was pretty fantastic," I insist, grabbing my purse from where I dropped it on the floor.

"Yes, it was." He gives me one more kiss before taking a step back. "Thank you. You always seem to know what I need."

"You mean a blow job in the middle of your office?" When he just smiles adoringly back at me, I add, "I'll see you at home, dear." With a wink, I release the lock on his door and step into the hallway as he returns to his desk.

"What the hell are you doing here?"

I look up to find Trevor standing directly in front of me, a snarly look on his hairy face. "Trevor?" I ask, confused as to why he's standing here.

And then it hits me.

The player Nate is about to trade.

The one he hates, who caused his injury and ended his career.

It's Trevor.

My stomach drops down to the floor as realization sets in.

I take a few steps forward, avoiding eye contact as I move around him to go to the elevator. An uneasy feeling settles in my stomach as I do my best to ignore his presence. I can feel the heat of his ire hitting me in the back as I walk away. I'm grateful he doesn't say anything more, but I can feel his eyes on me with every step I take.

Pressing the call button, I wait for the car to arrive and the door to open, anxious to get away from this man. Only when I'm safely inside the elevator car and descending back down to the bottom floor do I take a deep breath.

I can't believe the player being traded is Trevor. The same man who cornered me in the bar, upsetting me enough to accidentally call Nate. I guess the good news is I won't have to worry about running into him much longer. I don't know when the trade is set to happen, but I would assume soon. If I'm lucky, I won't ever have to see him again.

What a mess this turned out to be.

NATE

"TREVOR, HAVE A SEAT." I motion for the chair across from my desk. He saunters into the room like the cocky fuck he is. I would love to punch that cocky smirk right off his face, but that's not my current role. Right now, I need to get through this encounter as a coach, not as the man and teammate this fuck stole a career from.

He flops down in the chair. The look on his face tells me he doesn't like me any more than I like him. That's going to make this even more difficult and was part of the reason I struggled with the choice.

I knew the choice wasn't really mine, but at the end of it, I'm the one who has to execute the mission. All I know is I want to get this over with so I can go home and lounge on the couch with Oaklyn.

"Coach," Trevor sneers.

I push the trade paperwork across my desk. "The front office has decided to make a trade. We need a seasoned kicker, and Chicago is offering us one. You'll need to report to practice first thing Monday morning. We'll help facilitate as much as we can during the transition." I rehearsed what I was going to say and decided with Trevor it's best to just tear off the truth like a Band-Aid.

"What the fuck did you just say?" Trevor sits up straighter in his chair.

Looks like I now have his attention. "You're being traded. To Chicago."

He bolts to his feet and leans over my desk. "Are you fucking kidding me? Are you for fucking real? She did this, right? It's because of that whore?"

"Who are you talking about?"

"Oaklyn," he seethes.

"What does my girlfriend have to do with this?"

"Don't play dumb with me, motherfucker. Be a man and give it to me straight. She was constantly hitting on me, and I turned her down. She got pissed off and ran back to you. I'm going to the top with this." He points an index finger at me. His hand is shaking. He's so mad, spittle is flying from his mouth.

I stand, laying my hands flat on the desk, and lean over just as he did. "This has nothing to do with Oaklyn." My voice is tight, and the rage I feel toward the coward standing in front of me is roaring through my veins. "This is an upper management decision. As the head coach of this team, it's my job to inform players of trade status."

"Fuck you," he seethes. "This is all that bitch's fault."

Standing to my full height, I fist my hands at my sides. My chest is rising and falling rapidly with each breath I pull into my lungs. I'd like nothing more than to slam my fist into his face.

Not just for how he's talking about Oaklyn but for my career. Suddenly, the clarity of the trade that I've been looking for washes over me. It was going to be me or him. I would have tried to be the bigger person, but no way do I not know exactly what it is he's referring to where Oaklyn is concerned, but my guess is he's the douche canoe who had her in a frantic mess the night she called me when she meant to call Natalie.

I lift my fisted hand, only to drop it back to my side. I'm a professional. I can't ram my fist into his face. Instead, I take a deep breath and reach for my phone on my desk. I hit the button for security.

"Security," one of the guys answers.

"This is Coach Vaughn. Can you come to my office, please?" I ask.

"Right away, Coach," he says, and the line goes dead. I place the handset back on the receiver and listen to Trevor bitch some more. He doesn't ask who I called. Honestly, he's so pissed I don't even think it has registered with him that I'm about to have him escorted out of the building.

What a way to start off my first season as head coach. An unruly player who's ungrateful. We all know in this career a trade is possible. We all know we have to roll with the punches if it happens. This isn't new information to Trevor or any other player in the league unless a non-trade clause is included in their contract. That's a very rare occurrence.

"You can't do this!" Trevor screams. "You can't trade me because your girlfriend wants my dick."

"Enough!" I roar. "Shut up."

"Fuck you, Vaughn."

"You're under contract, Trevor. It's clearly stated that the Storm organization has the right to trade you at any time without reason. The decision has been made, and you've been notified. It's happening."

"I won't sign that."

I shrug. "It doesn't matter if you sign. The owners of both teams have their signatures on the trade. You're in breach of contract if you don't. Are you willing to pay that fine?" I ask him. It's hard as hell to maintain my composure, but I'm doing it. I'm not going to let this fuckstick get the upper hand here.

He's in the wrong.

I'm just doing my job.

Security knocks on the door, causing Trevor to whip his head around. "You fucking called security? Fuck you, Vaughn!" he seethes.

"Mr. Thomas, you're going to need to come with us."

"Fuck off." Trevor slings his arm to keep security off him.

"That's not how this is going to go." Both security guys come after him and manage to get him into cuffs. "We'll be escorting him from the premises," George tells me.

"Thank you, George. His entrance codes have already been deactivated. I'll have someone clean out his locker and have HR contact him to arrange for pickup."

"Don't touch my shit!" Trevor screams.

"Good luck to you, Mr. Thomas," I say, managing to keep my temper cool. I wait until I hear the elevator door close, taking Trevor's angry screams with them before grabbing my phone and keys out of my desk drawer, locking my office, and heading for the stairs. I need to get out of this building. I need to think. I need to call Oaklyn.

I think I've put the pieces together, all but why she kept it from me. I remember asking her specifically who the guy was, and she avoided the question. I should have pressed harder, but fuck, it was the first time I'd seen her in years, and I didn't want to push her away again. So I let it go, and now here I am.

Blindsided.

I run down the stairs and push open the back door. I keep jogging until I'm in my car and gripping the steering wheel. I don't know how I feel, but I know I need to go home and see her. We need to talk about this.

Pulling out of the parking lot, I head toward home. The one I share with the love of my life. The woman who kept a secret from me about one of my players. About a man I can't stand. The same man who stole my career from me. I have a million emotions running through me, and I don't know which one to latch onto when they're all screaming to be heard.

Before I know it, I'm pulling into the garage. I turn the engine off and sit here for a few minutes. I don't want to face this. I don't want the happy bubble we've been living in to be disrupted, but I know that's not life. Life is messy and unkind, and there are bad days. This is one of them.

Pushing open the door, I make my way into the house. I find Oaklyn sitting on the couch with her laptop, catching up on patient charting, I'm sure. "Hey, you." She smiles. "How did it go?"

"Why didn't you tell me?" I stand frozen about ten feet away from her. Normally, I'd rush to her side and kiss her hello. Not today. Today, I need answers. I need to understand what's going on.

"Tell you what?" she asks, tilting her head to the side.

"About Trevor."

"Oh, that. I wasn't hiding it from you, Nate. I knew he was going to be one of your players, and I thought it best not to get off to a bad start."

"Tell me everything." It's a demand, my voice cold and detached. I've never spoken to her this way before, and I'm already mentally kicking my ass for it, but right now, I can't take it back. I need to know.

"I ran into him a few times while we were apart. He kept asking me out, and I always said no. That night at the club, he cornered me. He wanted me to come to the VIP area with him for a drink. He wanted more from me, but I wasn't interested. I told you that."

"You just failed to mention it was Trevor fucking Thomas."

"It wasn't malicious, Nate." Her voice is soft and soothing, but there's also an air of desperation in her eyes as she tries to explain. "I didn't want you to have it out for a player. He was drinking, and nothing happened. He caged me against the wall, said a few unkind things, and I managed to push him away and leave. I called Natalie. Well, I meant to, but I called you instead."

I nod. Technically she didn't do a damn thing wrong, but I'm pissed that I was blindsided. If I had known about what he did to her or wanted to do to her prior to the meeting, I could have been more prepared. Hell, I probably would not have agonized over the decision that's been weighing me down for weeks had I known.

"Trevor is the player. He's the one who missed the block on purpose, and he was the trade."

She nods. "I ran into him in the hallway coming out of your office. I assumed that was the case. You mentioned the player was one and the same."

She stands from the couch and walks toward me. She approaches slowly as if I'm a caged animal ready to strike. I'd never lay a hand on her in anger. Never. However, when she reaches me and wraps her arms around me, I don't return her hug. Instead, I just stand here, her scent surrounding me as turmoil swims in my gut.

There is too much in my head. I can't think clearly, and I just need a minute. I need to decompress and organize my thoughts, and I'm scared to death that I'll say something that will hurt her and I'll lose her again. That can't happen.

"I need to go," I tell her.

She releases her arms from around my waist and takes a step back. "What? Where are you going?"

"I just need to clear my head."

"Where?"

"I just need to go." I reach into my pocket and pull out my keys. "I'll be back." I turn on my heel and head toward to the garage. Two minutes later, I'm driving away from my house with no destination in mind, at least not until my phone rings. I sigh when I see the name of the jewelry store that I ordered Oaklyn's engagement ring from. When I went to pick it up the first time, I decided to add engraving, which meant they had to send it back. That was fine with me. I wanted it to be perfect.

"Hello."

"Mr. Vaughn?"

"Yes."

"This is Harold from Hometown Jewelers. We have your ring here to be picked up."

"Can I come now?"

"Yes, sir. Just ask for Harold, and we'll take you to the back to inspect the ring before you leave."

"Thank you. I'm on my way." I hit the phone button on the steering wheel to cancel the call. I guess now I have a destination.

With the ring picked up and burning a hole in my pocket, I'm still not ready to head home. There is only one place that I can think of going. One place outside Oaklyn that feels like home to me. Pulling up to the stadium, there are a few cars here, but not many. I nod to a security guard I know well, Roger, who is working the door, as I enter my code and head inside.

I don't bother going to my office. Instead, I make my way to the field. I walk aimlessly onto the turf until I'm standing dead center on the fifty-yard line. I move to sit, popping my elbows on my knees as I bury my face in my hands.

Within ten minutes, my breathing has slowed, and I can think clearly. I know she didn't know it was Trevor who missed the block. She didn't know it was Trevor I was trading. I never told her.

I'm not mad at her. I'm mad at the situation. I was blindsided, and to hear him talk about her like that, it took every ounce of strength I could muster to keep from kicking his ass. Oaklyn is my entire world, and it went against everything inside me not to lash out to defend and protect her.

Reaching into my pocket, I pull out my phone to call her. I need to apologize and let her know I'll be home soon. I shouldn't have left the way I did, but I just needed a minute. I needed to reset.

"Thought I might find you here."

That voice. My head pops up, and there she is. As if just thinking about her brought her to me in the flesh. "Hey, baby." My voice is soft, something I wasn't capable of earlier.

"I was worried about you."

"I'm sorry." I clamber to my feet and hold my hand out for her. She places hers in mine, letting me pull her into a hug. "I'm so fucking sorry, Oak. I shouldn't have walked out like that. I was just mad, and I didn't want to say something that would hurt you and push you away." I cradle her face in my hands. "You're everything to me. The thought of losing you again sent me running. Again. I wasn't leaving, just taking a time-out."

"We're allowed time-outs, Nate. We're going to have arguments and disagreements. That's life. We're human."

"It was all on me. I felt blindsided. He brought that up, blamed you for his trade, and started spewing shit from his mouth, and I was so angry. Not at you, baby. I was sad you didn't trust me with who it was, but I never told you either. If you had known Trevor was the one who had a hand in ending my career or that he was the one I was mulling over trading, you would have known why it was important for me to know he was the one who accosted you that night."

"I'm sorry too. I never should have kept his name from you. I just didn't want to cause problems for you in your first year of coaching. We just reconnected, and not in a way either of us saw coming."

"Baby, I need you to understand something. There is nothing in this life that's more important to me than you. The job, sure, it's nice, but I don't need it. I have enough money for us to live a very comfortable life without it. There are other options for me. I don't need the league. Not if it means losing you or causing problems with us."

"I love you, Nate Vaughn." She leans up on her tiptoes, and I bend my head, meeting her halfway. Our lips touch, and the tension leaves my body.

All I need is her.

This isn't how I planned to ask her, but we're here, and this moment feels right. Taking her hands in mine, I gradually move to my knees. My old injury whines in protest, but I ignore it. Releasing her hands, I reach into my pocket and pull out the ring. She gasps, her hands moving to cover her mouth.

"One night there was a man who was struggling with where he was in life. He decided to go against the usual and pulled into a small dive bar on the edge of town. In that bar, he met the love of his life. It took some time for him to realize what he had was once in a lifetime."

I pause, swallowing back the lump in my throat. "Dr. Oaklyn Schmidt, you are my once in a lifetime. You're the brightest part of every single day, and when I hold you in my arms at night, you're my dream come true." With shaking hands, I remove the ring from the box, taking her left hand. I hold the ring up, staring into those beautiful hazel eyes. "Will you marry me? Have babies with me? Build a life with me? Oaklyn, will you be my wife?"

She's nodding, tears coating her cheeks before I can even finish talking. I slide the ring onto her finger, climb to my feet, and crush her in a hug. I thought I knew what it meant to be happy. The day I was drafted, I was certain there was nothing better. The day she called me by mistake, I was convinced that was it.

I was right, yet wrong at the same time. This day is one that will be on my list of bests. The day she takes my last name, the day she gives birth to our children, and I'm certain with her by my side, there will be so many more.

Pulling out of the embrace, she kisses me and stares down at her ring. "Nate, it's gorgeous." She smiles up at me, tears still shimmering in her eyes. "We're really doing this? Are we really getting married? We're going to have forever?"

I nod. "There's an inscription," I tell her.

Her face lights up as she slides the ring off her finger. There is a slight tremble in her hands as she lifts the ring to read the inscription. "'Watch and learn,'" she reads with a chuckle. "What am I watching and learning?" she teases.

"How I'm going to love you every day for the rest of my life. I'll show you every single day how much I love you more than the day before. You are my world, my everything. I love you."

"I love you too."

"You ready to go home and consummate this engagement?"

She tosses her head back in laughter. "Nate, that's the wedding." I raise my eyebrows, and she shakes her head. "I know, watch and learn."

There is nothing left to do but seal those words with a kiss.

EPILOGUE

Oaklyn

The next summer

"I HAVE A SURPRISE FOR you," I tell my new husband after taking what feels like a million photographs in the backyard of our home.

We're surrounded by our family and closest friends, all milling around the reception tent set up along the back of the property. It's the perfect June day. The sun's slowly starting to fall behind the trees as sunset approaches.

I'm standing near the trellis we had built in the yard that we stood beneath as we exchanged vows in front of those we love. My ivory satin dress is simple and classic, a contrast in design to the first few dresses I tried on. I learned really quick those big princess dresses weren't my taste at all.

This is the one that made me feel like the most beautiful woman in the world, and if the look on my husband's face and the tears brimming in his eyes when he saw me for the first time was any indication, I'd say I did well.

"A surprise? Is it in our bedroom?" He waggles his eyebrows suggestively. He looks positively edible, not that I expected anything less. Nate would look delicious in ratty, oversized clothes, but him in a pair of navy dress pants and an ivory button-down, sans tie? I almost ran up the aisle and threw myself at him when I saw him standing there.

"That surprise is for later." I wink. "No, we're going somewhere."

He looks toward the large tent before turning confused eyes my way. "We're leaving? Before we've even set foot inside our reception? I mean, I'm all for blowing this Popsicle stand, but—"

"We're coming back," I reply with a chuckle. "We paid a lot of money for that meal. I'm getting my steak."

He grins widely before stepping closer, lacing his fingers through my hair, and placing his lips against mine. Again.

He can't seem to keep his hands off me.

Not that I mind.

"Are we ready?" the photographer, Veronica, asks, a knowing smirk on her face.

"We are," I confirm, taking Nate's hand.

"Great. Car's out front, waiting," she states, reaching for my bouquet of red roses and white cala lilies so I can lift the bottom of my dress with my free hand. It only has a sweep train, but I don't want to step on the hem while walking through the grass.

As soon as we slip into the back seat of the waiting SUV, we're whisked away to our destination. Fortunately, it's just a short drive away, because the anticipation is killing me.

"Are you going to tell me where we're going?"

I bat my eyelashes at him. "You'll find out soon enough, husband."

He sighs dramatically, taking my hand and kissing my knuckles. "Yes, wife. Fuck, I love saying that."

"It does have a nice ring to it, doesn't it?"

Within five minutes, we're pulling into the private parking lot of the Storm's stadium, and my husband shakes his head. "What are we doing here?"

"I told you. I have a surprise."

The car stops in front of the security door and two smiling guards step out. They open my door and extend a hand, only to have Nate growl behind me. He jumps out of the other side and runs around to my side. "Take your hands off my wife, Robert," he states in a teasing tone.

Robert only laughs and takes a step back, hands in the air in surrender. "Marriage looks good on you, Coach."

Nate smiles down at me. "Yes, it does."

We walk into the stadium and follow the long corridor to the field. A few staff members are there, making it easy for us to maneuver through the concrete and steel building easily. Veronica hands over my bouquet and darts ahead, just like I knew she would, so she could be ready for our entrance.

When we reach the players' tunnel that leads them onto the field, I pause and face Nate. "I'm so glad I wore sensible shoes," I joke, holding my foot out of the dress and revealing my ballet-style slippers.

"Those are the best," he replies with a laugh. "They suit you."

"I didn't want to spend all night with sore feet," I tell him, turning and facing the field. From where we stand, I can see all the green grass, but not the place we're headed.

"What are we waiting for?" he asks, moments before the game announcer is heard overhead.

"Storm fans, are you ready?!" he bellows, just like he does at the start of every game before the players take the field.

"Holy shit, is that—"

"On. Your. Feet. It's time to welcome Coach and Dr. Vaughn!" he proclaims.

And with that, we make our grand entrance into the stadium and head out onto the field. The crowd is much smaller, but I can't help but laugh at all the hooting and hollering. Nate looks over, completely stunned to find his entire team, coaching staff, and office personnel in the stands, cheering us on. "I can't believe this," he whispers.

"Surprised?"

He pauses in the end zone and pulls me into his arms. "Completely. Thank you."

Smiling, I confess, "It wasn't all my idea. I wanted to come take photos here, since this is where we got engaged, and when Phillip and Rogan found out, they asked to do something special for you by inviting the players to congratulate us."

He shakes his head, wraps his hands around my waist, and dips me back. His mouth seals the deal, earning him another round of cheers. "This is the best surprise."

"I'm not done yet, cowboy."

He stands me up and we finish making our way to the fifty. Veronica has been snapping photos left and right, posing us for more formal portraits. When she feels like she's gotten enough, she gives me a nod and steps away. The crowd in the stands all wave as they make their exit, Jax giving me a thumbs-up before he goes.

"I didn't even see him leave the reception," Nate says, shaking his head. Jax is his best man and cut out while we were taking photos at the house to make sure he beat us to the stadium. Now, he's on his way back to the house to continue the celebration.

I retrieve the small bag on the ground where Veronica left it and hand it to Nate. "This is for you."

Confusion is evident on his face. "We already did gifts."

"I know, but this one is special."

He glances down at the custom watch on his wrist I had made for him. The black face has both the Storm logo and the physician logo and is inscribed with today's date.

"Trust me."

He nods, pulling the pink and blue tissue paper out of the top and setting it on the turf. He reaches inside and pulls the small white piece of material from within. He holds it up, his eyes wide. "Is this—"

"It is," I confirm, barely able to get the two words out before he's whooping and pulling me into his arms.

"We're having a baby?" he asks, his eyes wide with excitement.

"We are."

"Holy shit, Oak. This is…" He pauses and glances down at the small onesie in his hand. On the front is the Storm logo, and since he hasn't seen the back yet, I take it and flip it over. There in big black letters are the words *Coach's #1 Fan.*

Then he's pulling me into his arms again, his mouth descending in a bruising, fierce kiss. "I love you so much, Dr. Vaughn."

"And I love you, Coach Vaughn."

another EPILOGUE

NATE

I KNEW THERE WOULD BE more moments. More days when my love for my wife would be so overwhelming, I wouldn't know how to express what she means to me. Each day I love her more than the last. However, the last twenty-four hours have been nothing short of incredible. I don't have the words to express how I feel. That's nothing new because saying that I love her doesn't seem like enough.

I stare down at my son, who is sleeping peacefully in my arms, and then glance at my wife, who is doing the same in her hospital bed. Twelve hours of labor. Twelve hours of watching her suffer through contractions and pushing to the point of exhaustion. My wife is a fucking rock star. I hated that there was nothing I could do but hold her hand and tell her how strong she was, how much I loved her, and thank her for giving me this gift.

Our son.

Lucas Nathan Vaughn.

My heart feels like it could explode in my chest with how full it is. I've heard stories about how the love for your child is life-changing. When my parents found out, Dad pulled me to the side and congratulated me, and told me to prepare myself for love like no other. I argued the fact, telling him I had already felt that love with Oaklyn. I'll never forget his words, especially now that I'm living them.

"Son, loving your wife and your child are two different worlds. The love is equally as strong, but when you have a part of you and a part of the woman who owns you walking outside of your body, it's a feeling even I can't explain."

It makes me feel better that even my dad was speechless from parenthood. I understand my parents' worries growing up and their concern for me so much more now that I'm a father. Lucas has only been with us for a handful of hours, but I know there will never be a day that passes that I won't worry about him. I chuckle softly, knowing my mom will be thrilled that she gets to say, "I told you so."

"What's so funny?" Oaklyn's sleepy voice greets me.

"Just thinking about how my mom is going to love telling me she was right."

"About what?"

"That as a parent, you never stop worrying."

Oaklyn nods. "How is he?"

"He's perfect, baby. So fucking perfect."

"Hey, you're going to have to work on that mouth of yours. Our son's first words will not be f-u-c-k, Nate." She gives me her stern mom voice, and I grin. I can't wait until she has to turn that around on our little man.

"Why is that making you smile?"

I shake my head. "I was just thinking about you using that mom voice. You've already got it mastered for Luke here." I peer down at our son. "If he's anything like me, he's going to give us a run for our money."

"Oh, I have no doubt."

"That's why he needs a little sister," I say, my eyes going back to my wife.

"A little sister, huh?" she asks. A smile lights up her face. "Maybe let's get him home, and let me heal first?"

"What do you think, Luke?" I lift him in my arms. "You need a little sister, don't you? Tell Mommy we need little brothers and little sisters," I coo to him.

"Nate." Her voice cracks, and my eyes dart to her. There are tears in her eyes.

"What's wrong? Are you hurting?" I stand. "I'll get the nurse."

"No."

Her voice stops me. Instead of moving toward the corridor, I go to her side. With Lucas in one arm, I take my free hand and tuck her hair behind her ear. "What's wrong, Oak?"

"Nothing is wrong." She smiles and wipes at the tears trailing down her cheeks. "I love you. I love our life. I just—" She waves her hands in front of her face. "Hormones." She laughs.

"I love you too. I love our life. Thank you for this. You did all the work, and I felt helpless that there was nothing I could do but thank you, baby. For loving me, for giving us this precious little boy." I bend down and kiss her.

"Knock, knock," a nurse says, entering the room. "How are you feeling, Momma?" she asks Oaklyn.

"Good. Sore, exhausted, happy." She smiles.

"He's handsome. Are you all good with him, or did you want me to take him to the nursery so that you both can rest?"

"No." I'm quick to answer. I pull Lucas a little closer to my chest. "He's good here." My wife and the nurse both laugh, but I don't care if I'm being ridiculous.

"All right. If you change your minds, you just press this button" — she points to the side of the bed — "and we'll be right in."

"Thank you," Oaklyn and I say at the same time.

"You have some guests. Is it all right to send them in?" the nurse asks.

Oaklyn looks at me. "My parents, your parents, and my sister went back to our place to get some sleep. I don't know who it is."

"Best friends," the nurse replies.

"Yeah, send them in," Oaklyn agrees. The nurse nods and steps out of the room.

"You sure you're up for more visitors?"

"They're our family too, Nate."

"I know, but you and this little guy need to rest."

She smiles softly. "I have no doubt that my husband will be waiting on me hand and foot, and Lucas will sleep through anything, including being passed around by his pseudo aunt and uncle."

Just as she says the words, the door pushes open. Natalie peeks her head inside, and tears instantly fill her eyes. "Hand him over, Vaughn," she says, making her way toward me. She pauses, and goes to Oaklyn, bending over the side of the bed to give her a hug, then continues to me. "Let me have him."

"He's mine." I grin at her.

"You have to share."

"Fine. Watch his head."

She playfully rolls her eyes. "I've held a baby before, Nate."

"Not this one."

My wife and her best friend crack up laughing, and that's when Jax chimes in, "Ease up, Daddy." He's been standing by the door, taking it all in.

"She's holding half of my heart, man."

"Aww," Natalie coos. "Did you hear that, Lucas? Your daddy is a big, ol' softy."

Jax walks to the bed and bends to kiss Oaklyn on the cheek. "You did good, Momma."

"Lips off my wife," I say with no heat behind my words. "Get your own." Everyone laughs as I move to sit on the bed next to Oaklyn, carefully wrapping my arm around her. I kiss her temple, soaking in this moment.

Jax eventually convinces Natalie to give him a turn holding Lucas. He stares down at my son in his arms, and when he finally glances up, I swear I see his eyes shimmering. He gives me a tight nod before dropping his gaze again. My best friend likes to pretend he's a badass and that he doesn't want a family of his own. One day he's going to find his Oaklyn, and he'll understand.

"I love you," I tell my wife softly.

"I love you too." She smiles up at me. "We can do this, right? I mean, I know it's too late, but he's our responsibility. We—"

I cut her off by pressing a soft kiss to her lips. "We've got this," I assure her.

"Nate—"

"Watch and learn, baby."

A beautiful smile lights up her face as she nods. "Watch and learn."

the END

Thank you so much for taking the time to read
Watch and Learn.
We hope you loved Nate and Emerson as much as we do.

To learn more about these two authors visit their websites here:
www.laceyblackbooks.com
www.kayleeryan.com

ACKNOWLEDGMENTS

There are so many people who are involved in the publishing process. We write the words, but we rely on our editors, proofreaders, and beta readers to help us make them the best that they can be.

Those mentioned above are not the only members of our team. We have photographers, models, cover designers, beta readers, formatters, bloggers, graphic designers, author friends, our PA, and so many more. We could not do this without these people.

And then we have our readers. If you're reading this that means you took a chance on a new to you author, and we cannot tell you what that means. Thank you for spending your hard-earned money on our words, and taking the time to read them. We appreciate you more than you know.

Special Thanks:
Becky Johnson, Hot Tree Editing.
Deaton Author Services and Kara Hildebrand, Proofreading
Y'all That Graphic – Cover Design
Golden Czermak – Photographer (Main Guy Cover)
Chasidy Renee – Personal Assistant
Jo, Sandra, Jamie, Stacy, Lauren, and Erica
Bloggers, Bookstagrammers, and TikTokers
Tempting Illustrations, and Graphics by Stacy
The entire Give Me Books Team
And our amazing Readers

www.ingramcontent.com/pod-product-compliance
Lightning Source LLC
Chambersburg PA
CBHW072347020726
47506CB00004B/1032